THE
TESLA TRAP

THE
TESLA TRAP
At The World's
Columbian Expo

Book III
of the
WARDENCLYFFE TRILOGY

DANA REYNOLDS

Wardenclyffe Tower Books ™

WTB

WTB

ISBN 978-0-9884380-7-1

19627 W Vanzant Rd.
Springdale, AR 72764

Cover Art by Dana Reynolds and Megan Reynolds
You may contact the author at:
author.dana.reynolds@gmail.com

∞

If *Many-Worlds Theory* is true, events, locales or persons, living or dead in this book are a certainty somewhere, but resemblance to the universe you reside in is such a long shot, you may consider it entirely coincidental.

This book is for Belinda Eubanks,
my first genuine reader.

10% of the Author's proceeds
of this edition will be donated to the
Tesla Science Center at Wardenclyffe.
This book is not otherwise affiliated with the
Tesla Science Center.

For more information, visit
http://www.teslasciencecenter.org

BÖÖK THREE
of the
WARDENCLYFFE TRILÖGY

∞

CHAPTER ÖNE

"You would be wrong if you described The 1893 World's Columbian Exposition as an event unparalleled in all of human history. It is in fact, the most paralleled single event in all the multiverse. Blame the artist, if you need to blame anyone at all. It is the nature of art to create and destroy, and recreate again in countless cycles until the artist decides —by whatever means she does —that she is finished and satisfied and walks away.

Chicago's fair was and is and ever shall be the most important timework of the Gilded Age. It is the fulcrum upon which the twentieth century totters. And by extension, the twenty-first. Thuswise pray the artist gets it right!

I am her patron, and I am her subject. And as her subject, I am so oft revisited she has made a genre of me. I am the portrait at the focal point in her vast tableau, and I have paid dearly for that privilege. I have paid for it with my life, over and over again and it remains to be seen if I will survive the work.

    —The Chairman's Notebook
      Wardenclyffe Foundation Archives

∞

In the year 2083, Commonwealth of Arkansas

The small boy hesitated on the edge of the playground. The stream of children exiting the Primary Conditioning Center bottlenecked briefly and then parted to flow around him, shrieking with impatience to be let out for recess.

"Lauder! Move it!" his classmates called. He was roughly jostled as they passed and he suffered a few good-hearted punches and just one mean-spirited one, but the challengers slid on by without the satisfaction of any reaction at all.

The boy Lauder was at that moment transfixed at the sight of the old man sitting on the park bench beneath the tree. He was feeding the pigeons – just like he had been the day before, and the day before that.

Lauder was not meant to notice the old man. He was meant never to notice him again; and so it was strange that the boy was gripped with a dread curiosity and the sense he had forgotten something important. He studiously and furiously focused his thoughts in the old man's direction, but even his goog was silent on the matter. He threw inquiries against the nanny-wall, which was a big effort for such a small boy, but even then he could not find the reason he was so enthralled.

Lauder was not so lucky the night before. He had lain wide awake for as long as he could, keeping his eyes on the pale yellow glow of his nightlight, knotting his toes, flexing his knees, tightening his buttocks and squirming his shoulders down into the mattress just to feel real and awake and safe and far, far away from the man beneath the tree. But as sleep finally softened his thoughts and slacked his face against his pillow, he let down his guard and tweaked his goog on the very thing he'd been trying so hard not to think about.

It happens like that sometimes to the very young.

Remaindered in his goog's short-term memory was the data he'd found and wished he hadn't. The stuff he *wasn't-supposed-to-see.* When he realized what he'd done, he shut down so fast he forgot to purge, but not so fast that he foiled the uptake. It *took*, and it was stored, awaiting access. He didn't mean to think about it. He avoided the thoughts like a cat avoids a stovetop the second time around. But for all his trying, all it took was a stray neuron, soft as a down-feather adrift in slumber, settling to rest on the hair trigger of his goog, and in his sleep he downloaded. Downloaded it all. It poured into his drowsy brain like a ruptured sewer line into the shallow end of a kiddy pool.

In his dream the old man sat feeding the pigeons next to the schoolyard as usual, except his dream was augmented and his goog ballooned the scene in helpful intel. The implant told Lauder the old man was a.k.a. *The Murderer of the World,* and when the boy's attention fixed on that, he was shown how the elder had earned such a fearsome title. A sidebar suggested he access *conspiracy theory,* but before he could, the main focus began to hemorrhage worst-case scenarios.

Lauder could not wake up in time to shut it off. Shrieking commentators, whack-jobs and fear-mongers portaged their hysteria straight to his neocortex, embedding in the malleable matter of his brain.

That night, Lauder wet the bed for the first time since he was a toddler.

"'Tis all righty fine," his mother told him, but to his supreme embarrassment she informed the Primary Center. As a result, in the middle of a math test he was called to the office, and from there, sent to the infirmary. The relief he felt for missing the test was short-lived when he was asked to sit in the appliance the kids called *The Chair.*

They called it *The Chair* with appropriate emphasis of awe because nightmares followed after a child was strapped in and his first goog was implanted. The goog implant was nearly painless and the nightmares weren't a punishment by any means; Troubled dreams were just a symptom to be dealt with as the brain made its necessary adjustments. Getting a goog was a child's rite of passage, like losing a tooth. Everybody did it and everybody had nightmares at first. *Everybody.* But they rarely lasted more than a few days.

The nurse handed Lauder a lolli with a soft loop for a handle and he occupied himself by sucking on it while his brain was scanned. He was asked to think about kittens. He was then asked to goog 'kittens' and review the memes he liked the most. As he did, he couldn't help but giggle and kick his feet a little. His nurse looked pleased, and then she asked him, *ever so gently*, to think about his dream last night.

Lauder's giggles stopped and his feet went still. He felt cold and his stomach turned over and he let his hand drop with the sticky lolli still in it. It stuck to his pants but he didn't pay it any attention or worry about what his mother might say. He was too busy remembering the old man on the park bench. Lauder's pulse began to race.

The nurse frowned as she scanned the image of his brain, watching his neurons firing down newly furrowed pathways. Lauder could feel it when she patched into his mem and looked for the breach. It didn't take her long to find it.

Lauder's anxiety had to step aside for his rush of shame. He was caught. He could see it on her face. *It wasn't fair*, he thought at her. He'd never seen an elder in person before. He'd never seen wrinkles, nor veins like a 3D map overstretched with skin. He'd not seen gnarled hands nor a neck so corded it seemed his head was atop a bundle of sticks. Lauder couldn't help it. It was his goog's fault. How was he to know that particular elder, that old man specifically, had a mature-rated bio? He didn't know. It was the old man's celebrity, his god-awful history, and the giga-hits from the school libraries that allowed the intel to leak around the nanny-wall. It wasn't his fault forbidden domains deposited their cargo square between his ears. Right-to-die-ers. Wholly Rollers. Unitarian Terrorists. The One True Universe split into diminishing divisions. Screaming fanatics who couldn't grasp that infinity went both ways.

And most of all, worst of all: *Quantum Suicide.*

It terrified him: the idea that his world was just a shadow of the real one. It all started with that man out there, the one on the park bench feeding pigeons. Some called him the Father of the Quantum Suicide Solution. Some just called him the Murderer of the World.

"Oh deary me," the nurse sighed. She made the necessary patch in his firewall and erased the long-term from Lauder's cloud, but the damage was done. She couldn't erase *his* memory, but she bypassed the current furrow, buried it, and tidied up his goog the best she could. She would later tell his mother how resilient children were and how he'd outgrow it in time but only if his mother treated it lightly and didn't make a fuss.

The nurse upped prescriptive measures to his mother's goog that they might be followed and that was that. Lauder was dismissed to make his befuddled way down the empty hallways back to his classroom just in time for recess.

And now as he stood on the edge of the playground, he automatically ticked his goog, scanning the old man with renewed fascination and dread, but without recalling exactly why. His goog remained benignly quiet. *Access forbidden*, it told him when he persisted. The old man's I-Dee and all peripherals were even removed from his textbooks. The purge was complete and this time, the nanny-wall held.

But so did his curiosity.

Lauder crossed the playground and slipped up quietly to where the old man sat. He was afraid, of course, but he also wanted to see for himself. He knew what *aging* was from school because they'd studied it in biology. It was physical entropy suffered by all living things. All living things except man, that is. When he himself came of age and was in his prime, he'd be fixed like everyone else, and from that point onward, his body would renew itself. He'd be in his prime for the rest of his life, and if he avoided accidents, the rest of his life would be a very *very* long time. No one so far had reached the end of their natural span since the fix was in, not even the elders. Some people said it was forever. But the elders were old already when the fix was first released, so they'd be *old* forever, like this man here. It was sad: Lauder knew it was sad because his goog told him it was.

The pigeons quarreled on the ground at the elder's feet. With a wink and a grin the old man reached into a brown paper sack, which was nearly as wrinkled as he was. He withdrew a handful of sunflower seeds and tossed them near where Lauder stood. The birds were happy to waddle over to the boy. Lauder gave a slow and gentle kick just to see what they would do. They parted perfectly, some fluttered a few feet, but most just dodged and turned back again to grab at the seeds next to his feet as if he'd never given any offense.

"You'll have to try harder," the old man told him. His voice was like rustling husks of corn, but not unpleasant.

So, Lauder shuffled both his feet and watched the corresponding ripples of activity that telegraphed through the flock. Compelled to put more energy into it, he kicked up faster and faster until he was dancing a jig and flapping his arms. He yelled, "Go! Go! Go!" At last the pigeons reached the breaking point and they rose in unison, chortling complaints and flapping their wings so hard it scattered the seeds and lifted the hair on Lauder's head.

Lauder and the old man grinned at each other.

The elder removed his hand from the paper bag, dusted the clinging seeds form his fingers and extended it in a friendly offer for a handshake. He said, "My name's Sergei. What's your name, son?" but Lauder didn't answer. He was amazed at the man's hand, not by the wear of years on it, but by something even more improbable; There were no tattoo bars on the back of it. It was as bare and unmarked as a child's: as clean as his own.

"Where's your tats?" Lauder blurted out, forgetting his manners.

"Where's yours?" the old man asked him back, with just as much guile, which is to say, none at all.

"I'm too young to shunt!" Lauder was amazed he had to explain this. He only had the vaguest notion of shunts. It was, as far as he could tell, a revolving door only grownups were allowed to go through, and on the other side was *a better world*. Every time you went through it, you got another tat bar on your hand, and a lot of creds besides. Some people had so many tats they formed a solid square and those people were very rich. As he thought about it, he couldn't quite resolve a related word that presented itself: *Quantum Suicide.* It wavered at the edge of his consciousness and then evaporated.

The old man regarded the back of his hand and asked, "What does it profit a man to gain the whole world if he loses his soul?" It was the wrong thing to say. It was something the Wholly Rollers said. Something they were famous for screaming from their pickets.

Lauder's eyes widened as neurons only just buried by the school nurse fired and branched and networked to connect, and once connected, they lit pathways in his brain where the forbidden knowledge was stored. He accessed it now and in spite of the endorphins triggered by his goog to leak soporifics into his system, Lauder *remembered* and he was gripped with renewed terror. It was all the boy could do to surface enough wits to flee back to the playground, leaving the old man to stare after him.

It was 39 years before Lauder saw the old man again. On that day Lauder was determined to kill The Murderer of the World, but the old man escaped in his time machine.

Fortunately for Lauder, the time machine was left behind.

CHAPTER TWÖ

"I was not merely beholding a vision, but I had caught sight of a great and profound truth."
—*Nikola Tesla*
Wardenclyffe Foundation Archives

∞

On the road to Chicago, April 1893

"The Murderer of the World!" Esmeralda screamed and bolted upright in bed. She was tangled in her bedclothes and struggled to be free of them as she thrashed and babbled in her terror.

"Es! Es, calm down! Christ, you are shaking the whole wagon." Vladimir helped her get untangled and she bolted out of the bunk. He followed her, reaching for her in the dark. She wasn't hard to find: the space was small. He found her shaking between their bed and the pantry that served as both their kitchen and living space in the Gypsy van. Vladimir pulled her into his arms and stroked the back of her head.

"Come back to bed, it is but a fever-dream, that is all. It will pass. It is just a dream."

"He is coming!" she whimpered and buried her head in his shoulder.

"Who is coming?"

"The Murderer of the World. He's coming!"

"How can one man murder the whole world?" he reasoned. "Shush now. It was just a dream."

Esmeralda pulled back from him and found his moonlit eyes.

"No," she told him with a tremulous voice. "It was not a dream. It was a *Dream*." Her emphasis and meaning was clear.

"Then come back to bed and tell me," he said, gently tugging her back toward the bunk.

His wife pulled away from him, blindly running her hands across the kitchen shelf until she found the saltcellar, identifying it by touch. She threw off the lid, poured out a fistful of salt and began tossing it about the room, crying and praying all the while. Vladimir backed away and let her work. When she took another handful and flung it at their bed, her husband started to object, but he thought better of it. He could tolerate the grains of salt in the bedclothes if it would calm her. Tomorrow he would shake them out.

When his ears told him she was done, he managed to coax her back up the wooden step, over the carved sideboard and into the bunk. She had to hitch her nightgown up to her hips to climb in. Vladimir wished for more moonlight and thought how he might restore her spirits and relax her tension. With collateral benefits, of course.

Back in bed, he pulled her close and she lay with her head on his chest where she trembled like a captured rabbit.

"Tell me, my queen," he urged, while he stroked her hair.

Her dream was strange. There was a child whose mind was interfered with, yet it was not this *thing* inside his skull that frightened her, but the thoughts it gave.

"And what thoughts were those?" her husband asked.

"Unspeakable things," she whimpered, "Meant to come to pass in times to come, though many years hence from the present day. I have never seen the like before and to God's ear I pray, never again! If I saw such things with my own eyes I should pluck them out! Oh! I renounce my gift! Oh! May the saints take it back and remove these visions from my head!"

"No, not so," he whispered, "Do not speak so. One does not return a gift from God."

Esmeralda put her hands over her face, hiding in the darkness. Vladimir marveled. He had seen her cry and grieve with her whole heart. He'd seen her fly in and out of rages as easily and as often as she laughed. His wife was always quick with a barbed tongue or a bawdy jest, but she did not *despair.* Not before now. Vladimir tightened his arms around her because it was the only thing he could do.

He would not ask her again what things she saw. "How far ahead?" he asked instead.

"Ten scores of years, at least."

Vladimir relaxed. "Well then, see? You have nothing to fear!" He leaned in and kissed her on the head and pulled her hands away from her face so she could see his reassuring smiles. "Even our children's children will not live to know descendants in such times. There is strife and turmoil enough for us now. Let us tend to our own troubles. Let them tend to theirs."

She gripped his free hand to stop him from pulling back the strands of her hair that had stuck to the tears on her face. Her fingers were ice cold.

"You don't understand!" Her voice was nearly strangled with fear. "He's coming here!"

"Impossible," he flatly stated, but nevertheless, he felt the imperative to protect his wife stirring in his chest.

Esmeralda was not comforted. She gave way to great racking sobs. She was absolutely certain, then.

Vladmir nurtured his outrage against whomever it was that reduced his Es to such a state. *Who is this Murderer of the World that I might kill him*, he thought. To her, he just said, "Describe him to me."

She convulsed against his chest. "I do not know!" she wailed. "I quit the dream too soon. Stupid! So stupid! I've never been so afraid."

"Tell me what you can."

Esmeralda shook her head against him. "I saw a boy. I saw an old man. But I don't know which one of them it is."

"A boy or an old man murders the world? The whole world?"

Only her trembling answered him.

"Then we will watch for them both," he told her, and tried to keep his disbelief in check. He knew she was weary and her wits were stretched thin from the long trip. Once they reached the fair and made a permanent camp her constitution would be restored, especially when the money began to flow.

Three days more of steady traveling and their caravan would be at Jackson Park and they would grow fat again. There had been a drought of good fortune these past two years, and the harvest of coin was thin, but the place called the White City would draw coin like a great magnet. He didn't need Esmeralda's gift to see it. Those on the road with them strained under the weight of their purses and cast uneasy glances at the Gypsies as they passed. Vladimir knew many would come to Es before they were depleted. Glamoured by the wondrous sights of the World's Columbian Exposition and urgent to know more of their own personal fortunes, they would drop the last of their coins into Esmeralda's hand.

There would likely be old men climbing into their wagon, to show their palms to the Seer Queen, and some boys as well. If Es indicated one or the other was the phantom in her dream —man or boy —they'd not climb out again.

Vladimir stroked his wife's hair until her breathing came slow and even. He thought she was asleep, but she surprised him by speaking, her voice ringing out clear and wide-awake in the dark.

"He tears it in two. Right down the middle, like a house-maid rending old sheets into rags. Then he does it again and again. It keeps getting smaller and smaller until there is nothing left, and still he keeps on tearing. There is no end to the tearing, it goes on forever."

"Tears what?" he asked her.

"The world and everything in it."

He remained quiet.

"There is no end to it, do you not see?" she asked him. "Halving a thing forever, down and down, and always some tiny bit left to halve again."

Vladimir loved his wife. Loved her, and understood her to depths most men did not attribute to the fair sex, nor imagine they possessed. He knew she spoke a parable with the house-maid's sheet, and so he put his mind to the problem there, be-cause rending the world itself was not something he could imagine, nor could he comprehend any similarity between fab-ric and the world. But because she'd offered an analogy, he took it. In his imagination he felt the weight of linen in his hands, felt it resist his tug in opposite directions. He imagined how he must allow slack and then jerk his hands apart to start the tear. He heard the fibers snap and then let go, the sound ascending up the scale with a satisfying *rip* that sawed the air with its brief protest and he felt the corresponding buzz in his fingers. He saw the dust sparkle in the air before his eyes with tiny particles from the bursting threads.

As the actor in the theater of his mind, he discarded half the sheet with a flourish and took up the remainder and posi-tioned his hands like before. If the fabric was strong, he thought, he might feel the resistance down to his elbows as a slight ache. He tore again.

And again. And again.

He kept tearing until he held only the smallest scrap be-tween the thumb and forefinger of each hand, held it by his nails, because it was so small. He tore. Next, he had to put so much pressure into the bite of his nails his fingertips throbbed. His fingertips *were* throbbing, because his concentration was so vivid he was pressing his fingers tightly together as he lay in bed, next to his wife.

He tore again.

It was only in a fantasy that such a small piece should come apart, but he willed his imagination to comply. The next shred was so small he could only have torn it in his mind. He did. Again and again until only a single thread remained. He tore that too. He had to imagine what it was that made up a thread. Little fuzzy tendrils of flax or cotton, he thought, and he tore them as well, until only a single fiber of that remained, and that he tore also. As he continued, he felt the beginnings of fear because he could imagine nothing smaller than that single fiber. Then he thought again of the sheet, infinitesimally small, and his own tiny hands likewise growing smaller with each division they inflicted.

He felt helpless to stop. It bloomed into an obsession, this tearing. He wanted to throw it down, to leave it alone, but always, he could do it again. Halve it one more time.

And he knew this was only the briefest brush of the vaguest idea of what 'forever' meant and he was in its grip. The idea grew from the pit of his stomach into a great black incomprehensible *nothing* in his mind as he confronted the thought that could not be encompassed by merely thinking at it. It was like contemplating God or death or nothingness, but with none of their comforts. From this there was no end.

Vladimir flung it away from his mind to cling desperately to his wife in their bed, where they trembled together until dawn.

CHAPTER THREE

"You can find in a text whatever you bring, if you will stand between it and the mirror of your imagination."
—*Mark Twain*
  Wardenclyffe Foundation Archives

∞

Chicago, August 1893

In downtown Chicago, Sunner stood at the mirror in the milliners and adjusted the derby on his head. He turned his chin to the right to catch as much of his profile as he could, and then to his left. He admired the hat for the salesman, but his gaze settled on the reflection of his own eyes. Was he Sunner seeing Sergei there, or, was he Sergei catching a glimpse of Sunner? The segregation of their thoughts wavered and blurred around the edges, and Sunner carefully eased his focus away. Sergei did the same. Best let sleeping dogs lie.

When Sunner was in command of himself, there was little physical indication that Sergei was present inside him, and thankfully, the old man usually kept his opinions to himself. Today, he nearly felt normal, unique and singular, and for short periods he forgot. But forgetting was itself a trigger. It tipped him off, and made him remember again. Damned if you do, damned if you don't. If he could just *not think about it*, and *keep* not thinking about it. It was like trying too hard when learning to ride a bicycle. It worked better when you just got on with it.

As he considered his reflection, his eyebrow lifted and the corner of his mouth rose with it, but not of his own volition. Sunner yielded to being pleased with what he saw. No; He was more than that. He was positively giddy. His elder self didn't give a shit about the hat, it was his face that cranked up the happy.

"Not bad for an old coot." Sunner allowed.

Sergei had barely made it under the wire; He lived long enough that medical miracles arrested his age, but in his 80's it only promised eternal decrepitude. But now he was young again – If hitch-hiking himself at a younger age counted as that. For Sunner, the dimensional convergence with his elder-self was a headlong dive into his mid-thirties when he had been barely twenty. He was lucky. Had they met halfway in their cumulative years, he'd be pushing seventy now.

"And you'll be wanting a strolling hat as well. For the fair?" The milliner asked hopefully.

"Yes. Certainly." Sunner had no idea what a strolling hat was, but he was indeed going to the fair. He hadn't mentioned it, but he hardly needed to. Every out-of-towner in 1893 Chicago was on their way to the World's Columbian Exposition. He was no exception, even though he had come farther than most. He had come 111 years by Sunner's account, and 234 by Sergei's.

The strolling hat turned out to be a straw panama, with a neatly pressed navy blue band. He removed the derby and ducked his head so the salesman could adjust it for him. The hat stood out in bright contrast to his new dark suit. It was the kind of hat to complete the costume requirements of a barber-shop quartet. If he was asked to also purchase a white seer-sucker suit with red pinstripes, he was going to draw the line. Sunner checked in with Sergei, felt an inward shrug, and so asked the salesman, "Is it appropriate to wear this hat with this suit?"

"Only if you mean to impress the ladies!"

Sunner sighed in relief, reached up and canted the hat to a slight rakish angle. *There. Better.* He gestured to the derby laying on the table. "And that one I shall wear to the lectures at the Electrical College, yes?" Sunner looked at him apologetically, indicating clearly that he wasn't from around here. He needed very badly to know if he would fit in. If he would make a favorable impression on Nikola Tesla.

"I say, are you an electrician?"

"In a manner of speaking. Up from the country."

"Which country?"

Sunner cleared his throat, as though embarrassed.

The salesman patted him on the shoulder. "Never mind. Your accent is hardly noticeable at all. And yes! This hat will serve your purpose."

Sunner turned back to the mirror, relieved to have ducked the question. He'd been able to mimic the manner of speech in late 19th century Arkansas, as he had grown up hearing soft remnants of it on the voices of his neighbors. Chicago was something else again. The accent of the well-to-do sounded harsh and clipped to his ear, while the working class had an ethnic blend he couldn't quite work his mouth around.

He exchanged the panama with the derby again and ran his finger around the brim. His new jacket felt heavy in the summer heat, especially over the waistcoat and the starched long-sleeved shirt with the stiff collar buttoned in. He'd left the top buttons undone and his tie hung on a relaxed knot. He didn't dare loose the knot entirely. He left it so that he might reverse engineer it later; for in all his collective experience, neither he nor Sergei had ever learned to manage one.

Even in this slightly disheveled state, he thought he looked pretty good; Too old to be a student, but a young industrialist, perhaps. Or a prosperous engineer in the employ of one. He had to get his story straight.

"What do you think?" He seemed to be asking the question of his own reflection, but he wasn't. The answer came as a light double-tap against his shoe that sent a corresponding electric tingling up the nerves in his leg. He guessed that meant Lilly liked it.

"I'll take them both," he said and dug folded bills from his pocket. It was nearly the last of money Lilly had liberated from the booking agents at Kansas City's Union Station on their trip up on the train.

Both hats together were $5.50. Sunner counted out six dollars, hoped the tip was sufficient, and stuffed the rest back in his pocket. He didn't want Lilly to see how few bills were left. He didn't like her foraging for money. It seemed much too dangerous an occupation for one as frail as she was, invisible or no.

He was handed two hatboxes, each with a braided silk cord that served has a handle. They were large and awkward, and he gave the empty one back, since the derby was still on his head. He might have just clamped the panama under his arm, but the frown of the milliner forbade it.

As Sunner left the shop, he held the door open longer than it appeared necessary before stepping through. It was exactly as long as was needed for the three of them: Lilly, Sunner, and Sergei. And the damned hat-box, of course.

CHAPTER FÖUR

*"I am part of a light, and it is the music. The Light fills
my six senses: I see it, hear, feel, smell, touch and think... A
bolt of lightning can be an entire sonata. A thousand balls of
lightening is a concert."*
—*Nikola Tesla*
  Wardenclyffe Foundation Archives

∞

The Electrical College, August 1893

Lauder knew how to enter a place like he belonged there,
but there was no need to tap those skills today. This was familiar territory. Electricians. Physicists. Engineers. Industrial ti-
tans. Newspaper reporters. All men eager to throttle the nine-
teenth century to death to get it out of the way. It was not unlike re-entering Edison's workshop in those giddy days when
he and Mr. Brown believed they could change the shape of the
world. Lauder felt a pang of nostalgia. *Actual nostalgia.* He
had been in the past that long!

He strode easily into the lecture hall at the Electrical College and took a seat at the far end of the top row. The audito-
rium was a kind of amphitheater, with chairs on risers around a
lowered stage that abutted the back wall. On the stage was a
long table that held various apparatus covered over with a
white sheet that provided a degree of intrigue about the objects

it concealed. From his seat, Lauder could see both the stage and the faces of most of the audience. He let his gaze sweep the assembly but saw no geezers. His use of the word 'geezer' had relaxed over the years. A white head or a bald pate was no longer enough. Indeed, there were a handful of those scattered among the audience, but he dismissed them at a glance. The geezer he was looking for was ancient. There were none so old here today. Not too surprising, but a disappointment nonetheless. The elderly in this day and age were frail folk and must spend their time indoors, preparing to die. Or, so he imagined. Not so the Murderer of the World.

"I believe you are in my seat?"

Lauder glanced up in annoyance. "You are mistaken."

"See here? I have a ticket that says..."

"This is my seat." Lauder said flatly and turned his face away.

The man gazed at his ticket again and tentatively counted chairs from the aisle. He was apologetic, and even bowed slightly as he pressed the point. "I am sorry, but the ticket says otherwise."

Lauder's brows lowered to where he had to tip his head to see out from under them. His eyes glittered but his voice took on a mean and lazy nonchalance. "Check again, pard."

To his surprise, the ticket was thrust before his face. The lack of subtlety of this age was a constant trial. Lauder sighed as he took it, consulted it gravely, and then tore it up.

"I'll have you know I paid good money for that ticket!"

Lauder gathered himself, shifted forward and rose to his full height, yet he was clearly not giving up his seat. Looking down on the man now, he watched with satisfaction as the contester went pale and retreated a step. Lauder tapped his temple, commending the man for his wisdom, however lately arrived. He smiled, winked, and sat down again. The next time he looked up, he saw the man had prudently withdrawn.

A few rows down a similar exchange was being made. A shoulder was tapped. A head shook 'No,' but then cocked up in surprise. There was a reluctant conversation and bills were pressed into the seated man's hands. He considered what he held, but didn't move. More money was thrust into his lap, which he gathered up with a kind of hypnotic reluctance. Lauder watched with marginal interest to see when the man would break, watching for the shift when resolve would give way to the presented windfall. The man's shoulder's dropped when the tension if indecision fled. Lauder sniffed at this little drama, watching the man rise and clap the shoulder of the man who bribed his seat before he hunched his way to the exit. Nikola Tesla might be popular, but there was a recession going on, after all.

The Dean of the Electrical College was a rotund man wearing professorial robes. He made his way to the podium at the appointed time and delivered a long and trying introduction for the guest of honor. The audience gradually settled into polite attitudes of listening, although most eyes were on the closed door that led to the stage from the adjoining room. The dean at last came to his laborious conclusion to a mild clapping that cued the door to swing open. When the Serbian inventor emerged to take the stage the clapping turned into a thunderous applause. The hall rose to a standing ovation.

Lauder did not rise. Instead he hunched lower in his seat and rested his cheek in his hand, letting his hair fall forward to shadow the remainder of his face. Tesla walked gingerly to the podium in cork-soled shoes, and stood silently, waiting for the applause to die. When it did, he remained silent, gathering the quiet in attention to himself. In his platform shoes he was likely as tall as Lauder, and that was saying something. But where Lauder had the cultured DNA of an athlete, Tesla was a slender reed. His suit hung as limply from his shoulders as it would from a hanger. Nevertheless, his charged presence bespoke a self-confidence rooted in absolute certainty.

Tesla's eyes fixed on a focal point beyond the room. He didn't meet the eyes of any present, let alone Lauder's. It was as if he stood alone and was merely thinking. The hush in the hall stretched. In time, the volume of expectation became too costly and a few began to fidget. A wave of awkwardness passed across the audience. Men glanced at one another. A few heads turned to rustling fabric as shoulders were shrugged. A derisive sniff telegraphed across the room, was taken up and passed on. This was followed by an epidemic of throat clearing and murmured apologies. Still Tesla stood. He seemed taller than before. Imposing. Like the discomfiture in the room was energy he drew in and amplified. This was remarked upon in whispers that rose and fell like the wind.

When it was silent again, totally silent, Tesla drew in a deep breath, and the audience did likewise.

"The courses of nature are not beyond the intellect of man, should he apply himself to understand." Tesla announced. His accent was thick enough that men leaned forward and strained, although the Serbian pitched his voice to its limits.

"In connection with resonance effects, I would say a few words on a subject which constantly fills my thoughts, and which concerns the welfare of all. By that, I mean the transmission of intelligible signals, or, perhaps, even power, to *any* distance *without* the use of wires." He paused to let that sink in. "I am becoming more convinced of the practicability of the scheme; and though I know full well that the great majority of scientific men will not believe that such results can be practically and immediately realized..."

Lauder detested this kind of formal oration. The drawn-out inflections and over-enunciation made the words dither and hang, with pauses in between that stretched too long. Though it was a necessity to deliver the words to the back row in a large room without the benefit of a microphone. Lauder winced and shifted his gaze away from the stage, glad for once of the constant static from his offline goog. He let his attention drift to his node: let the white noise envelop him.

"...Though we have no positive evidence of a charged body existing in space without other oppositely electrified bodies being near, there is a fair probability that the earth is such a body, for by whatever process it was separated – and this is the accepted view of its origin – it must have retained a charge, as occurs in all processes of mechanical separation..."

Lauder wasn't interested in Tesla or what he had to say. Instead, he took another careful inventory of the room, registered each face one by one, working methodically but without much hope. With the last face catalogued, he came to the conclusion that today, as usual, Tesla had proven inadequate bait in his trap.

But, this day, he was wrong.

Three rows below him, in the seat he had bribed, Sunner was taking furious notes, while Sergei, the geezer cohabiting his skull, went unrecognized.

CHAPTER FIVE

"Necessity knows no law."
—Mark Twain
   Wardenclyffe Foundation Archives

∞

Chicago

Lilly stood with her back against the bricks in a narrow alley. Above her, laundry was strung in a cats-cradle that worked back and forth along pulleys at every window to four stories up. The hapless way they hung reminded her of prayer flags strung in art-student dormitories over hand-lettered signs of *'Free Tibet!'* in another time, another place.

There were several doors in the alley. Most with dilapidated stoops nearly obscured by trash bins and laundry. She'd been standing there for a about twenty minutes; long enough to work it out that the basement windows at street-level were actually coal chutes.

The door she faced had leaning wooden stairs, dished in the center from many footfalls. There was no landing at the top and a precarious awning leaned overhead. The awning was covered in tarpaper and looked like it might come loose from the wall the very next time the door was slammed. In contrast, the doorknob was unexpectedly ornate and next to it a braided red cord fed through a hole bored through the casement. Two men had exited so far. One had entered, obliged first to pull the cord three times, listen for the faint bell and wait for the lock to click. He had seemed anxious and fidgety, whereas the two who had exited looked sullen. Heads down, hats low. Hands in their pockets.

Lilly pegged the place as a gambling den or a whorehouse. Either way, there would be money inside; money to take without regret.

She started to come away from the wall but another figure stepped into the alley and she pressed back again, but not to be out of sight. She was most definitely *out of sight*. The accident in Sunner's lab left her out-of-phase and invisible to the naked eye; She pressed back to be *out of the way*. She hated the slippery-gut sensation of passing too close to someone. Even worse was the nerve-jangling circuit-jamming electric storm that would happen to both of them if they came in solid contact. This almost never happened, unless she made it happen. Most of the time she skulked at the edges and stood in corners, becoming an expert in traffic patterns and places people almost never moved into. She was beyond their narrow band of sensory perception, and the space she occupied had a kind of natural repulsion. Though she generated an uneasiness that people tended to avoid, places like this had unique challenges. Drunks, drug addicts and children were not reliable in this regard. She had to be extra careful in the city.

If Sunner knew where she was, he'd be furious; but Sunner was at the Electrical College to meet Tesla, and she knew his pockets were nearly empty. Her method of funding their odd little family was a mystery to him, and she liked it that way. She liked controlling one small aspect of their enterprise, and it was unnecessary to keep a straight face when he questioned her about the money. It is hard to interrogate someone who isn't really there. The only problem was, she felt bad about taking other people's money. She really did. She chose her marks carefully, trying to take it where its absence wouldn't be keenly felt. But money was money, and money or the lack of it changed things, and who could say what the consequences would be? The art of time travel was not unlike being a diver trying to cut the water with a minimum of splash.

She couldn't find the word 'paradox' in Granny Idee's bible that she and Sunner used as a codex to communicate with each other, but she eventually made her meaning clear, taking the long way 'round by using phrases that could be taken as metaphor. When Sunner's explanations failed to satisfy, Sergei within him came to the fore and rose to the challenge. Inevitably his responses were even more perplexing than Sunner's. He spoke of 'normalizing dime-streams' and 'multivariate possibility matrices' that could only be summed up in the end, as 'It really doesn't matter'. Except it mattered to her. She might be sailing an ocean of possibilities at any given moment, but she'd be damned if she'd let her passage leave a big wake. She lay awake at night wondering if money she took might have been used 'down the road' to buy medicine for, say, Mother Theresa's grandmother, who might have died without it.

"There *is* no 'down the road'!" Sergei insisted, but that didn't help much.

The figure entering the alley was a policeman. This gave her pause. She knew from painful experience she could be shot. Even a 'warning shot' fired no-where in particular might turn out to be exactly where she was standing. She decided to stand directly behind the policeman as he mounted the stairs to her doorway of interest.

He pulled the cord the requisite three times and the latch clicked. They barged in together, Lilly so close on his heels she felt queasy.

It was dark inside. A paraffin lamp illuminated a glass globe, but little else. Before it, a ledger was open and a woman sat poised, her pen lifted and ink beginning to bead on her nib. She regarded the policeman and tapped her pen in the inkbottle, discharging the black teardrop, and set the pen in the crease of her record book.

"It's not yet the mid o'the month," she complained.

In the gloom, unmistakable sounds drifted down a dark and narrow stairway, confirming for Lilly what she expected as soon as she entered the heavily perfumed dark: this *was* a whorehouse.

The policeman cocked his head and grinned. "Tithes is tithes no matter the day. You seem to be doing regular trade, even midday, such as it is."

Lilly's heart kicked up a notch. Money was about to change hands, and she meant to have some of it for herself. She moved around the table, looking for the money box, and saw what the policeman did not; A pistol lay across the lap of the woman.

"You know it isn't so," the madam said. "The fair bleeds the city like a wound, and when it is over we'll be dry. My girls aren't pulling half their weight, but have to eat regular nonetheless. No one wants a skinny bag o'bones, and we're all hungry here."

"Times are tough all around, Sal. Tithes aren't what they used to be, either. We're all feeling the pinch. Even me."

"I don't see you earning yours on your back."

He shrugged. "You're still open for business, aren't you?" His meaning was clear. "I earn my cut. Same as you. C'mon Sal, fork over your taxes and the roads stay paved to your front door."

A baby started to wail from somewhere upstairs. From the darkness of the parlor a man grumbled. "Christ, Sal, if that don't put me off. If I wanted to hear babies cry, I'd go home."

Lilly hadn't even seen the man sitting in a parlor chair in the corner, presumably waiting his turn.

The woman gripped the table and pulled herself to her feet. What Lilly had thought was a pistol turned out to be the head of a cane. The woman grasped it and hobbled to the foot of the stairs. "Give it a tit!" she yelled up into the darkness. "Or you'll be trading that mite for a loaf of bread!"

"Tell you what, Sal. Why don't you just wet my whistle, and I'll give you a couple more days."

"Do I look like I have money for liquor? Those that want a sip of courage stop off at the corner first. Men don't come here to drink."

"I wasn't asking for a drink."

Lilly now understood each were doing lines from a play they'd performed together many times. It was going to be a while before the till was opened, if at all.

She could wait around here, or...

Curiosity won out. She stole up the dark stairs, hoping not to meet anyone coming down. The stairs opened into a large room, strung with sheets to partition off individual beds. The windows were heavily curtained and the sheets flickered from candlelight. No doubt the business conducted here looked better in the half-dark of candlelight, even at mid-day. Maybe especially at midday.

There was nothing titillating here. She wanted to see, just to see. It was far cry from a teenaged fantasy of being invisible in the boy's locker room. The sounds behind one of the curtains reminded her of Donna's pig rooting in the mud, and she might have laughed except there was no humor here. She did not so much as peep through the gap in the sheet.

Lilly heard the baby and was led on by its persistent fussing. The next sheet hung slightly open. Inside a young woman shushed the baby at her breast, its basinet half pulled out from under her bed. The prostitute's head was bowed so that her hair hung in greasy strands over her face, but Lilly could tell; She was young. Horribly young.

I'm stealing from widows and orphans, she thought.

Disheartened and ashamed, Lilly fled back down the stairs. The policeman was folding money into his pocket. He got what he came for after all, and Lilly had missed her chance at the moneybox, but she'd not have taken it now if they had asked her to.

She changed her tactic and followed the policeman out into the mid-afternoon heat, and tailed him as he meandered his way block by block, checking in with every establishment, legitimate or not. Each time, Lilly stayed outside and waited. It was farther than she planned to go today, and her head swam and her legs trembled with fatigue. What limited nutrition she got from goat's milk was strictly budgeted and she was deep into the red now, to say nothing of her thirst. She had a canteen at her hip; never went anywhere without it. Uncapping it, she sniffed and wrinkled her nose. The milk was diluted with as much water as she could stand, but still it had gone off in the heat. She sipped it anyway and shuddered, panting to exchange the sourness in her mouth with as much fresh air as possible.

Another block, and there was the police station. The cop she was following did not stop except to lean in, exchange a few words and then continue on down the block. But he had led her to her destination. The entire station was a narrow room on a ground floor of a small stone building. It was manned by a skeleton crew of two. Although she was glad to see the pair of policemen were subdued and lethargic in the heat, Lilly left her illusions at the whorehouse; These were not keystone cops and they were unencumbered by the protocols of her own century. Aroused to her haunting, they could do anything, and they were armed.

Lilly had eased through the open doorway with a pounding heart and stood against the wall behind one of the men who was leaning back in his chair, balancing on its two back legs. She thought he dozed but just as she took her position to watch and get the layout of the room, he lurched forward. But instead of bolting from his chair and reaching for his gun, he bent over and aimed a stream of brown saliva at a spittoon, which was as nasty and encrusted as a brimming chamber pot. Satisfied, he sighed deeply, rearranged himself on the chair and leaned back again. Lilly endured a fit of trembling, as though it had been an actual close call. Shaking made her head swim. She was running on fumes, here. Weak and uncertain, she hoped this would be her last caper for a while. By slow degrees she reclaimed her nerve and at last ventured to explore the room.

The second cop sat scribbling on a disarray of paper at a table. There was a large lockbox underneath the table, bolted to the floor with a hammered iron strap. It was, for all practical purposes, a safe. Lilly pinned her hopes on it. She imagined it bulged with the tithes of whores and the paid indulgences of tourists and other miscreants. It was locked with a mean looking padlock. She checked for a corresponding key ring. She even checked for a hook on the wall near the jail cell, in case it was hanging just outside reach, Hollywood-style. The cell was little more than a cage, only large enough for a standing man and unoccupied. Its door was ajar and its keyhole was empty. But it did give her an idea. Might they keep the keys to the cell and the safe together? She eased over to the cell and swung the door wide with a bang.

This brought a harrumph of surprise from the dozing policeman and he instinctively reached to his breast pocket in a 'touch wood' gesture. *There,* she thought. *The keys are in his pocket.*

Lilly maneuvered around behind him as he settled back. She took a deep steadying breath and laid her hand his shoulder, meaning to do more than just unbalance him on the back legs of his chair. He startled, flailing arms and legs to counterbalance but to no effect. With a yip and a crash he toppled over. His partner bellowed out a hearty laugh, but cut short when the sprawling man convulsed and appeared to be choking on his chaw of tobacco. The man at the desk bounded up, leaving his paperwork and his position by the safe. He hauled the sputtering and coughing man to his feet and began whacking him on the back.

Staggering and disoriented, the choking man cursed and shrugged away from the blows he was receiving, waving helplessly, trying to show he was okay. Undaunted, his partner kept chuffing away at his back.

In the confusion, it was easy for Lilly to lift the keys and make quick work of the safe.

She carried out three fat stacks of bills, but had only one of them left by the time she got home; the two other stacks were carefully packed into an infant's bassinet under a bed in a whorehouse.

The leftovers would have to be enough.

Back on the street, Lilly stumbled along at the shoulder, where people usually weren't. She figured she was at least two miles from Mary Murphy's white clapboard house. The sun was sliding to the west and she wanted to beat Sunner home, but more than that, she wanted to *make* it home. Her grinding weariness was such that she was forced to consider it could go either way. She thought of Granny Idee, who might or might not notice she was gone. Sunner most definitely would, because he wouldn't rest until he had some indication from her that she was present and accounted for. Mary, on the other hand, didn't know she existed. Mary was a middle-aged spinster who was easily convinced to accept them as borders when she was fanned from her swoon with a handful of 20-dollar bills. Part of the bargain was use of her kitchen where they quickly resumed their production of goat-milk yogurt and kefir and fresh potted cheese, the only food Lilly could stomach thanks to Pi, her trans-dimensional milk goat.

Mary was old-school. She still had a stable in the back, which garaged her buggy and the horse that sometimes pulled it. The elderly mare was indifferent to sharing her stall with a pampered goat, time traveler or not. She and her mistress were well-matched and made little demands on each other. With the goat came extra rations, and sometimes even carrots. The horse did not complain. It mostly dozed. Pi settled in like she'd always lived there.

It was a great relief when the house came into view. Someday this might be one of those over-shaded Victorian neighborhoods wealthy Chicagoans lovingly restored. Right now it was raw and stark without a tree in sight. Lilly was glad to be back.

She slipped in with no trouble. Idee and Mary sat in the back-yard under the shade of the eves, heads bent together over a basket of pea-pods and a bowl of peas, pausing now and then to sip sweating glasses of lemon water. In spite of the heat and the lowly occupation of shelling peas, Idee wore her new dress, buttoned up to her chin. Her feet were likewise buttoned down in new pointed shoes with impractical one-inch heels. The old woman peered at the work in her lap through her brand-new spectacles with the natural aplomb of a hillbilly granny with her huge reserve of 'make do'.

Lilly tiptoed past them into the kitchen, unslung her canteen and regarded it with regret. She could not afford to waste one drop of Pi's milk. Every calorie was a precious and irreplaceable unit of time. She located the jar of fresh milk in the icebox, and set it down in front of her at the ready.

Take your medicine. She told herself. She closed her eyes, brought the neck of the canteen to her lips and gulped down every foul drop without stopping to take a breath. She gagged, shuddered, set down the canteen and grabbed the fresh milk and allowed herself three sweet swallows before she sat it down too, panting. The rest was carefully replaced in the ice-box for later. She left the canteen in the dishpan. Mary would wash it later without complaint. It's what they paid her for, and liberally, but as Lilly staggered up the stairs to lay down and wait for Sunner's return, she knew he had no idea how hard money was to come by, even for her.

CHAPTER SIX

"All the circumstances that happened to lie in the snow-ball's path would help to build it, in spite of themselves."
—Mark Twain
Wardenclyffe Foundation Archives

∞

Chicago

Sunner warned Lilly that Tesla's fame came from bathing himself in lightning, as he had once shown her from the book, *Tesla. Man out of Time*[1]. Lightning still terrified her, and for good reason. For her present circumstance, yeah, but also for the death of her first husband. The time fugues she once suffered when it struck nearby might only have been panic attacks. Or they might have been an indication of her natural talent for time travel – or a natural talent for screwing it up, given how she hadn't quite made it to the present dimension. It was the peculiar circumstance of her make-up; Lilly attracted lightning the way some people drained batteries or spooked horses.

So she did not attend Tesla's lecture, which was good, because she wasn't there to witness when Sunner blew their chances.

As for lightning, Tesla disappointed his audience. He did not produce dramatic cascades of arcing electricity. His main demonstration was turning on his brilliantly luminous carbon button lamp. With no more fanfare than the twitch of his mustache, it simply *came on*. But because Tesla ignited it without wires of any kind, it commanded a standing ovation. Afterward, he lectured on resonances and the behaviors of ether inside the lamp. Not ether the gas, but as a substance that was thought to make up the space between the known elements. Sunner chaffed at this until Sergei presented him with the knowledge that his own house would someday be powered by an etheric kite. Sunner shut up.

When the talk was over, Sunner leapt to his feet and pressed through the crowd, eager to introduce himself.

"Mr. Tesla! If you please?" His voice was lost among the many clamoring for attention. Sunner waved his sheet of notepaper over his head, but it was only one of a snowstorm of waving papers. Tesla retreated from the crowd.

Sunner wormed his way after him, and finally cornered him in the backstage hallway.

"Mr. Tesla, I want you to take a look at something: The resonating properties you describe… when applied to a body, a *human* body, might the cumulative effects…"

Tesla's eyes flicked to the diagram and equations Sunner had just jotted down, and his brow furrowed. He read them more slowly and he blanched.

"Sir, you detain me," Tesla said.

"I beg your pardon, but this is a matter of life and death!"

"Indeed it would be. You will not entrain me into plans for an improved execution chamber, do you hear? Tell Mr. Edison or Mr. Brown or whomever you work for, death is not to be *improved*. It is quite sufficient when left to its natural courses. Good day, sir."

"No, you don't understand, this has nothing to do…"

But Tesla preferred to suffer the press of the crowd than to suffer fools. He plowed through the advancing crush of students, reporters and hopeful scientists. Holding his hands above his head, he cut his path with the sharp angles of his body, leaving Sunner cursing himself for his stupidity. Sergei agreed.

A matter of life and death? Jesus Christ! What were you thinking?

Sunner arrived late back at Mary's house. He entered his softly occupied room. His anger and dismay still raw. "Plan B." was all he said to Lilly, and jammed his head onto his pillow after punching it twice.

As yet, there was no Plan B.

The next day, Sunner went to the World's Columbian Exposition by himself.

Time was stretching thin. The fair opened in May. It was then mid-August and it would close in October. They had no way of knowing if Tesla planned to stay to the end of the fair. Westinghouse hadn't. Edison was gone to Maryland to oversee his movie studio and was busy filming his hammering horseshoes and sneezing for the camera. The War of the Currents was over for him. Edison's new passion was sealed when he witnessed fairgoers eagerly paying 25 cents to peer into his kinetoscope for 15 seconds of moving pictures.

Sunner knew that Tesla and Westinghouse were about to be awarded the project to install their generators at Niagara Falls. He couldn't remember when exactly, but the papers predicted soon. Lord Kelvin was asked to preside over the award and would kick the coveted project over to Tesla. But when? The moment that happened, he was sure Tesla would be gone. Where to, he didn't know. But Tesla was here now and they needed to rally with another plan to get his attention.

So, Sunner went to the fair alone to see what they were up against. Quite a lot, it turned out. When he saw the immensity of the fair, his knees went weak. The World's Columbian Exposition wasn't merely a fair: It was a *city*. He had pictured it as a kind of State fair, but the difference was like comparing Chuck-e-Cheese to Disney World.

He stood aghast at the massive buildings that stretched beyond the boundaries of his imagination.

"We're in Rome," he said to himself. His self agreed, and added for good measure, *Dinotopia*.

When he returned to tell Lilly and Idee of its stunning scale, Idee sat and said nothing. Lilly was so still he had to ask her if she were there. Her answer came after a long pause; banged out, tense and angry. He didn't understand why.

Idee just drawled out a resigned *"Well..."* And made a great show of lurching painfully and slowly out of her chair. "I done sit too long." She complained. "It stoves a body up, all that sittin'. Ain't used to *not doin'*. Too much biding is bad for the constitution." She looked pointedly at Sunner. When he had nothing to say she sucked loudly at her teeth and said *"Well,"* again and shuffled slowly to her room at the end of the hall.

Granny Idee's disposition hadn't improved overnight. She glared at Sunner across the breakfast table the next morning, where she sat dressed in her new frock, bustle and all.

"My, my, Mrs. McIntyre, aren't you a picture?" Mary Murphy gushed, as she carried in their breakfast. Her voice was dripping syrup, but her gaze was narrowed at Sunner. "Doesn't your Nana look lovely today?" she prompted.

Sunner shot her a look.

"Seems a pity to be all dressed up with nowhere to go," Mary sighed. "If I had such a fine dress as that, I'd want to show it to the world. Why, I'd head to the largest crowd of people I could find and just parade up and down to be admired."

Sunner knew an ambush when he saw one. He opted not to answer and became exceedingly interested in buttering his toast.

Idee didn't let him off the hook so easily. "I reckon you'uns a-goin' back to that fair again?"

Sunner lay his knife down carefully on the edge of his plate. "Now Idee..." he began, "You know how it is."

The old woman was perched on the edge of her chair, ramrod straight in her corset. When she saw no invitation was forthcoming, she leaned toward him and seemed as dangerous as a tree about to fall.

"We's a goin' with ye, and that's all they is to it."

Sunner splayed his fingers out to her, expressing his help-lessness, but Sergei rose up behind his eyes to give a stern reply.

"*Ida Mae,*" he said her name very quietly, making it clear by whose authority he spoke. "It is out of the question. I need you here to watch the goat."

Idee recognized the speaker and fell silent.

Mary Murphy tut-tutted at him on behalf of the older woman. "Where are your manners, laddie? You can't have dragged Mrs. McIntyre all this way to be a goatherd, surely?"

Sergei ignored Mary. "You know what's at stake," he reminded Idee. The gravity in his voice stoppered Idee's reply, but the steam of her ire continued to build. Her lips went white as she pressed them into a thin line to hold it in. Sunner and Sergei braced for what was coming, but it came from the other end of the table.

Mary smacked her palm on the table so hard the china rattled. "Jesus, Mary and Joseph!" she cried, and then quickly crossed herself in apology. "'Tis a goat, is all. I raised eight children and lost nary a one. I believe I can keep an eye on your beastie one single day so you can take your Nana to the fair."

Sunner felt a solid kick to one of the legs of the chair he sat on. Lilly was making her point and it was a clear vote for women.

"*No,*" he answered Lilly.

"Disgraceful!" Mary spat, thinking his answer was directed at her. "A goat over your own dear Nan."

Sergei gave way to Sunner's sigh. "Please, Mrs. Murphy. It isn't like that."

"Just tell me how it is, then?" Mary fumed.

"Yes, Mr. Tillman, do tell." Granny Idee leaned back and crossed her arms. She tilted her head to see him better over the rim of her new spectacles.

Lilly nudged his chair again. It wasn't a gentle nudge.

Sunner shifted in his seat, looking aside with what the other two women might see as distracted annoyance, but was a clear rebuke to Lilly. He knew what her kick meant. She'd made it clear that morning. She'd placed Idee's family bible on a chair in front of the bedroom door. It was open to the book of Ruth and his ticket stub from the World's Columbian Exposition was used to underline the passage that read *Whetherffoever thou goeth, I ffhall go.*

With it was a stack of paper money squared neatly and tied with a string, proving how capable she was.

His first response at seeing the money was anger. *Was she insane? How could she go out alone? What if something had happened?*

"There's way too many people," he said. "The crowds are ridiculous. It's far too risky. And seriously, how in the hell do you think you are going to get in with a goat?"

Idee scowled. "I reckon we made it this far."

"By *necessity*. But Idee, come on, we're so close now..." He was pleading for reason. But what about their situation was reasonable? "I have *one job*. I've got to get Tesla to help us. Whatever it takes. How am I going to do that towing a goat and a...and a..."

"And a what, exactly? And a what?"

Sunner's expression rippled. Sergei tried to temper his young self, struggling for discretion.

"*Pearls*," he burst, pointing with exasperation at Granny Idee.

"I beg your pardon!" Mary Murphy gasped. "At my table!"

"No..." Sunner raked back his hair in frustration. "Idee's pearl buttons..."

While Mary blushed, Idee looked at the long buttoned cuffs on her left arm, while her right hand touched the pearl buttons fastened in silk cloverleaf eyelets running from her waist to her neck. The trim used one small pearl button each half inch. It was the finest dress Idee had ever seen and she indulged in the guilty pleasure because for once in her life, money was no object.

"I knowed it. It's too 'stravagant," she said with remorse.

"No, Idee, no. It's not that. It's just the pearls, you see: Tesla has a thing about pearls. Let me tell you, the man has issues – *phobias* – and I don't know what might set him off. But I do know this: You come at him wearing pearls and you'll kill the whole deal."

"What's phobias?"

"He gets the jibber-jabbers."

Granny Idee nodded slowly. "I kin get another frock."

"She can wear one of mine!" Mary declared.

"But *the goat*, Idee. You can't drag that goat along. What would he think?"

"Like I cain't do on my own!" Idee burst. "I been doin' on my own many a year jus fine. Mayhap not so many as you'uns with all that back-and-forth, but I gots my own self through all on my lonesome and for a long time afore you'uns showed up. Go tend to Mr. Tesla and put on all the airs ye like, but me and Lilly, we's a goin' to the fair and that's all they' is to it."

"You are not taking Lilly to the fair," he said.

Sunner's cup jolted. Tea splashed over the rim. He barely managed to grab the teacup and rebalance it in its saucer. Placing a protective hand over it, he cleared his throat. Intentionally or not, it sounded like a growl.

"You've no need to take the blamed goat!" Mary wailed. "I can look after it. I'll bring it into me own kitchen if that'll be satisfying you!"

"I'm sure you could take fine care of her, Mrs. Murphy, but we won't leave her. Not ever."

"Lord have mercy!" Mary slumped back into her chair, thoroughly disgusted.

Idee stood, uncorking her outrage. "You know what they is callin' it? *The Eighth Wonder of the World*, that's what. And I'm a-here to tell you, I already missed out on the other seven so I ain't missin' this'un. The Eighth Wonder is too big and too near to pass over on account of *what ifs* and *better nots*. You'uns is so used to lookin' ahead, or lookin' back, you is missin' what's right here, right now. Open up and see the sight afore your eyes, Mr. Tillman. Front ways or back ways, we gots today to live and no other, and I don't mean to spend another one of mine porch sittin' when the fair is just outside the door. No offense, Mrs. Murphy."

"None taken," their landlady said.

"I'm a-here to tell you: Unlike *some people*, I ain't gettin' no younger, and Lilly... well, Lilly ain't no invalid and you gots no call to keep her shut up like one."

Under the table, Idee's dog Spitfire barked encouragement on general principle of joining any commotion his mistress got herself into.

Sunner looked askance at the dog. "Lilly has to stay with the goat, Idee. You know that. It's just too risky."

"Who's Lilly?" Mary wanted to know.

Idee stomped her foot. "They's a comin' with me, and that's the last word! Lilly and the goat together!"

Sergei shoved Sunner to his feet to confront her. "Idee, I forbid it!"

Idee's jaw dropped and Mary looked wide-eyed between the two of them.

"You ain't my Magnus," Idee whispered in a rage so complete it stole her voice.

"Of course not." Sunner stammered, taking back the reins of his self-control.

"Only my Magnus has the rights to say such-and-so to me an' you ain't him. I'm a goin', Mr. Tillman, and 'lessin you locks me in and ties me up, I'm a goin' *right now*."

Idee pulled back just a hair to watch his expression falter from the internal struggle between Sunner and Sergei.

She looked satisfied. "You with me, Lilly?" she asked. The table banged twice, and Mary hiccoughed in surprise.

"Here now, Mr. Tillman! If you chip my china, it is coming out of your rent."

"Well that's that." Idee summed the conversation in her favor and sat back down, passing a pinch of sausage to Spitfire, who took it and licked her fingers clean.

Sunner felt only the slightest twinge of regret as he slipped from the house without Idee, and presumably, also without Lilly.

He walked a ways down the street, then stopped, listened, walked again, ears straining. Once he said, "Lilly, if you are following me, so help me the first thing I'm going to do when you pull through..." But he didn't finish. He had the distinct and foolish sensation that this time, he was just talking to himself. He wasn't sure how he could tell the difference, but he could.

He had a second full day at the fair. Mostly, he hung out in the Hall of Electricity, keeping an eye out for Tesla. He loitered near Tesla's exhibit which was a roped off section of floor directly across from the massive Westinghouse generator that bore his name. Sunner had to restrain himself from wondering about like a kid in a candy store, like a geek at a steampunk convention. Tweaked to the max, he held firm, but he never quite managed to wipe the grin off his face. It was an expression shared by just about everybody there.

Tesla made his appearance around mid-morning and Sunner sobered. He was suddenly very worried about all the ways he might blow his second chance. He decided just to watch Tesla for a while, making a study of him all the long day and into the evening. When Tesla finally left his stall, Sunner followed, feeling like a stalker, but wanting to know where the great man hung his hat at night, thinking he might orchestrate an accidental meeting over dinner. Under his breath he practiced saying, "Say, if it isn't Mr. Tesla! Fancy running into you!"

From somewhere inside his skull, Sergei groaned.

Keeping as close as he dared, he followed Tesla out of the main entrance. It was later than he thought. It turned out to be a languid summer evening, only slightly cooler outside and he was glad for the fresh air. As he followed Tesla to the broad promenade, exterior lights were just coming on. They came on in a cascade, one building after another bolting out of the dark. It was indeed the Eighth Wonder of the World. As it registered what he was seeing, Sunner shambled to a halt and stood transfixed, completely forgetting his errand as the White City blazed with glory. This is what ancient Rome might have looked like, had it been strung with a million lights. The incandescent bulbs gave the buildings a slight yellow cast that glowed in supreme optical contrast with the deep violet sky. This was the first time, the *very first*, that so many lights burned together at once, and for no purpose except for the beauty it afforded. The thoroughly illuminated White City was reflected in the grand lagoon and as if that weren't enough, fireworks leapt up from the peristyle and streaked across the sky. When Sunner snapped out of it, he realized Tesla had slipped away.

But the consolation prize was *this*. Idee was right. 'Open up and see whats afore your eyes. We gots today and no other.' He owed her an apology, because she was right, and because; *damn*, it was beautiful, and he didn't mind taking the time out to appreciate it. He wished Lilly was there.

When Sunner returned home late that night, Mary Murphy met him at the door, her expression making it clear something was wrong. She wrung her hands and wailed in remorse, her accent becoming more Irish, the more distraught she became. Sunner gripped both her shoulders and fought the urge to shake her until she finally made him understand Idee and the goat were gone; as if the entire episode at breakfast never happened. As if she hadn't taken their side. As if she hadn't walked two doors down to her neighbor who owned the buckboard to pay him with one of the $20 bills Idee pressed into her hand that he might take them to the fair.

Sunner sprinted upstairs at the news, calling Lilly's name and groping through their rooms like a blind man.

He was furious. He was frantic. But there was nothing he could do but wait and swear. He paced the night through, Sergei cursing Sunner, and Sunner cursing him back. Adrenalin was like heroin in his veins, and it clawed at his heart and made him shudder like an addict, but none of that brought them home. Not that night, nor by daybreak.

What the fuck? Idee must have collapsed. Died. Was arrested. Got lost, went back to Arkansas... or worse. It wouldn't be the first time someone disappeared at the fair. The papers were full of stories like that.

A Western Union man arrived before breakfast with a telegraph. Taking it in his shaking hands, Sunner read it with disbelief. It was from Idee, inviting him to join them, not at the fair, but behind it, at a Gypsy wagon under the banner of the Red Hand.

CHAPTER SEVEN

∞

The Gypsy Camp

Not knowing why Lilly and Idee failed to returned from the fair had cost him. Sunner's usual penchant for obsession had sometimes bordered on paranoia back when he was a young man in the twentieth century working on his secret project in the barn. This was worse. This was a full-bore bender on the fermented anxiety Sergei distilled for a lifetime. So when he finally located the Gypsy camp and spotted Idee sitting by a campfire, nursing a mug of coffee, he didn't know whether to hug her or strangle her. He considered trying both at the same time.

Idee sat on a big brocade pillow atop a cut stump that was pulled close to the fire to help her ward off the morning chill. A wool blanket was draped over her shoulders and her white hair was in disarray in the universal attitude of someone who had spent the night out camping. She spied Sunner and lit up with a radiant smile.

"There you'uns are, you rascals!" Idee called.

Vladimir the Gypsy was stooped over the fire. He looked up, dropped his fire-poking stick and closed the distance between himself and Sunner with a few expansive strides. He greeted Sunner with a slap on the back and pulled him into a crushing hug like they were lifelong friends; The kind of friends money can't buy, except it had. An entire pillowcase full of money, in fact, taken directly from the Columbian Expo's main box office.

When Sunner extracted himself from the hug and from being kissed on both cheeks, Vladimir was even richer from the contents of Sunner's pockets.

"Welcome, Mr. Tillman! Or should I say, "Sergei the Amazing?"

Before Sunner could respond to this, the Gypsy wagon opened and a barefoot beauty floated down the steps in a cloud of layered skirts and shawls.

She beamed at Sunner. "You must be our new Sergei the Amazing!" she echoed.

"Sergei the Amazing?"

"The identity your Grandma-ma has just paid so well for," she said.

"I beg your pardon? My name *is* Sergei."

"Of course it is!" Esmeralda laughed, and kissed him on both cheeks like Vladimir had, and then after a brief appraisal, kissed him hard on the mouth for good measure. It was the kind of kiss that caused him to abandon hope and seek out Vladimir with his eyes to beg his pardon, while holding his fingers splayed and empty behind Esmeralda's back to clearly demonstrate to all they were minding their own business, and still the kiss went on. Up close he could see the lines of middle age around Esmeralda's dark eyes, and he was even more disconcerted to see her eyes were open and shrewdly taking his measure.

When she broke off, she said, "You are older than you look."

"Is that so?" was the best he could manage. He did not voice the same observation about her.

"Let me have a look at your hands," she wheedled and her fingers traveled down his shoulders and were at his wrists and tugging them gently toward her before he regained his composure. He stepped back quickly and shoved his hands in his pockets.

"Another time, perhaps," he said evasively. He remembered his prerogative to check in with Vladimir, who was in no way showing any offense, but seemed, like his wife, to be sizing him up with friendly interest. Sunner cast his eyes about the yard, clearly wanting to check in with Lilly as well, and offered a hapless smile directed nowhere in particular.

"Another time, certainly; I have foreseen it!" Esmeralda smiled up at Sunner, and stepped back to readjust her shawls. "Lilly has told me a little about you at least," she said.

His astonishment at being kissed after the assignment of his name took on the weight of this new revelation, and he dropped it helplessly at her feet along with all pretenses.

"How...?" he stammered.

"My wife, Esmeralda, descendent of the Seer Queen!" Vladimir interjected with panache and a deep bow.

Esmeralda added a curtsey and said, "At your service."

"That thar Gypsy gal kin see our Lilly, an talk to her an all!" Idee told him. "Ain't that a pickle?"

"A pickle," Sunner repeated, looking at Esmeralda who was laughing, like she was sharing a joke among girlfriends, and maybe she was. Or maybe she wasn't. He wasn't convinced.

Sunner asked, "You can see Lilly *now?*"

"Of course I can." She smiled at him.

"Can you describe her?" he tested.

"She stands with her hands on her hips and is provoked and she says: '*We finally find someone who believes us and you're being a prick.*' And as for her appearance, she's a wormy looking girl: wears her hair loose like a child and dresses like a Moroccan hookah dancer, bare legs and all. It is good you cannot see her." She glanced at Vladimir. "*Most unseemly.*"

"Wormy?" Sunner asked.

Vladimir burst out with booming laughter.

"But, where is Pi?" Sunner asked Idee. She cocked her head toward the wagon. Underneath, the goat was tethered along with the dog, Spitfire. The animal housekeeping was all set up. They burrowed together in a nest of hay, purchased from the Wild West Show, he was told.

Sunner took all this in with a dumbfounded expression that didn't often cross his features.

The Gypsies led him to the fire, pressed a mug of coffee into his hands and brought him up to speed while Idee smiled smugly and nodded at the parts that involved her. They explained how Sunner and company were already outfitted with a wagon, a tent, and a plum position 'on the wall', having bought out a magician with part of the pillowcase full of bills. It was their scheme that Sunner should take his place.

"A magician," Sunner marveled. "*Huh.*"

With Vladimir's help, Idee had literally bought the shirt off the magician's back, the one with its hidden pockets and false seams. They also procured his top hat and tails, and the flamboyant silk cape, along with some rudimentary tools and props. Vladimir and the original magician split the profits, and they parted happy and wealthier men. Furthermore, Vladimir was now their new business manager.

The magician's stage also had a large painted sign. It read, *Sergei the Amazing.*

"But my name *is* Sergei," Sunner sputtered again and his elder's voice came echoing from the distant corridors of his mind: *Which came first, the chicken or the egg?*

Sunner swallowed hard and tested the edges of a mild hysteria as he considered the origins of his unlikely first name. His parents named him after Sergei, but Sergei was himself. Where had the unlikely name first come from? It couldn't be *this*. This didn't happen until *now*. So why did it feel so connected? What accounted for that creepy sensation in his gut?

"My name *is* Sergei," he repeated stupidly. He was taking this pretty well, all things considered, though he was glad he was sitting down.

When Vladimir dropped the top hat on his head and gave it a firm tilt, it was a perfect fit.

Of course it was.

CHAPTER EIGHT

"The White City was and is a spectacle more grand than any before it, populated with as great and diverse a collection of mankind as had ever been peacefully gathered in one place, or — if you'll forgive the misnomer — one time."
—The Artist
A retrospective of 4D works from the Wardenclyffe Foundation

∞

The World's Columbian Exposition, September 1893

In the cavernous Electricity Exhibition Hall, Nikola Tesla stood with arms folded, observing the shuffling herd of humanity from the far corner of his stall. A woman pulled along in the wake of her husband's cigar smoke captured his attention. She drifted to a halt and stood gaping beneath the sign that read *Electric Kitchen of Tomorrow.* The tiny light bulbs that formed the words blazed forth like the annunciation and in its glow she practically swooned.

Tesla watched as her husband indulged her; watched him wait as his wife reached out to stroke and covet the electric toaster, the electric fan, and the electric oven. When they moved on, the man's back was a little straighter; he walked with a little more self-importance.

Tesla saw how women plucked at the exhibits with their fingers and devoured them with their eyes. He imagined them committing the fair to memory, that they might examine its many wonders later in the solitude of their domestic industry. With hands busy and minds adrift, they'd relive the fair in daydreams and yearn for a better tomorrow.

Tesla saw how men strode these halls like conquerors, paying and receiving homage to man's triumph over nature. Each exhibit was a validation of what they suspected all along: Nature in service to man! Man in service to God! Their gazes slid over the cunning devices laid end-to-end on Tesla's table and they nodded: *Quite so. Quite so.*

Yet, like moths in summer, they were drawn past Tesla's tables toward the light of the gaudy tower of bulbs that pulsed to music and held aloft the name of Edison. From there they followed the pounding drum of machinery from deep within the bowels of the building, as though being called to a tribal gathering of bully investors. The mechanical monstrosities thrummed the floor beneath one's feet, and quickened the beats of one's heart, while working loose the very screws that held them together.

An earnest young man fresh from one of the new Electrical Colleges interrupted Tesla's revere and stepped forward to present himself. He had to press against the velvet rope to capture the inventor's attention. Another acolyte of the *Guild of the Flaming Sword,* Tesla knew, and prepared himself to indulge the youngster up until the point he uttered the epithet *Wizard of Lightening*, for that he could not abide. The young man held aloft his calling card. Tesla sighed, indicating the brass tray into which he could leave his card with the others. The young man did so, practically genuflecting as he laid it down with both hands like an offering. Tesla obliged him with his deep Eastern European bow, but would not shake his hand.

Tesla was indulgent only up to a certain point. He let the student fawn over his devices, as long as he touched nothing. Tesla tensed when the young man leaned as far as he could over the banister and tested the space that kept the elegant inventions safe beyond stretched fingertips. Tesla decided this one would not be granted an audience behind the railing, though he could show a thing or two, and thus suffered, he might depart the quicker. He might hurry away flustered, or float away in a hypnotic daze, as few could linger long under the burden of such astonishments. But this morning Tesla could not summon the energy to give the admirer more than a curt nod, after which he pointedly looked away. The message was received. When next Tesla looked, the student was gone.

Tesla repositioned himself by the neon light which he had blown and shaped with tremendous care onto the name of Zmaj: A love letter in a single glowing word to his homeland and its beloved Serbian poet. It was a courtly offering to gentler old-world muses in opposition of those muscular American gods in whose service he now labored. Passersby that realized the glowing rod contained a word would whisper it with puzzled pronunciations and glance uneasily at the dark man who brooded beneath it. Next to Zmaj, another neon light comforted onlookers by merely saying "Welcome Electricians".

A small boy caught his eye and Nikola stepped forward and bent down. With a conspiratorial twitch of his mustache and a little bounce of his brows, he threw the switch to the Egg of Columbus. The copper goose egg that lay serenely in its metal bowl came alive and Tesla was delighted when the boy shrieked with amazement and then fell silent.

The egg began to vibrate, amplified by the bowl until it reached a kind of breaking point; whereupon it bounced, rolled over and began pivoting around its smaller end. It rolled at first as one might expect, and then end over end, faster and faster until all gentleness was shaken off and it danced so wildly it hurled from one side of the bowl to the other, just short of flinging from the edge. Finally it stabilized and went smoothly in its course. Spinning like a top, it hovered on its point, a whirling dervish, soundless but for the *shush* of polished metal. It should have been unheard against the uproar of the building, but by a magical grace all other distractions fell away and it was just Nikola and the child beholding the gravity-defying egg in the wondrous company of one another.

The boy's mother broke the spell: *This was the Devil's business*, her features plainly said. Tesla could read it in her eyes as she jerked her son away. The boy's protests were lost in the din that welled up and he was lost in the crowd like someone drowns in a river.

Nikola Tesla sighed and withdrew from the rail. Standing again to his full height, he folded his arms and was resigned again to endure, except he noticed a rudely dressed man of late years who was so frantic to capture his attention, he resorted to jumping up and down. To get his regard, the old man had even pulled off his slouch hat and was waving it with the exuberance one usually reserved for parades. His bewhiskered face crinkled up in a grin when he caught Tesla's eye. He clamped his hat over his wooly hair and pulled it low on his forehead, all the while winking and beaming.

It was Mark Twain.

Tesla broke into smiles and was across the stall in three strides. He bowed over the hands held out in greeting.

Twain's hands were left empty so he clasped Tesla's sleeves at the elbows and shook his arms instead. "Nicky! Nicky! Here you are!"

"Mr. Twain!" Tesla said with real warmth, but he kept his own hands at his sides.

"Shush. No. *Incognito*," Twain explained. "Call me Sam. Or use Mr. Clemens if you must, else I'll be collared and placed under a bell jar for display like all these other dusty artifacts." He looked around from under the drooping rim of his hat. "Except in here, of course. Everything's new and sounds like Judgment Day! How do you stand under the strain of this infernal noise?"

Nikola grinned and dug the beeswax plugs from his ears for Sam to admire.

"I thought you were abroad," Tesla said.

"Yes, I am abroad! I was! I will be again! Just attending to a little business before my return."

Nikola glanced down and away to cover any indiscretion over Twain's financial troubles. But Sam Clemens was patting him affectionately on his shoulder. "Nicky, you are as guileless as a kitten. Don't you fret. That's all taken care of now. My debts are all settled but for one, and that is yours."

"But Mr. Clemens, you owe me nothing. It is I who shall remain ever in your debt. As far as I am concerned, you saved my life. That is, your wonderful book rescued me as I was in mortal decline after I…"

"No, don't say so." Sam interrupted. "Such things are best let alone. You were but a boy, and your brother? Well, horses spook and boys flung headlong don't always get up again."

"Dondi would have been twice the man I am, had I not startled his horse."

They both stood together in silence while Tesla mastered the tremor that had crept into his voice. He had to look away before he could continue.

"Because of Huckleberry Finn, I resolved to live and not to die. That is a debt I can never repay."

"Yes. Well, yes." Sam clasped Tesla's sleeves again, and had to look away to hide the shine in his eyes. "But, also, *no*. If I return to Switzerland with one penny un-repaid, Olivia will pin my ears back. *With real pins*. Never marry a virtuous woman, my boy. They are as humorless as God, but without his forgiving nature."

Sam Clemens paused to sniff his mustache. "But see here. I have a benefactor now. Took care of my debts with a stroke of his pen. All he wanted in return was my soul, and that is in such sorry shape I'm certain it will be returned forthwith." He paused again to make sure Tesla was following his humor and was only thinly rewarded when he saw the corners of Nikola's mouth briefly shrug his mustache, but above this, Tesla's eyes glittered with amusement and so Sam was appeased.

"No, son," he continued, "I am flush for the first time in a decade. Just one more circumference of the globe and I shall return in high style. Why, I've lectures booked across the world. They are holding theaters for me in South Africa and New Zealand too, can you imagine?"

"This is gratifying news. I am very happy for you."

"Don't be! The only difference between a sideshow barker and myself is the size of the audience and the quality of accommodations! But, at least by this time next year, I should be back in New Haven and writing words meant to be read, not shouted to the back row."

Nikola didn't know what to say, so he just nodded.

"Say, have you eaten?" Sam wanted to know.

"It is but mid-morning."

"That's not an answer. I could count the ribs under your waistcoat. How are you holding up? When was the last time you slept?"

"The fair ends next month. I will sleep then." Tesla offered a smile.

"Let's dine together, Nicky. Break your fast and let me indulge my second breakfast."

"I cannot leave my booth," Tesla protested.

"Nonsense. Do you see Edison over there? Neither do I! He doesn't babysit his exhibit and neither should you. Where is your assistant? Who is in your employ?"

"They are working, as they should be," Tesla told him.

"What about you? Shouldn't you be working?"

"But I am working."

Clemens looked at him for a moment and then broke into a grin. "Ah, yes. The men upstairs. They never sleep, do they?"

Tesla paused, translating the phrase into his native Serbian. "Oh I see. The men upstairs." He tapped his temple. "Yes. Very good. But I *do* have an assistant that comes in at night to watch the exhibit after hours. Things sometimes go missing from the hall, but I've been lucky. I've been vigilant."

"Come with me now, Nicky. Let's get some vittles down your craw. You look ready to drop."

"Really, I cannot leave..."

But Sam was already grabbing a startled young woman by the elbow who appeared to be without escort. "Miss? Excuse me, Miss? My young handsome friend here begs a favor of you."

When she blushed and looked away, he patted her shoulder reassuringly.

"You see, he must take leave of his exhibit for an hour or two and would be so grateful if you could grace it with your presence in his stead. Your only duties will be to scold anyone who touches his little machines, and should any inquire, inform them Mr. Tesla shall return in the afternoon."

Her eyes flitted over Nikola and rested on his hand that was without a wedding ring.

"It will not be without recompense," Sam continued, and took from his jacket a wallet and peeled a whole dollar off for her. "I shall give you another if when we return none of this equipment is missing."

She looked left and right, worried about the impropriety of accepting money in public, but the lure was too great. A dollar would buy her a ticket on Ferris' great wheel. For two she could ascend in the captive balloon and have her picture taken in the basket. Equally tempting was the reward of being in the debt of this handsome bachelor. In the end propriety collapsed in defeat and she took the dollar.

"I shall do as you ask," she said, looking shyly and slyly up at Tesla.

"Look sharp," Nikola told her, clearly worried. "Not a finger on anything. Not even your own. These are electrical devices, you understand. *Very dangerous*."

"No sir. I shall not touch a thing, and shall forbid anyone else."

Tesla wasn't satisfied. He leaned down and pointed toward Edison's tower. "See those men over there?" he asked her.

She looked at the toughs manning the exhibit and nodded.

"Especially them. Thieves and scoundrels every one. If they so much as approach my counter you are to scream until someone comes to your aid."

His intensity made her sorry she had taken the dollar.

"Pay him no mind," Sam told her, and on the side of his head where Tesla couldn't see, he circled his finger at his temple.

This only made her look sorrier still. But a dollar was a dollar, and two were even better, so she entered the booth with her hands knit together so as not to accidentally brush up against any of the electrical devices, and stood at its exact center, not looking happy at all.

"This is foolishness," Nikola fretted. "A stout fellow perhaps. She is but a lamb for the wolves."

"Give her a smile, boy, and she'll defend your territory like a she-bear with cubs. Go ahead. *Turn on some charm.*"

Tesla gave her a tight smile and a curt nod.

Her eyes widened with alarm.

"Oh yes. That cuts it!" Sam laughed and banged him on the back. "Well, perhaps she'll do you some good service anyway out of Christian charity, if not for greenbacks."

"We shall see."

"No need for a long face. I have something to distract you. You remember that scheme we discussed before I last embarked?"

"I remember everything," Tesla said woefully as they eased into the flow of humanity making their way though the building.

"Everywhere I go, it is electrification this, electrification that!"

"Is it?"

"I am not making reference to industrialists and businessmen, mind you. I speak of the upper classes. The people of leisure who are burdened with the chore of lightening their fortunes on curiosities to fill their tiresome hours of idleness and to amuse their friends."

"I see."

"Olivia and the girls are even now guests of a Madame R. in Geneva —a lovely and hospitable widow who is the dominant goose in a gaggle of other ladies of that enviable state which is the patient wife's reward. They waddle up and down the continent seeking cures and treatments and endure every tomfool quackery and suffer unspeakable indignities with the cheerfulness and enthusiasm of brides picking out trousseau."

"Indeed." Tesla was more amazed that Sam never seemed to run out of wind.

"Even my Olivia is not immune to the attraction of gewgaws that do what-all for the health and which evidently enliven the spirits when the sparks are applied."

"Oh, dear."

"Exactly. But do attend my point. There is a vast market of like-minded ladies girdling the globe, as it were, and coincidentally they congregate the very venues I am appointed to, and attend the same functions and soirees, as it were."

"Do they?"

"They do indeed. And I am sorely taxed with the society of them. They flock around and ask interminable questions, on and on, until I am frayed out. They require of me endless polite conversations, which are for all practical purposes dress rehearsals for my paid performance, but there is no profit in it, is there? They pump my well dry and give me naught in return. But I tell you, Nicky, if I were to but wave a play-pretty before their goosey beaks, one that sparked and shimmy-shammied and most especially if it was a portable contrivance of the oscillator with which you once cured my constipation, our fortunes would be made."

"Do your bowels still trouble you?"

Sam waved away the question, because his eyes alighted on what looked to him the device he had just described. "See here!" he cried, and climbed the step to a platform where a chair was displayed. "This is the very thing! A therapeutic chair. Is it yours? Oh do tell me you have taken my advice and you hold this patent at least."

"Mr. Clemens..."

Mark Twain threw himself into the seat and admired the straps and wires. "I should wonder if it should not be suspended above a commode. What do you think?"

"Come down from there, Sam. Please."

"A bit bulky for cargo, but could it be disassembled and reassembled by a competent fool? What am I thinking! A pamphlet will do fine. I could wire you the orders and let them contend with the assembly when it arrives. Think of it. You need not manufacture a single thing until after the funds were collected. This enterprise is entirely without risk!"

A young man in a Salvation Army uniform stepped forward. "Pardon me sir, have you pondered the state of your immortal soul?"

"Daily sir, and twice on Sunday," Sam replied tersely. "But my pardon is not granted. You have interrupted a conversion with my friend."

"It is your *life* which may be interrupted, as were the lives of the poor repentant souls which sat before you in that very chair."

"What have you got here? A Salvation chair?" Sam laughed. "Look here, Nicky. You've set your sights too low. While you've been dithering to move men's bowels, this chap has learned to move a man's conscience!"

The Salvationist was nonplussed. "You jest, sir, but indeed it is a chair of Salvation for many, just as the cross was both a device of death and yet upon it hung the redemption of mankind."

"How is that? You give them such a bully jolt that it implants the fear o'God? Ha!"

"More so, sir. This chair delivers them into the very presence of their Judge and Redeemer."

Sam sat very still as the color drained from his face. "You don't mean to say..."

"Come, Mr. Clemens," Nikola said and extended his hand to help him up but the older man needed no assistance.

Sam leaped from the electric chair as if his maker had tickled the switch.

"I have the solemn duty as chaplain to the condemned," The Salvationist told them. "To declare God's wondrous grace to the chief of sinners, even to such as these; please take this tract. Or, I will tell you my account first hand, if you are not in a hurry."

"We are indeed in a hurry," Sam said, and tugged at Tesla's sleeve, but his tall friend was regarding the uniformed man carefully.

"We have met before," Nikola Tesla said. It was not a question.

"I have been in the Lord's service here for some months." The reply came with a small bow. "Perhaps you have seen me about."

"No," Tesla said. "I am not permitted the luxury of forgetting a face or a name. Or, tryingly, anything else. You were a principle in the War of the Currents between our then employers. You staged public executions of family pets to perjure the name of Westinghouse in connection with the execution chair. You are Edison's dog killer, Mr. Lauder."

Because Tesla did not also say, 'You are the Wholly Roller time traveler,' Lauder was still for a only beat before he let a beaming smile transform his face into what might pass for the warmest of receptions for a long lost friend.

"Glory be to God!" Lauder shouted. "You see now before you a transformed man! I once was lost, but now am found. Was blind, but now I see!" Lauder cocked back his head, whaled in a breath and began singing in an ear-shattering tenor: "I am washed in the blood! Washed in the blood! Washed in the blood of the Lamb!"

"Bloody Salvationist," Clemens muttered. "Shake your stumps, Nicky. Hymns aren't meant to be endured more than once a week and not ever in the shadow of such an unholy device."

"I couldn't agree more," Tesla said. They left Lauder to his solo and inserted themselves again into the relentless surge of fairgoers which would not be encouraged to go faster or slower, but required an individual to find the current that matched his pace or shift to the eddies and backwaters along the edges. When they were carried past Edison's preeminent exhibit near the door, the assistants there nudged one another and made rude gestures but Tesla ignored them.

"Who was that man?" Sam finally asked of Lauder, but Tesla had sunk into a brooding silence and chose to ignore him too.

Outside, they paused in the towering hemicycle that sheltered the immense statue of Benjamin Franklin holding his kite. A white pigeon careened around the circumference of the interior space and settled on a high ledge.

Tesla gazed up at Franklin's statue and spoke at last. "In Belgrade I was given a vision which I took to be from God. I was walking in a park near sunset, and the sun became for me the great wheel-work of the universe."

Sam Clemens read the words inscribed above Franklin: *He that wrenched the thunderbolt from heaven...*

"And I saw in it the laws of nature, and more, I understood in an instant how to capture the natural courses of electricity. I fell into a trance, as oft described by saints in holy audience. It was an epiphany, and I was struck blind and dumb, as was Paul of Tarsus on the road to Damascus. For me, the infirmity lasted only for a short while, but do you see? The polyphase motor sprung fully formed in my imagination at that moment. It was a divine gift, meant to be for the benefit of all mankind to relieve the burden of labor and suffering from men and beasts alike. Yet, that man inside, that repugnant wolf in sheep's clothing; he has employed those same powers as an instrument of unspeakable cruelty and death. How can I abide such corruption? How can I redeem my soul from these devils, I ask you?" His voice echoed off the vaulted alcove above them.

He got no answer, and Tesla expected none. Instead the tall inventor launched himself out of the protected entryway of the Hall of Electricity, and walked at a furious pace across the Court of Honor. Sam Clemens struggled to keep up.

When the vigor of their pace began to crack the plaster of Tesla's oppression, Clemens changed the subject. "Where are we to dine?" he asked, a little out of breath.

"There is no decent public dining hereabouts," Tesla answered. "Just oyster bars and bean houses, cheap food at exorbitant prices. We shall dine instead in England. The dining room there is acceptable."

"England?"

"Victoria House. The consulate of the British Empire here on the grounds. I also lodge there. Very exclusive." He glanced apprehensively at Sam's attire.

Sam didn't seem to notice.

"Very well," the older man puffed. "Perhaps I shall find a room there as well."

He was caught up short when Nikola stopped in his tracks.

"You have no room? Mr. Clemens there is nothing for it. You shall stay with me. The fair is teeming, and moreover it is impossible to find a room of any reputation in the city, as it is booked to the end of October. Besides which, Chicago proper is over seven miles away. The train carriages are overcrowded, and the lines are impossible. Everything has been booked since last spring."

"Money talks," Sam assured him. "And I am not without some reputation myself."

"And then you will be incognito no longer and unable to move freely about the fair. No, I beg you. You shall stay with me. I insist. The bed is over large. You will be comfortable. I never sleep but four hours or so, and then deeply and quietly. You will never know I am there."

"I wish I could say the same. My Olivia would attest I am no good bedfellow. I snore and thrash and your four hours will be ruined. But I accept, for you make a good argument and I am accustomed to going about unmolested during the day. It is the great attraction of the old country: There I am just another American tourist and beneath contempt, and so left alone, at least until I draw out my purse." He was not telling the truth. His fame in Europe was greater than he enjoyed in his own country.

"It is settled then," Nikola said, and lead the way down the promenade, alongside the inlet from Lake Michigan. When they rounded the end of the cascading falls of the Grand Basin, they paused at the Columbian fountain, where gods sat astride thrashing seahorses slapping the snow-white 'Barge of State' with their fishy tails in exuberant sprays of water. Bare-breasted muses rowed the barge, atop which the goddess Columbia was seated on a throne. Winged Fame stood heroically above the prow and muscular Time struggled at the stern, wrestling his scythe into service as a rudder.

"Wait until you see it at night," Tesla told Clemens. "It is illuminated with colored lamps, set underwater to catch the movement of the water. Sealed of course, to protect them. The waterworks are Edison's," he conceded, "but I have just submitted a superior fountain patent which..."

"It's a sight to see *now*!" Sam sputtered. "It is a fountain to make a Roman blush!"

"It is the largest in the world," Tesla conceded. They stood together in silence while each contemplated that in their own way. Tesla finally sniffed and shifted when it had been long enough in his estimation and they pressed on. They went against the tide of sightseers around the North Canal and cut back behind the massive Manufacturers' and Liberal Arts Hall to the Lake Shore Avenue.

The buildings of the White City towered above them. The broad avenues accommodated canals down their centers that were filled with watercraft. Two years ago this had been nothing but swamp, and now it was a metropolis of the largest and most impressive architecture in the world. Witnessing it buoyed Tesla's spirits, and he indulged a little pride that it was his engines that powered it. The fair was a testament to what man could accomplish when the greatest minds came together in one accord. The future was going to be a wonderful place. Of that he was certain.

Tesla noticed Sam was slowing and so he signaled one of the Seminary students who piloted an unoccupied wheeled chair. Nikola placed a whole silver dollar in the student's hand and Sam sank gratefully into the chair. Tesla could now resume his natural pace. The young man pushing had to hump it to keep up.

Victoria House was in the old English Tudor style. It was a temporary Embassy flying the Union Jack out front. In a prime location, it was just off the paved beach near trees that were miraculously spared during the excavation of Jackson Park. Sam was gratified to see it was a handsome place, exactly the caliber he would have preferred and was accustomed to from his self-imposed exile in Great Britain. Nevertheless, they were stopped at the door where the doorman whispered urgently to Tesla, casting doubtful eyes on his companion.

Tesla stiffened in indignation and said loud enough for Sam to hear, "May I present the Reverend Rudolph Tesla, my father, visiting from Serbia. If he is not welcome here, I shall transfer my lodgings to Bavaria."

The doorman looked startled and then recovered before he bowed low and gave them the entree wave.

"Britain has always been kind to me," Tesla said with a shade of sarcasm. They both passed through into a paneled hall that was obscured in a haze of cigar smoke. This was an exclusive retreat, by invitation only. A men's club, for all practical purposes.

A pair of heavy doors opened into a large dining room where most of the tables were empty as it was but mid-morning. The maître d' led them in and stood by as the staff put a fresh cloth over the only table that was undressed. The table was next to the window overlooking the newly planted English gardens. It was exclusively reserved for Tesla while he was in residence. Nikola stood in careful observance as a woman in white hurried to stand in her appointed spot. The maître d' presented her with a flat box and she lifted a pair of pristine gloves from where they were wrapped in tissue paper. She donned them by touching only the cuffs before she retrieved polished silverware from the felt-lined drawer of a heavy sideboard the maître d' opened for her using the key he had around his neck. She laid out the tableware on fresh linen napkins on both sides of the plate, and set down another napkin stack. She stepped back awaiting further instruction.

Sam Clemens said nothing of this strange ballet. He had witnessed it before when dining with Tesla in New York at the Astoria. He was sorry his friend had not relaxed his eccentricities in the intervening years.

They were seated. A slight agitation riffled through the staff, but a glance from the maître d' demurred them and they did not ask Sam to remove his hat. At least they did not ask aloud. Clemens grinned at them and tossed it into an empty chair. Tesla wasn't the only one present with eccentricities.

Sam wore his expectation to be accommodated so well that he was obliged, even when he was on the lam.

Steaming finger bowls were set before them, each with a lemon slice floating in the center. Sam followed Tesla's lead, daintily dipping his fingertips and wiping them on the towel held by the valet.

Nikola began wiping his crystal goblet with the first of his napkins. The maid swooped in to take the napkin from him the moment he was finished, and a Negro waiter poured water into his polished glass. Tesla raised it to his nose and sniffed.

"This has been boiled?" he asked.

"Yes indeed, sir." The black man had the impeccable accent of the British upper classes. "Twenty minutes and no less."

"We have not been here but for five," Tesla said coldly.

"Yes sir, but it was taken from the boiler and was cooled for you in anticipation of your dining with us later this evening."

Tesla sniffed it again and ventured a sip. The waiter stood by holding unnaturally still.

He's lying. Sam thought. He was quick to recognize a fellow member of the fraternity of like-minded scoundrels and burst forth in a loud voice, "Well, let's have some here, boy!" He meant to draw attention from the duplicitous waiter to avoid a delay of another half hour.

The waiter leaned in and poured with taut restraint. Sam took a big swig and smacked his lips and then noisily gulped down the rest of his glass. He whipped his napkin in the air to unfold it and patted his mustache dry and then tucked it under his chin. Tesla put down his glass to watch this display with amusement. Sam's diversion had worked.

The waiter began his recitation: "Gentlemen, if you will tarry but an hour, we shall have roast beef. Creamed corn. Potatoes. Sauerkraut..."

"Do you have a nice mutton stew?" Sam asked. "I am right fond of mutton stew."

"Begging your pardon sir. We have just the one meal at noontime, and it is not yet prepared."

"What *is* prepared?" Tesla asked, worried about leaving his booth in the hands of that girl for any longer than necessary.

"Eggs, sir. Also with them: calf brains. Bangers. Scones..."

"Cream," Tesla said. "I shall have a dish of cream and a scone. Have you any fruit?"

"Yes, sir. We have a nice apple dumpling, but it is yet baking."

"I require an uncooked apple. Unpeeled. A sharp knife and a bowl of scalding water."

"Yes sir. As you wish."

"Eggs scrambled with calf brains!" Sam said rubbing his hands together. "And good stiff coffee."

"Very good, sir."

"And more napkins," Tesla added.

"Of course, sir."

The waiter backed away and Sam said to Tesla, "You have them bamboozled!"

"They are accustomed to my ways."

"I think rather they are paid to put up with you."

Tesla gave a slight shrug. "I pay my bills..." and then was immediately sorry, but Clemens didn't seem to mind, or had the grace not to show it.

"... And they make allowances," Tesla continued. "They had a little trouble in the power plant." He tapped the floor with his shoe. He was indicating the generator in the basement. "Regrettably, they chose to ship and assemble their own rather than rely on the power we are generating at the fair. 'Pride of the monarchy. Services by appointment of HM.' That sort of thing. I remedied the situation. Saved them a fire, no doubt. At least I can sleep here trusting my own handiwork," he gave a thin smile. "A situation I would not enjoy in the city."

Tesla nodded to the electrical chandelier hanging in the center of the dining room. "I remedied that situation too. Astonishing that an Empire with the likes of Lord Kelvin cannot produce a decent bulb." He commenced polishing his spoon with a fresh napkin in preparation for his bowl of cream.

"It is all very nice. Top of the line," Sam agreed.

"Had you cabled me, I could have prepared you a better reception. I might have secured you a room and you certainly would have had your mutton stew."

Sam was looking at him in astonishment. "But it *was* you who cabled me!"

Nikola Tesla lowered his spoon. "How do you mean, Mr. Clemens?"

"Wait," Sam said, and produced his leather packet. He pulled out an envelope and handed it across the table. Tesla cleared away his dinnerware and raised the flap on the back, laying out the contents on the table in front of him.

"This was waiting for me at my hotel in New York. After my meeting with Mr. J., the benefactor I spoke of. The one who is managing my accounts."

One of the objects in the envelope was a newspaper clipping from the Chicago Tribune, titled *The Wizard of Lightening,* an article on his talk at the Electrical Congress at the college just last month, in August. Tesla's eyes skimmed the article. He had not read it before now, but he remembered the reporter that had dogged him the day of the lecture while he was arranging his equipment on the stage. He'd asked him the usual questions, and none of them important. Tesla had worn his thick cork shoes on stage that day, making him tower nearly seven feet tall. *That* made it into the article, of all things. The rest of the article had a slight petulant tone: Tesla hadn't bathed himself in lightning as he was famed to do. No; The demonstration was discreet. He was done with the kind of showmanship Westinghouse encouraged. The War of the Currents was over as far as he was concerned. It was never any contest. The elegant and simple courses of nature prevail as they always do, without favor to the preferences of men.

He set aside the article and picked up the telegram. "This was delivered to you in New York?" He asked. "I had no idea you were in New York."

The Western Union telegram read:

NIKOLA TESLA REQUESTS THE HONOR OF YOUR PRESENCE AT WORLDS COLUMBIAN EXPOSITION CHICAGO ILLINOIS STOP

"Also were tickets to the fair, and paid accommodations on a Pullman sleeper. And *this*." Sam Clemens tapped the formally engraved calling card, which Tesla had laid out neatly next to the telegram.

"Yes. I've seen this before," he said. "I have a stack of these at my exhibit. People leave me calling cards all the time, but this one ... I get two or three like it each day."

The card read: Sergei the Amazing. Mentalist. *Electromancer.* Prognosticator without peer.

"I was accosted by an atrocious woman just as I entered the gate this morning, who handed me yet another one," Sam told him. "She was dressed like a grand dame, but had an Arkansaw twang that could curdle milk. And get this. She was leading a goat on the end of a silver chain. Damnedest thing I ever saw."

"Arkansas?" Tesla asked. "Adjacent to your Missouri?"

Sam bristled. "Heaven and hell are districts with more in common than Missouri and Arkansaw. It's a wilderness no-man's-land between industrious Missourians and the Gentile South. It is a state without purpose. Just wastrels of humanity neither here nor there nor this nor that..."

Tesla raised his eyebrows.

"... And yet here is this old hill woman right in the midst of the White City, a regular mountaineer dowager all gussied up like an industrialist's mother-in-law! And she claps her iron hand on my shoulder and proceeds to remonstrate on our appointment with this Amazing Sergei, and proceeds to give me directions..."

"I've never seen this Sergei, and I assure you, I am familiar with all the environs of the fair."

"They are not in the fair, you see. That is what she was yammering about. They are out back by the Wild West Show, although I think the Indians may have broken camp once alerted to the low caliber of their neighbors. *Arkansawers!* Bah."

Nikola Tesla turned the envelope over in his hands. *Mark Twain* was written in neat script across its front. The return address was engraved, but it was just the name of an organization. No actual address.

"The Wardenclyffe Foundation?" Tesla asked.

"I thought perhaps an underwriter of yours?"

"You are mistaken."

The waiter came and set the bowl of cream on the table next to the envelope, the foot of the bowl made a small *ting* as it touched the edge of the spoon Tesla had been polishing. Nikola pushed away from the table abruptly.

"Waiter, remove this and prepare my table again. And this time, bring my water hot and steaming from the boiler, after a full twenty minutes. We shall wait."

Sam sighed and sat back in his chair as the staff stripped the table bare. He resigned himself to a long lunch, and ordered a whiskey to tide him over.

They brought him brandy instead.

CHAPTER NINE

"1893 was unique: No 'nations rising against nations'. No 'wars or rumors of war'. Not one. Why? Because right then, for one blessed moment, there was enough. *That wouldn't be true again for close to 200 years."*
—*The Chief Engineer*
Wardenclyffe Foundation Archives

∞

Behind the Midway Plaisance

As the daylight faded, the river of voices along the Midway Plaisance became distinctly male, and no wonder; that's when Little Egypt and the celebrated harlots began their undulations. The sleazy tune they danced to could scarce be heard against the cheers and whistles of the men who thronged to watch. Nearby, a preacher leapt atop an apple crate to assign them all to hell's eternal flames, seemingly intent on driving them through the infernal gates on the strength of his indignation. Instead of contrition, he was answered by a renewed roar of enthusiasm for the show. The preacher met the challenge by hurling himself headfirst into a volley of red-faced damnations, but was cut short when a blood-curdling cry astonished him to silence. He turned to see from whence it came and witnessed Bedouins galloping up the Midway on their fierce little horses. They shook their curved swords in the air, making the tassels dance and catch the last glow of the sunset. Their war cries disintegrated into laughter at the dismay by which they were regarded. Encouraged, they wheeled and charged the crowded boulevard again, flashing teeth and steel.

Tesla and Twain were among the pedestrians that scrambled to get out of the way, but there was nowhere safe to go. In avoiding the horses there was danger of straying in front of an elephant under the nervous prodding of its turbaned mahout. On the far side was the white-sand track where reindeer sledges raced under the cracking whips of the Norwegians. Polynesian women scolded the Bedouins from the confines of their rattan porches but their voices were drowned when black savages from darkest Africa set upon their drums. The Africans dared the crowd to come closer to see if it were true; that they had no children in their number because they ate them, and not because they had succumbed to the ghastly Chicago weather, as had so many of the Esquimaux. Such was the Midway Plaisance.

∞

Mark Twain, who was traveling incognito under his given name Sam Clemens, jabbed his tall companion with an elbow and grinned. Tesla only winced, which was all the encouragement Clemens needed. Sam had done this several times already, as if his elbow were required punctuation to any ethnocentric prejudice that met his ear. Because Tesla knew several languages, he catalogued a longer list of epithets, but did not bring them to Sam's attention. He did not share the glee in which they were shouted, nor did he share the relish in which Sam received them. The Midway seemed perpetually on the verge of a brawl to him, and he wanted nothing of it. He would not be here at all if Sam had not insisted on the basis of the mysterious invitation he had received from the Wardenclyffe Foundation.

Because the press of humanity eased under the Ferris wheel, the two men moved to take advantage, hoping to make some headway. There weren't many brave enough to walk under the wheel, and Tesla noted the ground was littered with bolts that rained from above in the first days it was operated.

He found it impossible not to duck when the coach-sized passenger cars swooped downward from the crest 260 feet above. When the pedestrians squealed and ran, Tesla and Twain were among them. Sam laughed and even Tesla indulged a sheepish grin as they looked up at the wheel and marveled.

"A crowded city might make use of apartments built such and so," said Sam. "See here, a clever landlord could charge every tenant for the ground floor, plus a premium for the view."

"Let us hope Mr. Ferris is not the unwitting architect of the shape of things to come."

"How so?"

"This wheel-to-nowhere, you see."

Sam removed his hat to get the brim out of the way and looked up at the wheel. "It is folly to boast a swift ascent. Is that your point?"

"When one is cast down afterward to lose all progress in his estate, yes."

"Nicky, you are a pessimist."

"I am the opposite of that. I am a realist."

"So says both pessimists and optimists."

"Only because they have a limited view of reality. When one sees the full course of nature, one can be nothing but a realist."

"So they are both correct."

"They are both mistaken." Tesla said flatly.

"Well, count me a willing passenger on the tide of optimism. Prophets such as yourself promise salvation by science and I believe you. By God, I do."

Tesla nodded, basking in the heat of Sam's convictions. It would be 180 years before that fevered dream would finally come, but as Tesla stood on the threshold of the new century, gazing up at the wheel, not even he expected to wait that long.

The evening breeze off Lake Michigan touched them. It stirred a little, but did not lift the pall of smoke and haze that had drifted down from Chicago and her stockyards. It brewed more richly over the hills of manure pitched behind the Indian camp of Buffalo Bill Cody's Wild West and Congress of Rough Riders.

Sam wrinkled his mustache and fished in his pocket for a cigar.

"Please, Mr. Clemens. Must you?"

"I'd take an airing if there was any to be had, but I fear the breeze may give up from sheer discouragement."

Tesla sighed in agreement and withdrew a handkerchief from his breast pocket and pressed it to his nose.

The wall around the midway was their final obstacle to the district of makeshift slums on the far side. There wasn't a way over the wall without risking their necks, but it could be breeched for a fee via one of the many holes punched through. Any competent rascal could finagle a shortcut without too much compromise to his personal fortunes.

Sam Clemens was such a rascal, and paid only two pennies for passage through a narrow fissure in the back room wall of an espresso house. To get there, he and Tesla had to pick their way through turbaned men who lay on a patchwork of small carpets, stepping carefully over samovars and hookahs. The two were not afforded any interest at all, as they competed with a pair of dancing girls who commenced to drop their veils. In the back room a weasel-faced man grinned and moved aside a curtain after receiving his toll. Behind it was an irregular gap that looked greasy around the edges.

Sam went headlong through the breach as enthusiastic as a miner at the end of his shift and grinning like a boy up to no good. Tesla followed, easing through toe-first. One manicured hand lifted his crisply ironed trouser leg over his polished shoe like a woman might lift her hem above muddy ground. His other hand still clamped the white handkerchief over his mouth and nose. His eyes were not happy.

They emerged into the tent city on the backside of the Midway, entirely unaware that they were being followed.

Sam made a quick comparison of this district with the Midway Plaisance. He determined the same business was conducted and the same satisfactions could be had as on the midway, at least for those who weren't too particular. The patent-medicine barkers, whores, pickpockets and fortunetellers were of a lower quality, perhaps, but every bit as enterprising.

The location was strategic: The rutted track that ran through the middle of the disheveled tents was the only avenue to the Wild West Show and thereby caught the traffic going both ways. Cody's roustabouts ensured no one fleeced the sheep on their way to the show. But afterward, the crowds returning to the Columbian Exposition were *fair game*, as it were.

Tesla and Twain pushed upstream through the latest crowd trudging back from the afternoon show, having just endured one of Cody's spectacles. Three hours of trick riding, shooting, and feats performed by educated horses left them dazed and wanting for nothing but a way home to a cool bed and dreamless sleep. After this and a full day at the fair besides, they were wrung out of amazement and wonders.

Sam noted flimflam men decamping the tents and entering the pedestrian current like hungry wolves. Sam pitied the lambs in this weary flock and set his own expression in a stern scowl and took Nicola by the arm, both to claim him as his own and to steer him away from the sneak thieves.

Sam Clemens had nothing to fear. Although Tesla looked like a dandy, Sam cut the figure of an obvious pirate and appeared as world-savvy as any con man on the game. Furthermore, a third man tailed them, as any street urchin could plainly see.

∞

This third man was Lauder, and he was not wearing his usual Salvation Army uniform. Tonight he was doing his best to blend in with the crowd. He wore a battered derby low on his brow and his jacket was ragged and patched. He shuffled like he did in the early days, when his temporal aphasia had him mistaken for a drunk, when the static from his offline goog made him bark his words to compensate for the howling tinnitus in his head.

At the Salvation Army Mission in New York, his fellow derelicts had christened him Rip Loudly when he asked what year it was. That was before he learned to ignore the zephyrs in his head and modulate his voice. Yet six years later, after traveling 236 years into the past, he still had not accomplished what he set out to do: find the other traveler — the first traveler, the *Murderer of the World* — and stop him cold.

In those six years since he arrived, Lauder had risen to the rank of Captain in the Salvation Army. It was as good a cover as any, but a little too conspicuous tonight. The crowd was thick, and he must-needs keep close to the man he was following without drawing attention to himself. He believed that Tesla would lead him to the Murderer eventually. *Like drawing unto like, and so forth and suchlike.* Once found, Lauder would fulfill his self appointed mission and the Murderer of the World would never have the chance to split the universe asunder. Lauder was about to accomplish what the Wholly Rollers only dreamed about. He would keep the one true universe whole.

Lauder was aware his intense focus elicited uneasiness in the confidence men who noticed him. He repaid the attention with a dark and threatening glare, exacting *honor among thieves.* It was clear he wanted his prey left well alone until he could make his move. In this regard, he was not challenged.

∞

Tesla and Sam Clemens walked quickly, unaware of their tail. Sam kept firm hold on Tesla's arm; pressing him past tents where it was likely the pickpockets recycled their booty. In one he saw a reclining maiden of the Celestial City holding an opium pipe between her dainty teeth. Her eyes were vacant, but they followed the two men nevertheless, causing her to shift slightly on her cot in a way Sam found disconcerting. Next-door, stooped men were taking turns gazing into a lighted box, watching flip-card photographs of ladies preparing to bathe. Tesla came to a standstill when he saw the wiring trailing through the dust and snaking over the wall to steal power from the fair.

Tesla's brow creased.

"Mr. Clemens, do you see..."

"Not here, Nicky. Not now."

"I'll wager you the postcards are illuminated by a stoppered bulb. A Westinghouse bulb, stolen from the fair."

Sam Clemens collared him and steered him away before he got them into a jam. Sam might be old and rumpled, but despite the arthritis in his writing hand, he looked as though he might still be able to deliver a roundhouse blow, especially if he had backup. He looked like he might even enjoy it, if just for old time's sake. But Nicky, bless him, was no backup, so Sam hurried him along out of harms way.

"There. Up ahead," Sam said in encouragement.

A tight knot of people pressed around a flatbed wagon, which was being used as a stage. Atop this, a caped magician was performing. He was at this moment bending the stem of a spoon held aloft with only two fingers at the base. Startled cries and nervous laughter erupted from the crowd.

"See here!" Sam Clemens pulled an engraved calling card from his pocket. "This is it. That's *him*."

Tesla wasn't looking at the magician but at the painted canvas backdrop that bisected lengthwise the stage of the wagon. It was illuminated by gaslights from behind and glowed against the deepening evening. Across the top in script suitable for Barnum and Bailey were the words: *Sergei the Amazing. Mentalist. Electromancer. Prognosticator without peer.*

The words were the same as on the card Sam held in his hands, but Tesla didn't care about the card or even the name on the canvas. His enthralled gaze was locked on the painted scene beneath it. It was a cityscape that accomplished what the White City had not. Where the fair was built to an aesthetic 2,000 years gone by, this painted metropolis bespoke a future that would tax the imagination of Jules Verne. Multi-colored buildings rose smooth as obelisks and so high they touched the painted clouds. Here was a church that stood atop its own spire, the nave encircling the top. There were girdered towers hurling forth zigzags of lightning. They forked outward, striking both buildings and rockets, the latter rising like Chinese pyrotechnics on thick clouds of smoke. Tesla stood amazed to see windows along their side.

Peopled rockets! To what suicidal end? He marveled. Other rockets with wings plied the skies horizontally. Also cased with windows, they appeared to be pulled through the air by screws while chased by the forked lightning from the towers. Trains plied roadbeds held gracefully aloft in the air. These were not unlike the intramural train of the fair except they were without locomotive or tracks and were sleek as bullets. If the trains weren't transportation enough, floating across the landscape were bubbles with more people inside.

But what brought Nikola Tesla to a full stop was painted on the right panel. Round in the sky and throwing off rays like the sun was his own A.C. polyphase generator, the very electrical diagram as submitted for patent. A broad ray flared from its base to encompass the figure of a man trapped in its light with his head thrown back like Christ receiving the Holy Ghost, in orgastic rapture. The figure might have been he. Obviously it was intended to be.

"What mischief is this?" Tesla scowled.

Next to him, Sam was hopping up and down on his toes, trying to see over the crowd.

The magician was describing the contents of a woman's purse to her as she gazed into it, nodding slowly in a daze.

"But that's not all, is it Madame?" The magician asked her. "Something is missing, is it not?"

The woman dug through her small satin handbag and looked up alarm. "My coin pouch! Someone has taken it!"

Sam nudged Tesla low in the ribs. "Now watch. This is showmanship," he told him.

Tesla's scowl deepened. He had seen this man before.

∞

As Lauder made it his business to go wherever Tesla went, and scrutinize everyone Tesla spoke to, he was alerted by the inventor's expression. Lauder turned his eyes to the magician. Slowly, recognition dawned on him as well, but it took him a few moments to place him as the man who had ardently questioned Tesla after the inventor's talk at the Electrical Congress the previous month. Lauder remembered Tesla had quit the interview abruptly, evidently fearing for his patents. Lauder had thought nothing of it at the time. The man he was searching for, the Murderer of the World, was an old man. A *geezer*. This man was obviously in his prime, had barely warranted a glance. But Lauder did remember his intensity and now here he was again, in the most unlikely of circumstances. Lauder gave the magician a new regard, full of suspicion and calculation.

Apparently, so did Tesla, for his scowl flushed to crimson.

"Fear not, Madame," the magician told the woman with enough volume to carry to the back of the crowd. "Your coin pouch is not lost; missing from your purse, perhaps... but present in my hand." He threw back his satin cape and flourished his gloved hand where all could see and produced the pouch out of thin air. He then fell to one knee to deliver it back to her. The woman yelped and was reluctant to take it back. Even when he leaned close to present it, she hesitated, fingers poised as if it might now be contaminated by mysteries.

"I assure you and everyone present, I have not presumed to collect my finder's fee." He gave her a charming lopsided grin and winked to the crowd and was rewarded with laughter. The woman gingerly took the purse back, but with two fingers as if it might be hot. Then she bowed her head over it and flicked through her coins until she seemed satisfied with the accounting. After which, she blushingly held up a penny to the magician.

"You exemplify American womanhood." He bowed to her. "Charming as well as thrifty." He paused for the laugh.

Sam was nodding. "Did you see that? – Move. Set-it-up. Pause. Deliver the snapper! Oh yes, he has got it. Smooth as silk, bold as brass. Are you paying attention, Nicky?"

Tesla said nothing.

The magician leapt back to his feet with a suddenness that was startling, and held up the penny for all to see. "I shall, as all good Christians, store my treasures up in heaven," he announced to command everyone's attention. When all eyes were his, he flicked the penny into the air, spinning it end over end where it sparkled in the gaslight. The penny hovered at the crest of his toss and then vanished. There was a great intake of breath and applause erupted. The crowd thickened before the stage.

Tesla said to Clemens, "I'd like to see under that wagon," but he did not press in with the crowd.

The magician threw back his cape and doffed his top hat, wheeled it down his arm and caught it with a deep theatric bow. In a single movement it flipped back into place on his head. At that moment the four gaslight foot-lamps flared up and caught the satiny sheen of his hat and cape in a fine light.

Sam grinned up at his friend. "You don't get the wherewithal for that on a penny pinched from a lady's purse. Hands in your pockets, Nicky."

"I am aware of the ways of the world," Tesla replied.

Sam grinned at him. "You know the *hows* of the world. I know the *ways*." He laughed and shook his white head. "But I'll be hung if you or I know the *whys*."

Nikola indulged him a brief smile, which Sam had to infer from behind the handkerchief that was still firmly clamped over Tesla's nose and mouth.

"Now, you see how he is dressed?" Sam continued his instruction.

An eyebrow arched at him in warning.

"Oh, your clothes are fine, but this dandy knows the right getup is your best staging."

"I would not wear a cape," Nikola said flatly, "except to attend the opera."

Up on stage, Sergei the Amazing was holding aloft a light bulb. It glowed brightly in the deepening dusk. Nikola was pained to recognize another of the stoppered bulbs, made in the hectic weeks before the fair's opening when Edison refused the use of his own patent bulb because General Electric had not won the commission to illuminate the fair. This workaround bulb was inferior but it glowed more brightly on alternating current, which allowed them to be strung as dense as pearls on a necklace, outlining each building of the White City.

Sergei unclipped the bulb from its wire, and it continued to burn.

Tesla sniffed. "Child's play," he said. "It is he who is wired. There is a generator beneath his stage and a hidden connection. A plate beneath his feet. A small wire brush through his shoe perhaps..."

Sam jabbed him with his elbow. "Watch yourself. You're getting green around the gills."

"Nonsense..."

They both went silent when Sergei tossed the bulb into the air and it continued to burn. Until then Tesla had been annoyed. Now he was furious. Somewhere under that wagon was a high frequency generator and the magician was standing in its field, allowing wireless illumination of the bulb. It was the very thing Tesla was demonstrating at the fair. The first of its kind.

A second glowing bulb appeared and the Magician began to juggle, though not particularly skillfully, and only with the two bulbs, but the point was made. As he flipped the bulbs into the air, he bantered with the crowd, turning their cries of wonder into indulgent laughter until he looked out to the far edges of their number and locked gazes with Tesla. The magician faltered, nearly dropping the bulbs. He had to lunge to recover them and with a self-effacing laugh he bowed deeply to his audience to a smattering of applause.

Unseen by all, the performer began to sweat, but not nearly as much as Lauder who now dared to press in with the rest of the crowd. He no longer had his passionate focus on Nikola Tesla and his friend, Sam. His eyes were alight on Sergei now and burning with an excitement that might have dimmed the bulbs by comparison. In the flash of the magician's startled expression, Lauder knew. He'd seen that look before. On an older face perhaps, but he recognized it as surely as the magician in his turn had just recognized Tesla. Sergei the Amazing, indeed!

His name. Right there.

How could Lauder have overlooked such an obvious confession?

"Thank you all for your kind attention," Sergei told them. "But what you have seen here is not magic; I am but a fabricator of tricks. A rude illusionist — " He borrowed another of the pauses that Sam admired and dared to glance again at Tesla. "— Yet, here at this fair are truly great and remarkable men whose miracles you may already have witnessed. I implore you not to become dulled to these marvels, because I do them such disservice.

"However, I have talents they do not; to wit, I am a prognosticator *without peer.*" He gestured widely with his gloves to indicate the painted canvas wall that proclaimed the same. "The scenes behind me are but a poor representation of what I have seen of the future that awaits you, your children and your grandchildren, built upon the foundations laid here at this very fair. You are witnesses to the birth of a new and wondrous age, and it is an honor to salute your good fortune."

The crowd began to stir restlessly. They were fed-up with this kind of pontificating. If the show was over, they prepared to shuffle away. They were starting to remember how tired they were.

Nikola looked askance down at Sam. "And now we come to it. We shall find out what he wants. Be on your guard."

The magician upped his volume. "Before you take your leave, I beg you to afford me another moment. If you please, I would like to demonstrate to you how I know this is so. I am not a futurist by a gift of birth, nor by a boon bestowed by an elder seer. Through the tinkering of my meager sciences, I have opened a doorway to the actual future, and through that doorway I am visited by a citizen of the very city you see painted behind me."

He had their attention again.

"I should like to open that doorway again tonight, as that person is anxious to meet such an esteemed company. She — yes, it is a member of the fairer sex —speaks of the White City as do we of Athens or Cairo or of that holy city, Jerusalem."

"Here it comes," Sam Clemens winked at Tesla.

Tesla agreed. "For half a dollar admission you may listen to an actress babble about a New Jerusalem. I would wager on it. He is an obvious charlatan. Let us depart."

He was about to turn away, but the magician captivated him again by rolling a wheeled dais to the front stage from between the scenery curtains. On it was a rice-paper scrim stretched tight across the center. On one side of this sail, he set a small table and a lighted globe, which burned especially bright. The sky was now a deep indigo, dark enough that the globe cast his clean shadow on the sail when he stood between it and the table. The globe did not appear to be wired, and its light was many magnitudes brighter than a single bulb, like an arc lamp.

"My carbonite globe!" Tesla hissed. "I told you that young woman would not guard my exhibit! He has stolen my globe!"

"Easy, Nicky. Let's just see how this plays out. We can collar him after it is over." Sam was obviously enjoying himself. He had no idea of the singular rarity of the globe.

Tesla was livid, and barely managed to contain himself.

Sergei set a straight-back chair on the opposite side from the table and lamp. He seated himself in it and removed his shoes and tossed them aside. His feet were bare and white on a plate of copper at the foot of his chair. "Madame McIntyre, if you please," he called off stage. A grandmotherly woman, dressed near as smartly as the magician, parted the scenery and emerged.

"That's the one I told you about!" Sam burst. "She's the one who gave me this." He fanned the calling card in front of Tesla.

She was pushing a serving cart, and on it, an ominous apparatus. It was a box with a row of small bulbs, which weakly blinked off and on. On the top was a big jaw switch with a wooden handle. The old woman moved with an unnatural slowness, for maximum dramatic suspense. She put her cart before the magician and lifted from under it a metal helmet, attached with wires to the box. Sergei the Amazing handed her his top hat with his usual flourish, and took the helmet and adjusted it to his head with a leather strap under his chin.

"Ladies and gentlemen. This procedure is not without risk. I ask for perfect silence whilst I prepare myself and align to the resonances of our visitor. She will be unable to pass entirely into this sphere, but you will see her, though only I through my helmet will be able to hear her. However, once she appears, you may ask her anything you like, and I will answer on her behalf. Now, silence please."

He gestured to the old woman. "Madam. The lights," he said, and the old woman took a three-foot T-rod and fit it into the pipe-valve feeding the gas footlights around the edge of the wagon bed. She twisted it to turn them off. The illumination of the fair glowed over the wall, but the position of the wagon snug to the dark side afforded the white scrim a brilliant glow from the globe, undiluted by the lights from the midway. Sergei the Amazing was facing the audience on one side of the scrim; the table and globe were on the other side.

When the tension of the audience reached its mark, he reached out a hand that visibly trembled and threw the switch. The bank of lights on the device went bright and then blew out together with a loud bang, causing the onlookers to jump and cry out. Sergei's body went rigid and his eyes rolled up into his head, and then he began jerking and kicking like a man in an electric chair.

Even Tesla held his breath.

The matronly assistant struck a pose of peril, one hand before her face, warding off the scene before her. It was poor melodrama, as though walking slowly onto the stage had exhausted her reserves for the dramatic. Nevertheless, when Sergei finally slumped into his chair a woman in the audience screamed.

At the edge of the crowd, Lauder watched with avid fascination.

The magician allowed the moment to drag and let doubt settle firmly on his audience before he rewarded those watching with a twitch, first in one hand, and then in the other. To the relief of his audience, he slowly recovered his posture, but his movement was unnatural and puppet-like, as if the helmet itself had lifted him. He sat ramrod straight and stared forward with wide unblinking eyes. "Hark! She comes!" he gasped.

The light from the globe guttered for a moment, pulling all eyes to the to the other side of the scrim. It guttered again, and as everyone stared at this disturbance, the globe vanished.

But the light remained.

A shadow danced against the bright paper sail. This was a signal to the assistant, who again approached the dais and this time kicked it like a potter's wheel. The dais began to slowly revolve and the crowd cried out as the scrim moved perpendicular to the stage and they could see the clear outline of a woman holding in her hands the starburst of light. But there was no woman and there was no longer any source of light. The disk continued around, revealing all angles of a shadow with neither a light nor figure to cast it.

Even Nikola Tesla's vast budget of logic was spent.

Sam Clemens was fit to bust with the thrill of it.

"Yer questions, please!" the old lady shouted. "Jist be askin' an theyuns' – *they will* answer ye iffin' they can."

The crowd that had so eagerly pressed forward was now mute. The unseen lamp shifted and the figure showed in profile, her lips moving, gesturing to her unheard speech. The shadow-figure appeared clothed in a kind of Grecian dress of material so thin it allowed the light to shine through and outline her form, leaving no doubt as to her gender. In silhouette, it was understood one breast was bared along with her arm and shoulder. The fabric was so thin she might as well have been clothed in cobwebs. Her toga was also short, and when she lowered the lamp, the shadow of her bare legs stretched fetchingly up the scrim. On her arm a heavy bracelet hung. Her hair was pinned at the back of her head but loose strands hung in tendrils around her willowy neck. She seemed a wraith and fragile, but also evoked the visage of a goddess, idealized as any in oils in the art galleries of the fair. Her image fit perfectly with the archaic White City, and appealed to the Gilded Age romanticism of the audience, if not their Victorian prudery.

"The Lady sends her greetings to the fortuitous people of Chicago in 1893," Sergei said, filling the silence. "From Chicago in 2130."

Lauder clamped his hand over his mouth when he realized the high thin whine he heard was himself.

There was a pause while the audience gathered their pluck and courage. "What is my name?" a man finally cried out in challenge. The shadow shook its curls.

"The Lady begs your pardon, sir, but she does not transmigrate thoughts and cannot speak to things of which she has no knowledge." The magician paused, as though listening. "However, she does beg the gentleman's pardon to tell her his name and that of his wife, for she may know their progeny, and would be honored to deliver greetings to them on your behalf."

"Jebediah Jobs!" the speaker barked out. The shadow appeared to strike a pose of astonishment, far more convincing than that of the matron, and the light source panned as she spoke with animation.

"The Lady ventures to guess you may be the ancestor of that same Stephen Jobs; who shall be an inventor of miraculous devices and who shall amass great wealth and power. And even if he is not of your direct line, know this sir, the name of Jobs will someday be spoken of in every household. Even so, in each home there shall be a device which is like unto the telephone, save it operates without wires and provides the very image of the person with whom you speak —not as a kinetoscope, but moving as in life in that very moment as a living stereograph. Also this device contains all the libraries of the world so that anything you may wish to know is yours, and may be read as a book. Indeed, it is no larger than a small book of psalms, and may be carried in your vest pocket! Thus you may indulge any symphony, or observe the great events in history. Even the comedies and tragedies of playwrights may be watched as though through a window with this device."

The man's wife laid her hand on his arm. "My father's name is Stephen. Perhaps the boy is named so after him?"

"That's my boy!" the man shouted to friendly laughter.

The magician responded: "Indeed, but even master Stephen does not approach the genus of a man in your company tonight."

"Here it comes," Tesla muttered. But Sergei did not pursue it and instead answered another question from the crowd.

"In which year does our Lord and Savior return?"

On the revolving platform, the shadowed figure bowed her head and became still for a moment. She returned to three-quarter profile and her speech could only be detected by the movement of her chin.

"The Lady respectfully declines to answer matters of faith, as that is the providence of the Lord. She reminds the people of 1893 that she is not a spirit herself, but merely a woman speaking from another time, which is her present. However, there are now – in her time – devices, which can and do speak with spirits, much as the telephone works today. In truth, she has brought one with her this evening to demonstrate. This device is called a Quantum Entanglement Transmitter."

At the edge of the crowd, Lauder nearly peed himself. All of his suspicions now confirmed.

Sergei's claim induced much murmuring and speculation. Tesla did not wait for them to gather their thoughts. He winked at Sam and stepped up, lowering his handkerchief to do so. "You have a device which gives you congress with the dead?" he shouted. Sergei the Amazing stopped staring blankly and let his gaze rest in sharp focus on the speaker. The shadow was nodding and needed no interpretation.

"You can do this for us now?" Tesla challenged.

The shadow nodded again.

"If you please," Sergei asked tightly. "With whom would you like to speak?"

"I should like to speak with a scientist. One given to great discoveries and insight. An individual, I should hope, still of great renown in your own time. A man dead roughly a hundred seventy-five years by your reckoning. Perhaps as much as two hundred." He paused for the benefit of Samuel Clemens at his side before delivering *his* snapper: "I should like to speak with *myself.*"

All heads pivoted to take in Nikola Tesla, standing tall and indignant, his fine nostrils flaring above his trim mustache as he pumped currents of vitriol through his dark eyes.

The shadow petrified, and Sergei the Amazing was struck dumb. The only sound in the company was Sam Clemens, who was bent double with laughter.

"I thought not," Tesla said coldly. He turned, this time fully intent on leaving, when the paper sail began to shake and flap violently up on the stage. All eyes, including those of Nikola Tesla and Samuel Clemens and Lauder, and even Sergei the Amazing were drawn to it. The globe was returned to the table, and the shadow gone, but one could clearly see the results of the lady frantically shaking the flimsy framework of the sail to get everyone's attention.

Tesla sneered and turned away again, covering ground with his long strides.

Sergei leaped to his feet and shouted in perfect Serbian: *"Mr. Tesla, I beg of you, your brother Dondi has an urgent message from beyond the grave!"*

Nikola froze. The chill coming off of him stopped Sam in his tracks. Tesla did not turn around but bellowed his furious response, and then was away, with Sam scrambling to keep up.

Lauder, however, remained behind.

CHAPTER TEN

"[Inventors] are the creators of the world."
—Mark Twain
Wardenclyffe Foundation Archives

∞

The Gypsy Caravan

"Lilly, wait!" Sunner cried, but she was already gone. He couldn't see her, of course, but he saw the crowd open up where she passed as they were repelled by her vibe and moved aside. From the wagon-bed stage he watched the wake of her passage, which pointed like an arrow to where Nikola Tesla and Mark Twain were striding away down the dark track.

He turned and kicked over his chair, sending it careening off the dais. His audience developed a keen interest in one another, concurring on the finer points of dismay and mortification and decided as one to make an escape as discretely as possible.

It didn't matter. The magic show was over. The gig was up. The curtain had fallen. Sunner would never again pose as Sergei the Amazing.

He left the stage, dove through Lilly's painted scenery and jumped to the ground off the back of the wagon and entered the tent behind it. He moved through the partitioned 'parlor' with its draped table and two chairs where Nikola Tesla should have been sitting *right now*, and listening to Sunner explain his and Lilly's plight over the guttering stump of a candle.

He thought his magician's tricks would be self evident to a man like Tesla. Thought they were enough to prove his competence: *See that guy up on the stage? He can bend light! He's not just dicking around. Better see what he's up to.* Then, the tricky part: proving he'd traveled back in time. It would have been a delicate conversation, but, screw it, he'd tackle him if he had to. Keep him there until all was explained. He even had a length of rope beneath the table. If he'd had to restrain him, he would have, by God, and by any means possible until the great man believed. Sunner would have *made* him believe. If all else failed, he'd have Lilly touch him. That would get his attention! The frequency of her resonation beat the hell out of sticking a fork in an outlet. Tesla would have been persuaded. *Would have been,* but now that chance was gone.

Sunner felt the noose tighten around his heart. Time was running out. Day by day Pi milked less. He could only imagine the effect this had on Lilly. She had to be starving. Literally starving. He insisted she do nothing all day, saving her strength for the performance at night, conserving calories the rest of the time. Her quiet stretches were more frequent, lasted longer. He spent them straining to hear her stir, hoping she slept. There was no way to know. Sometimes little gifts showed up. Things she pilfered from the fair, so she wasn't always sleeping. There was only so much he could do.

The goat traveled better. Traveled 'well', as one might describe a bottle of fine wine, but she was trans-dimensional enough that Lilly could drink her milk and survive, if only just barely.

The accident in Sunner's barn back in Arkansas had been sloppy, and *thank God*. The pigeon caught up with them also trans-resonated and could move cross-dimensionally, flying between the worlds. It was a homing pigeon. Even taken across time and space, the little sucker did what all pigeons did. *It flew home.*

If super-pigeon could make the round-trip, then so could they. And it did so without the benefit of Sergei's Hadron Cell. Which was hopeful, because the portable black hole Sunner and Sergei used was a tricky little bastard. They went in together, and came out the same person. Okay, they *were* the same person, technically, but separated by about a century of hard living. The nice Hadron cell fixed all that. Nature dislikes redundancies. She likes to normalize things. Conserve energy. Take the path of least resistance. Tidy things up. Nature is a bitch.

Sunner dove under the back flap to the 'family room' and rummaged through the drawers of his trunk until he produced a fountain pen and his notebook. He scribbled down the Serbian words Tesla had shouted at him, phonetically recalling them as best he could.

His memory was improving, but it was nowhere near the total recall he had before his neurons were scrambled like brains in a blender, as happened when he and Sergei were merged together. As time passed, it was settling out. He felt more distinctly *himself* as a single person, and less like a man possessed, or s*elf-possessed*, in the most literal sense. He still thought of himself as Sunner, yet it felt natural to be called Sergei by others, and the memories and experience of his elder self were at his disposal. Sometimes he was tempted to investigate if Sergei felt the same, to go deeper in and suss it out. Did Sergei also think of himself as the "I"? Just the thought gave him the willies. Schizophrenic flirtations were firmly dealt with when they arose. He had enough on his plate right now, *thank you very much*. He could deal with the interior dialogue. It was not unlike what anyone might experience when talking to himself. It was only when his two selves disagreed that things got dicey. Two wills pulling the body in two directions might be fun to watch, but it was paralysis and seizure at the same time. It happened only once, but it had come at a critical moment and nearly got him shot on the road to Bentonville. Both of him resolved it wouldn't happen again.

Sunner looked at the Serbian words he'd written until was satisfied he could repeat them. He would ask the translation from Vladimir, who had given him the first phrase to memorize: *Mr. Tesla, I beg of you, your brother Dondi urgently wishes to speak with you from beyond the grave.* It was their last and most desperate card to play, and he had played it badly.

He blew it.

Again.

Sunner decided his cot needed kicking, so he kicked it until he'd smashed it to kindling. He would sleep on the ground with the goat tonight, and that suited his mood just fine.

Sergei didn't argue.

Outside, Idee was calling, "Git along now. Thas' all they is tonight. He ain't takin' no more readin's. Iffen ye wants readin's, you'uns come back tomorrow, hear?" – even though the crowd had dispersed already.

Sunner softened a little. She was doing it for his benefit. Making a brave show that maybe all was not lost. Idee noisily completed her routines of closing the stage and by the time it was cleared, Sunner was changed and ready to go in his broadcloth breeches and a plain white linen shirt, tails untucked. He left off the collar, vest, suspenders, jacket and hat. It was hot and he needed very badly to feel himself for a bit, and not an actor in an endless costume drama.

"What in tarnation?" Idee scolded when she stomped into the tent, then she pulled up short. "Ye ain't a-goin' out like that are ye?" she asked him, adjusting her spectacles to prove she'd had a good look at him and didn't approve. She was all propriety now; a far cry from the Ozark Granny that first met him with a rock-salt blast from her shotgun. She stood glaring in her new chin-to-floor crepe green dress. This one had 100 onyx buttons (not pearl) and filigreed black lace at the neck and cuffs, which was her only concession to probable widowhood. "I work them crowds fer a month solid and you'uns goes and runned oft Mr. Twain and Mr. Tesla afores they's even set foot in this here tent. And lookie here. Ye done smashed yer bed to smithereens! And now yer goin' out a-lookin' like ye just jumped offin a boxcar. Jist look at how yer dressed!"

"Not now, Idee," he told her, and managed to give her a kiss atop her head as he squeezed past.

"I ain't cleanin' this up!" she yelled after him, but she was already stooping to do so and he was already gone.

∞

Lauder drew back when Sergei burst from the tent and stalked off down the lane. The magician looked quite different without his tuxedo and cape. Lauder waited a moment before trailing after him. There weren't many people left along the makeshift avenue for Lauder to blend in with, and there was too much light leaking over the wall from the fair to follow directly. Lauder had to slink from one shadow to the next. He had no weapons in his pockets, only his bare hands. He had followed Tesla so long without success these many months that tonight he'd suffered no premonition that this would be any different, so he had come unarmed –stupid of him. Now that he had the Chief Elder Enge, the Murderer of the World alone in the dark, what could he do about it? He clenched his fists rhythmically. Did he have it in him to kill with his bare hands? He considered it seriously and then thought not. He'd never killed a man before, unless you counted his role in operating the Westinghouse Generator at Auburn State Prison for Kemmler's execution. Or, *All-Burn,* as he'd come to think of it. Because Lauder was Kemmler's chaplain, he was asked to pray over his charred corpse after it was removed from the electric chair. His prayers had never been so earnest.

He'd ministered to Kemmler in the weeks leading up to the day when his sentence was carried out, the first of its kind, death by electrocution. Lauder had grown fond of the hapless killer. More than fond. Thinking of him now, he understood Kemmler was just another death to lay at the feet of the Murderer of the World. A martyr in the struggle to keep the universe whole. But for all that, *no.* Lauder would not trust his bare hands to complete his service to the Lord. He would wait and watch and choose his moment. He had all the time in the world.

∞

Sunner entered the Gypsy camp and pounded on the wagon door. Esmeralda answered with a sour whine, but it was Vladimir who cracked the top of the Dutch door and then threw it open wide when he saw who it was.

"Sergei, you scoundrel!" And then, over his shoulder, "Roll out, woman! The Tillmans are here."

"No, it's just me."

Vladimir raised an eyebrow. "Your phantom is not with you?"

"No. She's... she is... out," Sunner gestured vaguely. "Running an errand." It sounded ridiculous to his ears, especially against the anxiety clamoring for attention every second Lilly was gone.

"Never mind, Es!" Vladimir called back into the wagon. "She is not here. Just Sergei." He scrutinized Sunner. "It is early. You are not working tonight?"

"I am working. I did. Done now. Vlad, I need another translation."

"Certainly my friend. Just give me a moment." He pulled back inside, shut the door and exchanged complaints with his wife before the door swung open again and he stepped out of his narrow wagon, which squeaked up on its springs when he stepped off.

"Profits are down today," he explained, excusing his wife's mood. "The cards foretold it would be so for another week. Coincidentally the same week every month," he winked. "Too bad, as she is particularly insightful during her confinement.

"Come and sit by my fire." Vladimir indicated the section of barrel hoop on the ground that corralled the burned down husk of a tree stump. While Sunner found a seat, the Gypsy prodded the stump until it agreed to flare and burn sullenly, giving them a little more light. They didn't bother with the lantern. The glow from the fair was as bright as a full moon. The fire itself was just for conversation.

Sunner sat on a cut round from a tree trunk that would be another night's fire. He pulled a small bottle of port from his deep pockets and handed it across to Vladimir who took it and pulled the cork with his teeth and gave it a vintner's sniff. "Finer than gold," he agreed. "What do you need translated tonight?"

Sunner found he didn't need to consult the page torn from his notebook after all. He recited the phrase carefully, glad his memory was improving.

"That is it?" Vladimir remarked, surprised, and took a swig from the bottle. "The cards are wrong. Profits are up! I have made a good bargain tonight."

"What does it mean?" Sunner asked.

"*Tell your employer you have failed,*" he said with a shrug. "Was it the man with the dead brother Dondi?"

Sunner nodded through clotting despair. It was as bad as it could get. Tesla thought he was working for Edison.

"Not even a curse. He could not have been too disagreeable. Did he accompany this with a gesture of any kind? For another bottle I will interpret gestures for you!" The Romanian laughed and took another swallow from the bottle.

Lilly had spirited the drink away from the Agricultural Building, where the vintners of Italia had a vat of bare-legged beauties stomping grapes with their skirts pinned up to the height of their thighs and their breasts swaying free in their blouses. It wasn't the easiest heist for Lilly, as it was a popular exhibit, and the crowds were dense. But she managed to keep the cabinet stocked.

The Gypsy was asking: "Do you want a response? What do you want to say now?"

"Nothing," Sunner said. "I am out of things to say. I only needed to get him alone. For just a few minutes, but he is right. I *have* failed."

"That is no problem," Vladimir said earnestly. "You point him out to me, I will deliver him to your tent. When he regains consciousness, you will have your few minutes." He laughed expansively again. "But I cannot vouchsafe how receptive he will be!"

He held the bottle out to Sunner, who started to wave it off but changed his mind. He took a deep draught before he handed it back.

"Perhaps I will, Vlad. But not today. If it comes to that though, you may name your price." Sunner surprised himself. Would he resort to kidnapping Nikola Tesla in order to get his attention? He shuddered to realize he *might*.

He cursed again his lack of foresight. Hector's watch that Lilly wore made the time jump just fine. Why didn't he see it? He could have brought *anything.* A smartphone would have been his golden ticket where Tesla was concerned. How could he have not planned for this? *Goddamn Sunner,* Sergei thought. *Goddamn Sergei!* His other half added. Then by mutual necessity, both of his personalities stood down. It was hard enough to for his two selves to inhabit the same body without descending into bickering. Branching timelines is all fine and good heading out. Coming back, the logistics were a nightmare. One man. Two lifelines. One body. Two minds.

It was nothing compared to Lilly's problem. She wasn't here at all.

Sunner and Sergei, young and old, pulled themselves together for the problem at hand: *My kingdom for a solar calculator,* he thought. Given time and materials, he might even be able to fashion one, but he didn't have that kind of time. The fair would be over by the end of next month.

Tesla would be installing his turbines at Niagara next year, but where until then? Could Lilly keep going in the meantime and in full pursuit?

He stood up to go and Vladimir stood with him and slapped him on the back for encouragement.

"Cheer up, my friend. If you like I will get Esmeralda up to consult the cards for you. You will be enlightened. Not cheap tricks like your sideshow; *no offense.* Come. Put her to the test. Who knows what the future will hold?" Vladimir was studying him intently. He seemed to want very badly for Sunner to submit to a reading.

"Who indeed knows what the future holds," Sunner agreed with a straight face. "But no. Another time, perhaps. Thank you, Vlad. You are a good friend." He reached out to shake his hand.

"And you are a good partner!" Vladimir grasped both of his hands on Sunner's arm and then pulled him into a back-slapping hug.

When Sunner stepped back, Vladimir was displaying for him the contents of his pockets.

"A good partner, but a *rube*. I tell you, Sergei. You have flair, and you charm the ladies, but as a geek, you leave much to be desired. You come around tomorrow. I will show you how to defend yourself from the likes of me."

"There is no one the likes of you," Sunner told him, taking back his coins. He flipped one through the air to Vladimir, who caught it on the downward arc. "For the lesson," he said, and then walked away.

Vladimir added the coin to the other heavier one he had failed to return, and went back to the bow-top wagon whistling. With them he would purchase a better mood for Esmeralda.

Sunner walked not only in the general direction where Lauder crouched in shadows, but on a direct path straight toward him.

"Wait!" Esmeralda called from the wagon.

Sunner stopped.

Lauder froze.

Esmeralda was framed in the doorway of the van, a night wrap pulled around her shoulders. "Come back, Mr. Tillman," she called. "We have unfinished business." She peered out into the dark with obvious unease.

"Lilly isn't here," Sunner told her, and then realized it was unnecessary. Esmeralda needed no one to tell her that.

"I need to see *you*," she said. "Not your ghostly wife. I need to see you *now*."

Sunner didn't need Vladimir to interpret the imperative in her command. Nevertheless he started to insist it was an inconvenient time, but Sergei squelched it and Sunner found himself turning back to the wagon.

Clairvoyance, or *clear sight*, allowed Esmeralda to see what others could not. This included Lilly. Sunner didn't give credence to the super-natural, but he would allow for *extra-sensory*. Most humans only perceived about 1% of the electromagnetic spectrum of light. It was about the same for sound. He wished he could measure the Gypsy woman's expanded perceptive range. It might tell him where on that scale Lilly was. Where was she pitched? Could her resonance be described by tones? Esmeralda could certainly hear her. Through her intercession, Sunner could even have conversations with Lilly. *Real conversations* that assured him like nothing else that his time-trapped wife wasn't just a figment of his imagination and all of this a madman's dream. He didn't have the luxury to say 'no' to Esmeralda tonight or any other night. He would do anything she asked.

He stepped up to the wagon and Es pulled back giving him room to enter.

The habit to remove his hat had engrained itself. After he raised his hand, he realized he wasn't wearing one tonight and so tried to smooth back his hair instead. His recovery was foiled when the Gypsy woman captured his hand in hers and pulled him by it over to the lantern.

"I will see your hand now," she said.

Sunner and Sergei both had their doubts about palmistry, but neither of them would go risk surrendering their secrets. He pulled his hand back, but she held on with a surprising grip. Any more resistance on his part would turn it into a real struggle. He was aware of Vladimir at his back, between him and the door. Something here was not right. There was sudden tension in the air. One hundred and fifty three years of collective experience told him to yield. He relaxed his hand and gave her a sheepish smile. "As you wish," he said, but he was sure he had little choice in the matter.

To his surprise she didn't turn it palm up, but examined the back of it in the light. Her brow knit and she made an impatient gesture for him to surrender his other hand as well. He did. She compared them, side by side and pursed her lips, puzzled.

"What are you looking for?" Vladimir asked her.

"The sign of the trinity," she answered. "I saw a holy man. The mark of God on his hand." She didn't add, *a very bad man*, but it was implied so plainly it gelled the atmosphere around them.

Sergei's reaction prickled Sunner's scalp. "Describe this mark," he encouraged her. His mouth was dry.

"Trinity," she said. "You know. Treble. Triune. Trident — like this?" She held up three fingers.

"On the back of my hand?"

She took her three fingers and pressed their tips near his wrist and drew them with pressure towards his knuckles. When she removed them, three pale stripes remained. They began to turn pink right away. "Like *that*," she said.

Sunner was shoved aside inside his skull and Sergei took command. When he did, Esmeralda dropped his hand so suddenly, Vladimir put his left hand on the nightstick hanging by their door while his right hand palmed his switchblade knife, and his fingers caressed the release button.

"I am not that man." Sergei, not Sunner said.

"But neither are you the man standing here before me," she whispered. All the color had drained from her face, but she gave no signal to Vladimir. All it would have taken was a glance, a flash in her eyes, but she withheld it.

Sergei repeated as emphatically as he could, "I am not *that man*." But he began to perspire when the possibility of whom she might mean caught up with him.

Esmeralda kept her face a stone, but her eyes continued to probe.

Sergei opened the memory to bring Sunner up to speed. Together they recalled the photograph Lilly had found in the Pilot's House Pub in Redding, Connecticut, in 2010. The old one with Mark Twain and Nikola Tesla and himself seated at the same table, and with the words "The Lazy Eight" scrawled across the bottom. Evidence enough for a time traveler: the pun for infinity.

In the leading edge of that photo, in extreme foreground was just the hand of another man, with three tattoos across the back of it. Sergei knew them to be shunt tats: Marks received each time a citizen of his time entered a Quantum Suicide Machine, and emerged — or did not emerge — in the new dimension paralleled by the act. In one he lived. In one he died. To the one exiting the machine, no change was detected at all, but in the dimension in which he died, there was one less mouth to feed. It was Sergei's own invention. It was necessary. It was painless, and most of all it worked. Gradually the pressures of overpopulation eased. It was a better world, *or worlds,* because of it. But there were a few who didn't see it that way. Religious fanatics, mostly. Fundamentalist terrorists. The man with the three tats was one of these, he was certain. Sergei had first seen that hand reaching for him as he entered his — to be cliché — *his time machine,* and had managed to escape into the past and out of his clutch just barely in time. But maybe not. The photo was evidence he was followed, and now Es was telling him the same thing: a holy man. A *bad* man. Indeed. That described the fanatics perfectly. He knew them well. This man and his tribe had dogged him for nearly half his lifetime. But the photo was only a possibility now. Anything could happen.

"This man has lost his lover," she said. "For this he mourns and seeks and will stop at nothing to undo what has been done."

Sergei kept Sunner's face impassive. For the third time he said, "I am not that man." Although the description fit him so exactly he half expected a cock to crow at his denial. Her next question shocked him.

"Are you the Murderer of the World?"

He had to swallow to compose himself, realizing as he did so it would appear a duplicitous act.

"By my word, Madame, I am the opposite of that."

"This phrase is not new to you," she said.

Sergei opened his gaze to her, and held her with its sincerity. "This man, the one with the trinity on his hand, he and others like him call me that, but they are wrong. The tattoos are a mark of honor in my ... *organization.* They are given for heroic acts. But he has turned against us." He didn't dare to say more. He had said what he could while remaining within the boundaries of truth, because he knew she would know the difference.

They stared at one another for a long moment. "There are doves in your eyes," she finally said.

Sergei blinked in surprise.

Esmeralda looked at Vladimir then. Her eyes didn't flash. Her gaze was steady.

"He speaks the truth," she told him. Vladimir diminished in height by a full two inches as he exhaled the breath he'd been holding.

"But this other man. He is here. He is coming for you. I have seen it."

"I know," Sergei said with a resigned acceptance, trying to ignore Sunner who raged inside his skull.

"And as for you..." she poked a finger in his chest, "I still don't know who you are."

"I hardly know where to begin," he sighed.

Esmeralda pulled her night-wrap closer around her shoulders and shook her head. "It is late, and you are preoccupied. Come back with your wife, Mr. Tillman. We will all sort it out together. Perhaps I can give you new insight. This fallen hero of yours, we will watch for him together."

"Thank you," he whispered with gratitude. He took her hand and bowed over it: A stately gesture that was not in Sunner's repertoire, Sergei, however, pulled it off flawlessly. When he turned to take his leave of Vladimir, the Gypsy was nonchalantly cleaning his nails with his switchblade knife. Their eyes met and Vladimir gave him a lopsided grin and a shrug.

"And what would you have done, my friend, had your Lilly told you the Murderer of the World was in your kitchen?"

Sergei gave it solemn consideration, and told him the truth, "The trouble with the Wholly Rollers is, if they were right, I would be compelled to join them. Their actions would be just and admirable, if their convictions were correct."

"And you are certain they are not?"

"I am," he answered, and keeping his eyes downcast, he pushed past Vladimir and into the night.

"Curious," Vladimir said to the empty doorway after he had left.

"What is?" Esmeralda asked.

"If he is so certain, why does he not also wear tattoos?"

CHAPTER ELEVEN

"When angry count four; when very angry, swear."
—Mark Twain
Wardenclyffe Foundation Archives

∞

The Hall of Electricity

Lilly hurried. She retied her toga to cover both breasts as she ran through the crowd even though she could not be seen. She was quickly out of breath clumping along as best she could in her makeshift shoes with the cork soles. In her old life, *before*, she'd not worn high heels. The formal footwear of her artist tribe was ballet slippers or high-top Keds or in-studio it was either bare feet or flip-flops. Besides being awkward, she worried about the soles shredding on the gravel track. They'd been a bitch to cobble together, even though cork, like everything else, was abundant at the fair. Virtually everything which existed in the world in 1893 was here, and as long as it was not so big that she couldn't lift it and keep it from grounding to the earth, it was easily obtainable, thanks to her unique talent of making things vanish when she carried them.

She cursed the dozens of buttons securing her shoes to her feet and ankles, preventing her from kicking them off. She couldn't risk taking her eyes off Tesla to remove them, so she kept going, her gaze locked on his derby hat least she loose it in a sea of bobbing heads in the illuminated nighttime. Her task was made easier because Tesla was tall at least, and relative to the present population, so was she –even more so in these ridiculous shoes. Keeping him in sight, she bobbed and weaved around people who shied uneasily away from the queer-slippery sensation of her passing, and good thing; She'd not have lasted a day without being trampled to death otherwise.

She'd have preferred the normal arrangement, walking with Sunner to her right, Idee to her left and Pi on a leash just in front of her. Their little phalanx kept her out of harm's way, and the crowd parted just as well ahead of Pi's curving horns, although usually with starts and laughter.

Lilly didn't know what she would do once she caught up with them. *Plan B* was to capture the inventor's attention with magician's tricks orchestrated with Tesla's own technology. It had taken weeks to prepare. Sunner thought Tesla wouldn't be able to resist speaking with him after such a performance. When he saw he was wrong, he took a desperate gamble, striking close to Tesla's heart; He revealed he knew the great and terrible secret of his brother's death. It was a desperate ploy and, as it turned out, a stupid one.

Sam Clemens was slowing Tesla down, and thank goodness. Her head was already swimming with dark clouds that boiled at the edge of her vision and she was gasping for air. She was too weak and malnourished for such a run, but she pressed on until she was able to fall in behind them, close enough to hear them speak, had they been speaking.

They weren't. Tesla was striding in mute fury. Sergei's words pounding though his head: *"Your brother Dondi has a message for you from beyond the grave."*

Clemens made little wordless exclamations at this or that curiosity of the Midway, but for all his effort, he was unable to capture Tesla's attention or divert his simmering anger.

Their destination was beyond the midway. They were headed to the massive Electrical Exhibition Hall.

At this hour, the main buildings of the fair were abandoned but the walkways were packed. Sightseers were all outside take in the lights. The sweeping beams of searchlights played and bobbed over the irregular and ornate facades of the towering buildings that were also decked and frosted with so many bulbs it reminded Lilly of Christmas decorations. The beacons shown down from atop the peristyle that bridged the canal entrance from Lake Michigan and a small sailboat eased its stately way between its columns. Crowds gathered along the lagoon railing, admiring the way the fountains and schooners prettily disturbed the reflections of the dramatic illuminations and to watch the great lighted wheel slowly turn. This was when the White City was its most magical. It was obvious Sam wanted nothing more than to stop and let it shiver through him. He'd seen nothing like it in all his travels throughout the world. It rivaled even Athens by moonlight.

But Tesla didn't slow down. When they reached the Hall of Electricty, he took the stairs two at a time. Sam had to pump his legs to keep up. The Columbian guard at the door stood aside, accustomed to admitting the Serbian at odd hours.

"Mr. Tesla." The guard said with a touch to the brim of his cap. Tesla nodded curtly but didn't slow down. The door didn't open fast enough to suit him, so he squeezed through sideways as soon as he was able. Sam slid in with him and so did Lilly, but just barely, causing the guard to inspect the sweep to see what it had caught on.

Tesla strode to his exhibition space. His assistant was there, a young man in shirtsleeves who was studying papers atop a podium desk under one of the burning lamps. When the student looked up with a guileless half-smile and raised eyebrows, Tesla bore down on him and swiped his notes from the top of the desk and let them scatter to the floor.

"Inventory *everything,*" Tesla hissed. "Machines, bulbs, tubes, diagrams, fountain pens... *everything.*"

"Yes sir," his assistant stammered and hopped off his stool to begin.

Sam stood to one side, a silent witness.

So did Lilly.

Tesla was at his tall case, scanning the contents, and then he opened it and carefully removed his carbon-button globe. He cradled it like a new father holding his infant, and examined it carefully. It was his, whole and unmolested. The carbon-button still new and unburned. The magician had not stolen it after all.

"Get a lock for this," he said as he replaced the lamp, and took a silk kerchief and covered it, tucking it in. He fished a key from his pocket next and unlocked the file drawer and began paging through the diagrams.

"Is anything missing?" he called.

"Not yet, sir."

"The bulbs particularly. The vacuum tubes."

"All here."

"Are you sure? *The wireless transmitter?*" He cried out, growing more frantic, even though he could see it plainly right before him. He uttered a Croatian curse that would have amused the Gypsy Vladimir. He struggled against the realization that the only thing worse than having his property and patents stolen was to find them precedented. By a sideshow con man, no less.

"All here, sir," his assistant reported.

"Nicky," Sam said.

"Where are the sketches?" Nikola cried. "They should be right here!"

"*Nicky,*" Sam's voice was tight and full of caution. Tesla looked up.

Standing at the railing were three men, casually rolling up their shirtsleeves. Even without their jackets with the pinned gold medal with "Edison" on one leg of the ribbon and "General Electric" on the other, he knew who they were.

Tesla stood to his full height and glowered at them. They were grinning.

"I believe the Wizard has lost something," one of them jeered. "Misplace one of your lightning bolts?"

That was all the confession Tesla needed. He stood up and unleashed his indignation as effectively as a tall bowling pin might resist three balls boring down on him at speed.

Done with his sleeves, the stoutest of the three tossed his hat aside with a 'bring it on' leer.

Sam sighed and looked around for something with a good heft to it, but all of Tesla's devices were bolted firmly to their tables. Tesla's assistant was backed up protectively against the tube cabinet. Protective of himself, that is.

"Shit. Shit. Shit." Lilly ducked under the railing and entered Tesla's exhibit just a moment before the three toughs climbed over it to stand in cock-fight readiness. They sneered at Tesla and dared him to throw them out, or better yet, throw the first punch. Nikola's long delicate fingers balled into fists; he raised them, in fisticuff style, rigidly, like a child might pantomime fighters in the ring.

Sam and Lilly both groaned in despair. Edison's men laughed and raised their fists as well. They assumed stances that were as natural to them as walking.

"Bad idea, *dickheads.*" Lilly said, and reached for the nearest man.

He went down like all his strings were cut, without even a shout of surprise. His eyes rolled up in his head as he convulsed in one great chattering shudder and went limp. The second one stared at him in slack jawed astonishment just before he doubled over and vomited, then fell to his knees where he barely managed to remain upright. There he remained, swaying and counting the cost of any effort beyond his own abject misery.

Tesla watched them with wide-eyed wonder. His hands sank slowly as his attention exited the fighting arena and entered the laboratory.

The third man was screaming. "What did you do? What have you done? Stop it! For the love of God, man. Stop it!" Edison's remainder backed up and seemed to trip over his own feet and went down as well. Kicking and sobbing, he scrabbled backward on the floor as fast as he could manage. His face was desperate as he cried, "Turn it off! Turn it off!"

Tesla looked quizzically at his hands and after a moment of consideration, he carefully brought them together, stopping just before his fingertips touched. He gently tapped the space between his pads, and then gingerly let them connect as if he was testing his own currents. Satisfied, he folded his hands and rested his thumbs on his chin while his index finger tapped his nose: a necessary action to prime the pump of his brain. His lids lowered to veil his thoughts but his eyes missed nothing. They were blazing with curiosity as he waited to see what might happen next. At this point his assistant leapt over the back rail and fled deep into the building to hide.

The first man who had gone down now lay as dead. Lilly was unable to muster up the sincerity to hope that he wasn't. Not since Eustess Caney had fainted dead away had she seen such a complete and satisfying reaction to her touch. *Sometimes it really came in handy.* The man who had vomited recovered enough to retreat, but he didn't go more than five paces before he suffered a crisis of conscience and came back to drag the unconscious man with him, whimpering all the while.

By the time two Columbian guards arrived, it was just Nikola Tesla and Sam Clemens, staring down at the sick pooled on the floor, which was the only evidence that something miraculous had happened here. Mr. Clemens was looking down from where he stood balanced on the seat of a chair. Getting off the floor had seemed a good idea at the time.

"What in blazes?" A guardsman demanded.

"We had a little trouble with Edison's men." Tesla said softly. "Get someone to clean that up, there's a good man." He didn't look at them at all, but backed away to sit on a stool to ponder.

The irreverent Mark Twain carefully climbed down from the seat of his chair. He was muttering to himself as one might limber up before a embarking on a vigorous prayer, but he managed to stifle it by stuffing the butt of a cigar firmly between his teeth.

Having extracted nothing useful from the inventor, nor from his rattled companion, he guards left to seek the bested brawlers.

Lilly seized the moment. She went to the basket filled with calling cards and fished out those engraved with *Sergei the Amazing.* She knew exactly where they were because she planted them herself, every day, at regular intervals. She took the small stack and stood before Tesla who was staring blankly at the floor. He was deep in thought, still tapping the side of his nose. Lilly gauged the trajectory of his line of sight and tossed down a card. He startled, and gave a little grunt. The tapping stopped. She tossed down another. And another.

"Mr. Clemens, attend if you please. I need you to confirm something for me," Tesla said quietly.

Lilly waited until Sam was standing nearby. Tesla was pointing at the three cards on the floor at his feet. Sam squatted low, his hands on his knees to see what they were and she tossed down another.

"Great Scott!" Sam cried and fell on his ass, scrambling backward, crab-walking with unapologetic determination to get as far away from the phenomenon as he could.

But Tesla leaned in. He picked up one of the cards, tilted it to catch the surface in better light and re-read it to be certain. There was only a slight shift in his expression as he rearranged his accounting. "Dust yourself off, Mr. Clemens," he said. "We are going back to the sideshow."

Unseen, Lilly did a little dance in her cork-soled shoes.

CHAPTER TWELVE

"The future will show whether my foresight is as accurate now as it has proved heretofore."
—*Nikola Tesla*
Wardenclyffe Foundation Archives

∞

The Magician's Tent

Nikola Tesla finally sat across the table from Sergei the Amazing in the front room of his tent, just as Sunner had been imagining for weeks. A new candle replaced the old one, and it too was burned down to a stuttering nub.

Sam Clemens sat on Lilly's cot, elbows on his knees, propping up his head. He looked weary of the world, but completely wide-eyed and unsleepy. He was out of cigars so he chewed his mustache in a concentrated effort to keep his opinions to himself.

Idee was in the back room, listening intently and wringing her hands.

No one could be sure where Lilly was. She was as silent as someone who wasn't quite there, which was precisely the problem at hand.

"You can prove this, of course, Mr. Tillman?" Tesla said, at the conclusion of the account.

"Hells bells, Nicky, haven't we seen proof enough?" Sam growled from the cot. His head was spinning and he wasn't at all sure he wanted any more proofs tonight. Or rather, *this morning*, as outside the cocks were crowing.

"I have seen effects," Nikola told him. "I have not seen the cause."

Sunner grinned at him. "I will, but you must prepare yourself. It is startling at first."

"That's bloody likely," Sam moaned.

"You may be excused, Mr. Clemens," Tesla said, but Sam was shaking his head.

"I reckon you need a witness you can trust. If our friend here is a mesmerist, you need me. I am impervious to hypnotism. I have tried it before but I am a hopeless subject, I am proud to say. He will not pull the wool over *my* eyes." Sam sat up, steeling himself for a shock, scowling at it in advance.

"Very well, Mr. Tillman. I shall examine your proofs," Tesla said.

"Idee? Can you bring Pi in here please?"

Granny Idee emerged from the divider between the two-roomed tent, tugging on a silver chain. The chain was taut, and then went slack as the goat stepped into the room.

"What a magnificent goat!" Tesla cried, happy as a child. He abandoned his chair and fell to his knees and hugged Pi. He began to pet her while he murmured platitudes to her in his native tongue that he hadn't used since in the farmyard of his youth. He stroked her in an methodical pattern, eyes wary for hidden devices. In return the goat licked the salt from his neck and was pleased to make his acquaintance.

"Have you traveled through time?" he asked her, gently shaking her chin by her beard in his hand. "You seem solid enough."

Sam snorted. "Yes. Ask the goat. She will tell you the truth." He gestured helplessly at Sergei. "Is this all the proof you have?"

"Please examine her thoroughly," Sunner advised. Tesla did so. He carefully lifted her front feet, and pressed his fingers between the cleft hooves, and then repeated it with her back feet. He did the same between her horns and even removed her collar and set it aside, assuring himself she wasn't wired at all.

"All right," he said.

"Please move back. Don't touch her. And prepare yourself, because the goat is about to be attuned to Lilly's frequency and will cease to vibrate within our own visual field. *Lilly?* A little help?"

Pi looked up and mumbled a friendly hello, and then she disappeared.

"I need a drink," Sam said miserably.

"And this happens with her touch?" Tesla asked, enthralled.

"It does. Lilly. Release the goat."

She did. Pi stood regarding them blandly.

"Can she do this to me?" Tesla asked. There was eagerness in his voice.

"Not exactly," Sergei said. "You saw the results earlier this evening."

"But I would withstand it. I would experience this. Miss Lilly, will you indulge me?"

"No," Sunner said firmly. "There is a better way. The goat serves as a kind of buffer, as well as a catalyst. If you were to grip her horn..."

Tesla reached out eagerly.

Sam intercepted him. "Son," he said kindly. "Let me go first. It is the duty of the aged to protect the young. I am played out, or near to it. You have more to offer. Much more, if this fellow wizard traveled through time and distance to petition your help." He took hold of Pi's horn with a sigh, and shut his eyes.

"You need to open your eyes," Lilly told him.

He did and stared at her. She was a vision of the shadow they had seen on the illuminated scrim, her toga now closed in modesty, yet instead of appearing goddess-like and sublime, before him was a young woman, smiling girlishly, with freckles sprinkled across her nose. She resembled his daughter Susie; except she was older and was so thin her collarbones were sharply defined, as were the sinews in her neck. There might have been dark circles under her eyes, but the room was not lit well enough for certainty.

"I'm pleased to make your acquaintance, Mr. Twain," she said.

The tent and the others wavered as through seen through turbulent water. He was so taken with the moment, he wasn't aware of the tide of nausea about to crash over him. When it did, he let go and raced out of the tent.

"Mr. Clemens!" Tesla shouted and he and Sergei both followed Sam out to attend him. "Are you well?"

"I am," Sam said over the puddle of bile on the ground. "Never better." But he was grinning up at them, wiping his mouth with his sleeve. "If I am dreaming, do not wake me. Nicky, you must try it, but ready a basin. It is like riding a storm at sea."

Back in the tent, Tesla extended a shaking hand to touch the goat's horns. Pi didn't like this at all, but she seemed to make allowances for Tesla and stood braced on all four feet. Sam, Sunner and Idee watched Tesla flicker like he was a projection on a damaged film. He was patting the goat on the horn instead of gripping it firmly, testing the effect, before he took a firm hold and vanished.

He was gone longer than they expected.

Sunner said anxiously: "*Lilly? Let him go!* This is *Nikola Tesla*, for crysake!"

A moment later, Tesla staggered to his chair and sat down. His face was white but his expression beatific. "I shall do whatever you require," he whispered with a shiver. He raised his hand to his cheek to caress where Lilly's kiss still burned.

His expression abruptly changed and he too bolted from the tent. Sam and Sergei followed dutifully. When Tesla was done with his retching he dabbed at the corners of his mouth with his handkerchief, and said, "Sergei, have you attempted this wearing cork soles? I believe the dissonance may be a result of conflicting oscillations..."

"Yes. Yes I have," Sunner said. He was grinning with relief, and with the thrill of rolling up his sleeves alongside Nikola Tesla. He couldn't wait to get started. "— But she depends on the goat, you see. We didn't want to push it ... didn't want to risk harming the goat, that is."

Sunner spread out his notes on the table, which they moved outside to catch the first rays of the morning sun. They worked until the sun was high and the fair a roar of voices, and then they collapsed next to Idee and Sam, making do as best they could with two cots between the four of them. Lilly was curled like a kitten in the cast-off jackets on the floor, with Pi's leash knotted around her arm. They all slept soundly together until late in the day.

When Sunner arose, he saw Tesla was gone. He eased his way out as not to disturb the chorus of snores from Sam and Idee. Tesla was standing on the flatbed wagon, his hands in his pockets, studying the future city depicted on the backdrop.

"Lilly painted it," Sunner told him.

"Is it really like this?" Tesla asked.

"Some of it," Sunner said. "Some is whimsical. From a cartoon ... a hand-drawn kinetoscope ... a child's futuristic fantasy."

Tesla was nodding, like he understood.

Sunner started to laugh, shaking his head.

Tesla regarded him curiously.

"I'm sorry," Sunner said. "The moment was so ludicrous, and you were so serious. Here I am in 1893 telling Nikola Tesla about the *The Jetsons*. – When there are so many important things to discuss. It's just so..." He looked out over the tent city. There was a roar of cheers and the distant pop of blanks and the bugle call of *the Cavalry to the rescue* over at the Wild West Show. Indians whooped in response and the audience booed and hissed like a basket of snakes.

"I can imagine," Tesla said. And then he amended. "*Perhaps.*"

"*Perhaps,*" Sunner agreed. And they stood together in comfortable silence, Tesla gazing at the new world, Sunner gazing at the old, both marveling and trying to take it in.

Fifty yards away, Lauder glowered at them both.

CHAPTER THIRTEEN

"All people make mistakes, and many of them are of tragic proportions. The greater the sum of mistakes the greater the cost of saving them. But how much more expensive not to?"
—*The Chairman*
Wardenclyffe Foundation Archives

∞

The Hall of Electricity

"Chief Elder Enge!"

Sunner paused, then turned, and rummaged through the baggage of Sergei's memory as if for something misplaced. The steadily flowing static of voices folded over that one penetrating voice, and he could not tell where it had come from. Perhaps he had manufactured it, had pulled together a raft of interconnected syllables from the flotsam of sound. He stood in the main hallway of the Electricity Building, a snag in the river of humanity that was forced to part and flow around him. He looked from face to face but none of them held claim to what he thought had tickled his ear and teased his perceptions, of what he might or might not have heard.

Sunner/Sergei stretched and pulled apart to marshal their perspectives and mound them up, one against the other for comparison. He felt his brain then: two hemispheres, the great gulf fixed down the middle, and both of him calling across the chasm. He felt also like an amoeba, pulling apart, bisecting, as perhaps God had done, in order to not be alone anymore.

His feet were planted to stay rooted in his physical singularity as his minds debated, then gave it up for unlikely and seeped together again to find ease in the present and let the curtain fall on echoes of disparate futures. He moved along to Tesla's exhibit and put the imagined voice with any import or implications behind him.

∞

As for Lauder, he saw the magician pause when he called out Sergei's singular title: Chief Elder Enge. It satisfied him immensely. His voice had carried on a torrent of voices. It had registered and, if for only a second, captured his attention. His and no other.

All righty then, Lauder thought, *it was confirmed:* The Murderer of the World had indeed un-geezered himself. Decodgering was a side effect, perhaps, of his infernal QET machine. Lauder had kenned no suchwise change in himself, but he was fixed in his youth already. He was in the very the mode of his perfection with no need for tinkery.

The Prime Elder Engineer was now in his prime. Didn't that just tweak your mod?

Lauder stood at attention next to the electric chair in his uniform as he did every day. Some mistook it for the attire of a prison guard, and he didn't bother to correct them. He wearied of pointing to the Salvationist's 'S' on his lapel and he was fresh out of earnest explanations and encouraging smiles. The task of capturing the attention of the gawkers and relocating their thoughts from one instrument of death to another —that is to say, from the chair to the cross, was no longer his primary concern. Gathering in one soul at a time dimmed in significance when all souls tottered on the brink. He had more important work to do, and it was muchly more complex.

Lauder stood so still considering his options that a passerby poked him to ascertain if he were a waxwork figure. The prevailing argument was to the affirmative, as Lauder didn't flinch in the least, nor blink, and it was pointed out that no living person had a face as unflawed and unlined in its maturity. He was admired for his lifelike and natural appearance in the same hushed tones reserved for comments about the deceased laid out in a funeral.

But Lauder was busy in his thoughts. The fair was the wiki of the present world, and had served him. Heretofore he gamed it, scrolling at random, wandering around as in a halo park. He upped the lingo, inserted himself in role-play where nodes intersected with his daring-do, much-like like any ordinary game-play on the net. Except this was pure physi. This was happening in real time, off-line and in-the-flesh. The fair was a VR cheat, a physi-simulacra of the age. This was Act 1 of the Transcendent Epoch, where mankind first began building the signposts that warned the road ahead was forked. And forked. And *fucked sidewise* to infinity.

As he stood beneath the banner which read *The Instrument of Justice for a Civilized World*, he felt — and not for the first time — that the words on the banner meant himself.

From where he stood on the raised dais in an alcove on the east wall, he kept an eye on the 'Wizard of Electricity' which was Westinghouse and 'The Wizard of Light' which was Edison, but most of all he watched the 'Wizard of Lightning' which was Tesla, that effete man in the shadow of those better known inventors.

It could have been any one of those cobbers who drew out the Chief Elder Enge, but his money had been on Tesla, and he was right. Dithering in the Geezer's keep while Nidhi reverse engineered the time machine, Lauder read the book Sergei had left behind: *Tesla. Man out of Time*[1], and the irony did not escape him.

While developing the electric chair with Edison and company, Tesla called him out. Walked right up to him in the street, all smart-wise and unrighteous, as if delivered to him as by angles. This coincidence was, as the goog-gurus would someday say, *the spontaneous fulfillment of desire*. It put him on his toes; it smacked him upside his useless goog. It was as obvious as God's handwriting on the wall: the Serbian inventor was the one to watch.

He knew it by the way Tesla got under his skinny. Nikola Tesla gave him the creeps, that's all. Intuition was a practiced skill and by-and-by Tesla had indeed led him to the Murderer. But once found, Lauder had failed to act and the longer he dithered, the more complex-wise it became. Sergei the Amazing, the Chief Elder Engineer, the Murderer of the World — or whatever name he went by these days — was not the only threat. If left alone, Tesla himself might become the Murderer's accomplice. Or perhapsly it was the other which-wise up.

Tesla moved all oiliy through water, sliding like dark malevolence through Lauder's understanding of *the way things were*. Just days ago, when the inventor's gibbering fool of a friend sat wisecracking from the seat of the electric chair, Tesla recognized Lauder from the wayback: Harkening to when Lauder electrocuted dogs on street corners, making plain the dangers of alternating current. The crowds had been fulsome appreciative until Tesla stepped up and rebuked him. Lauder should have recognized it then as the challenge to duel. Should have kenned what he knew now. But where his goog used to whisper insights, now all he had was angels screaming over the endless white noise of static. If Gideon himself blew a trump in his ear, he might not have heard. It was no wonder he'd missed it then.

But he'd not missed it today.

His work on the electric chair had thus-wise drawn out the Murderer of the World, as he'd hoped it would. Tesla led him to a grotesque pantomime with a facsimile of that very device upon a stage: Sergei the Amazing, strapped in and calling it a Quantum Entanglement Tracer. Of course he did. Such-wise did Satan go, *to and fro* upon the earth. If ever the Holy Bible referred to time-travel, that was it: *To and fro.*

But how had the Geezer transfigured himself? How did he appear in the guise of his youth? And posing as a magician! Sergei's affectations of the dark arts were ludicrous in the extreme: He consorted with Gypsies. He conjured demons. He held congress with a goat, for Christ's sake, which would be lol-ha if it weren't so goddamned creepy. Lauder had even heard him whispering endearments to the beastie, though thankfully he'd been spared the sight of their fornication.

The Geezer was leveraging relics of the pre-scientific epoch, yet the metaphors were handy. It gave Lauder the vocabulary to describe the Murderer's compatriots. Like, the ancient witch-crone with her familiar, the hideous little cur that stayed at her heels. If the World Murderer found it amusing to affect the trappings of the enemy of Christ, then Lauder would indulge him and gladly.

Lauder witnessed the laws of nature perverted, saw extraordinary things and recognized them for what they were. Sergei was not merely the Murderer of the World; he was the *Anti*christ. The World Murderer was damnation everlasting and the future was a hell without end. In ever diminishing dimensions death was no longer a refuge. This Lauder knew for certain. When Arlie departed to a parallel, there was no hope of reunion, there was no 'bright and shining shore', there was no 'meet me at the river'. He was just gone, and gone forever.

Lauder put to rest any doubt of the Geezer's new identity. When he shouted, *"Chief Elder Enge!"* the one calling himself Sergei the Amazing responded.

It was time to act, and so he would, but care-wise and sneaky.

CHAPTER FÖURTEEN

"There are three great themes in literature. Love, redemption and the journeys of heroes. At Wardenclyffe, we favor the cases that apply all three."
—The Chairman's Notebook
Wardenclyffe Foundation Archives

∞

The Cold Storage Building

Sunner ducked through the flip-rail that closed off Tesla's exhibit space, accompanied by Mr. Hardy of the Columbian Guard. Hardy believed his duty this day was to vouchsafe that articles removed from the exhibit were to the order of Mr. Tesla, and nothing more. In actuality, he was a convenience for daylight and for heavy cargo. He was both an escort and a license to plunder anything Tesla could sign for or Sunner could buy. The rest they could pluck from this vast storehouse like low apples from an unguarded orchard, but only in the wee hours when the fair was thinly populated, and only as much as Lilly could invisibly carry out from under the noses of the Columbian Guard.

This was easier.

Mr. Hardy had the signed list and handed it to the attendant in Tesla's exhibit, a student from the Electrical College recently appointed to man the booth during the day, as Tesla was suddenly indisposed, and planned to be indisposed for the remainder of the fair. The student read the list and ticked off a few items and shook his head over others.

"Of course I have *these*, but not *that*. Nikola Tesla has no need of a commutator, and why would he?" He regarded Sunner scornfully and inaugurated *the look* that generations of geeks would reserve for *newbies* and the *illiterati* up through the ages ahead.

Sunner looked impatiently over his shoulder at the Westinghouse exhibit, and down the row to Edison's. "What about them? They're still using D.C. to some extent, right? Have you seen a commutator on exhibit?"

"See here, now," Mr. Hardy said, and grew to fill out his uniform. "This is not a mercantile. You are authorized to remove articles from the Tesla exhibit only."

"If Mr. Tesla needs to procure more equipment for experimentation, let him inquire at the college, or telegraph his lab in New York," the attendant suggested. "If you mean to mess with the Edison boys, you are on your own. I have no truck with them, nor they with me. They are naught but a team of rounders and toughs. You may have luck with the fellows at Westinghouse if you have a mind to. They know where their bread and butter comes from. I cannot leave my station on any account. I have my duty."

"Fine. Just give me what you have out of Tesla's locker," Sunner said and waved his bag at him.

"As you say, Mr. Tillman. But these are delicate instruments. You cannot mean to tote them off in a tow sack?"

"I do, indeed. We mean to disassemble them at any rate." He handed the list back to Hardy. "You can tick them off," he said.

Hardy looked hard at the list and then at the student. "That thing there. What is it?"

"An electric resonator gauge, sir."

"Is that this here?" Hardy pointed at the list and held it up for the student to read off. His effort was met with a deep sigh.

Sunner grew impatient and lifted a small magnetic coil from the cabinet while Hardy and the student sorted themselves out. He strolled down to the Edison camp and set it on the table where he was regarded with suspicion and amazement.

"What will you give me for this fine Tesla coil?" Sunner asked them. "Have you a commutator at hand?"

The men regarded one another and made their calculations telepathically. When satisfied, the one on the right made to inspect the contents of his pockets.

"Only commutator like it at the fair, I reckon," he said. "One of a kind, most like. Not that it is a big draw for the crowd, sad to say, but a man who knows its worth and who would have earnest need for it in particular would consider it valuable indeed." He regarded the small coil before him. "Of course, if that man be Mr. Tesla, it would be dear to part with, as it would cost my job in addition."

His partner drifted away till he was outside the bubble of aiding and abetting, and proceeded to examine the ceiling with considerable interest.

"Well, as you can plainly see, I am not Mr. Tesla, and neither am I in his employ." Sunner removed a packet from his breast pocket and fanned a stack of twenty-dollar bills over the embers of the man's eyes until they caught fire. "I need that commutator. And toss in a roll of wire, will you? Not that low-tension twine Edison is partial to, but that heavyweight spool yonder. The one with the asphalt coating." He peeled off a healthy portion of the bills and laid them out on the counter one at a time. "Do we have a deal?"

Edison's man held off nodding until he saw that Sunner's wallet was emptied out.

"Good." Sunner lifted up the Tesla coil he had put on the table.

"Hear! What about that?"

"Cash or merchandise."

"Cash," Edison's man sighed, and went to fetch the device Sunner wanted. "Not much good without the generator," he said as he picked up the bills and made the exchange. "But that is your business."

"*Indeed.*"

Sunner retreated back up the corridor and replaced Tesla's little coil safely back into the cabinet and locked it. It was only a model, but Edison's men hadn't known it.

Hardy was ready with the sack and Sunner added in the commutator and took a corner of the sack in both hands. Between the two of them they grunted the contents down the exhibit hall and out the door where a handcart waited.

Mr. Hardy walked afore to clear the way, lending his dignity to the procession and allowing Sunner to push the cart himself. Big of him. Sunner managed it by moving crosswise against the flood of pedestrians coming out of the great golden doors of the Transportation Building. It was easy enough until they peeled off between the Women's Building and the Oyster Cafe and turned down the rutted dirt roads that connected the service areas.

"A little help, Mr. Hardy, if you please," Sunner panted. The guardsman was persuaded to take one of the shafts and bowed his back alongside Sunner until they humped it through the ruts to one of the sliding delivery doors along the back of the five-story Cold Storage building. This warehouse was every bit as decorated as the other buildings of the fair and also the tallest, if you took its tower into account. The tower rose over 100 feet dead center above its roof and imitated the one atop the Madison Square Garden in New York, except this one disguised the smokestack that ventilated the coal furnaces needed for the ice makers. Four lesser copulas stood on each of its four corners, making it appear castle-like, albeit festooned with classical columns and repeating arches all around the fifth-floor deck. Arches also receded in diminishing echoes to embellish the ground-floor entrance. This was more than just a warehouse: the souvenir map went so far as to call it the Cold Storage *Palace*. It contained an exhibit of the Corliss engines that ran the Hercules ice plant and the entire top floor was an ice-skating rink, as lettering on the central tower advertised. But most of all, the building served the practical function of receiving and refrigerating perishables and provided the fair with blocks of ice, all of which were offloaded into hand trucks and trolley carts for distribution across the grounds late each night. On its north side, the loading docks were already busy receiving. Buckboards pulled up flush to unload tomorrow's food-stuffs and perishable exhibits, like citrus for the tower of oranges from Florida in the Agricultural Building, and fresh flowers to replenish the arrangements in the Domestic Arts Hall, and barrels of oysters packed in dirty winter ice for dainty lunches at one of the many oyster bars. A similar arrangement accommodated boxcars as it was also situated alongside the train yard.

At the first street-level dock, Sunner rapped 'shave and a haircut' on the door and Idee disengaged the latch to peek out as would become the custom in speakeasies 30 years hence.

"Give way, Idee. It's just us."

She pushed over the night latch and shoved the door wide. Sunner bade Hardy a good day and heaved the handcart in without him. Idee closed it behind them with a severe look at the retreating guard. The interior was dark. A few dim bulbs labored in vain to illuminate a passageway that was barely wider than the door, but whose ceiling rose all the way to the third floor where the refrigeration units exhaled chilly fog to cool the rooms below. A row of vaults extended out along the central hallway, and past that a narrow service stairway led up to the fifth floor where the ice skating rink was. The main entrance and grand staircase for visitors were on the other side of the building.

The rink itself was a bust. The marvelous refrigeration units weren't enough to keep such a vast surface frozen in summer and water dripped down into the storage vaults below, even when they covertly packed the ceiling crawl space above it with blocks of ice. It was too large and too ambitious and the arched walkway around its exterior let in too much sunlight. Even after they boarded all the windows to block the heat and light, the rink had to be abandoned as an attraction. A small sign hung from the front doors to disappoint visitors that hiked down in the summer heat to the south end of the fair on the empty promise from 10-foot-high lettering on the tower: *Hercules Skating Rink*.

The building administrator was pleased to rent the rink to Tesla, who paid for it by recycling money taken in at the main ticket gate (and out again) by way of Lilly's peculiar skills.

The rink was set up as a temporary workshop until a rail-car could be secured to ship their party and equipment and animals —Pi, Spitfire, and a stray kitten that adopted Sam Clemens —to Tesla's New York laboratory. A Pullman strike was brewing nearby in Chicago and unreserved cars were even harder to come-by than usual. Because neither Tesla nor Sunner was willing to postpone beginning their work, they set up here in the meantime.

The rink in the Cold Storage building proved perfect because it was insulated, grounded, and of course wired from the new massive Westinghouse Electric Generators of Tesla's own design, the most abundant and reliable source of power anywhere in the world. Westinghouse Generators did *not* power the refrigeration units. Their generators harnessed, of all things, the heat of a coal fire furnace at the center of the building.

Electric light blazed from the rink when Sunner opened the door to deliver the booty. Because the windows were boarded, Tesla had insisted on stringing five additional strands of lights across the big room to work by. When Sunner and Idee entered, Tesla didn't look up from his work. He'd barely looked up but to eat in the last few days, except when he collapsed on the pallet in the corner where he rested in brief stints while Sunner spelled him.

Tesla was happier than he'd been since the fair had opened.

"Take a look at this, Mr. Tillman," Tesla said.

The instruments on the worktable were shoved aside, and on it instead was a new pair of gentlemen's riding boots. Tesla had affixed thick blocks of cork to the soles with glue and wooden pegs and he was paring down the edges and sanding them smooth with the same care and precision he put in all his endeavors.

"Boots," Sunner said.

"*Insulation*. These are for Lilly, with my apologies. I needed flat soles and sturdy heels. She indicated these will do. The ones she used before were not adequate. It's the density of the cork, you see: It is a wonder you were not electrocuted before now. I'll have yours next, if you please."

"You'll be electrifying me as well?"

"It will spare your goat."

Sunner was already hopping on one foot to remove his shoe. "How do you mean?"

"I see no reason why you and Lilly should not connect at once."

Sunner stopped hopping.

"What is it?" Tesla asked.

"I'm sorry – I am sorry to assure you we have oftentimes been ungrounded together, and the effect is the same."

Tesla read his expression well enough. "Hand over your shoes, Mr. Tillman," he said kindly. "No need to be crestfallen. You have the commutator, I presume?"

"Yes, I managed to barter for it."

"Your goat Pi is a kind of commutator, you know. I believe I can duplicate the effect artificially, but you will need to be insulated."

"Align our resonance? Both of us? Together?"

"Perhaps I can."

Sunner/Sergei wrestled over displaying indignation or dismay. "Mr. Tesla, as I have told you, there are complex forces at play, I hardly think..."

"I have the advantage, you see," Tesla interrupted without affront. "As my perspective is not narrowed to the antecedents of your esoteric sciences, I can observe the thing with innocence and therefore am open to alternative possibilities. Complexity is an anathema to understanding. You are constrained by your knowledge. I have no knowledge and neither the constraints of the paradigm you abide by. I have only the observation of nature, and nature is indicating a rudimentary adjustment to your respective frequencies will permit you to resonate in harmony. *Mr. Tillman*," Tesla said earnestly, "you should be able at least to see your wife. Perhaps even to *be* with her..."

Tesla cleared his throat, "... as it were. We should be able to treat food and water accordingly."

Sunner and his passenger instantly were of one accord. "If you can achieve that, you will have performed more than we dared to hope for."

"I shall try," Tesla allowed. "I do have to subject you both to currents which will be a lower cycle for her and a higher cycle for you, but not to an uncomfortable degree, I dare say. However, I am afraid we will have to employ direct current. Hence the commutator."

Sunner shook his head and coughed to hide his laugh.

"I am aware of the irony," Tesla let a companionable smile twitch beneath his mustache. "You will not inform Mr. Edison."

"I assure you I will not."

"What are we not telling that blatherskite?" Sam Clemens drawled as he walked in with his kitten in the crook of his arm.

"That we have pressing need for his monotonous current," Tesla said, resuming his work. Sam came to his side to observe, shifting his tabby to his other arm as not to crowd Tesla who was unfond of cats.

At last he said, "You make a fine cobbler, Nicky, but I presumed a more mysterious alchemy."

"You and our host share that assessment."

"It is to prevent shock," Sunner said.

Sam sniffed. "Yes. Well. Please summon me when there is mortal danger and lightning bolts and other entertainments. Just give me an advance warning so I may empty my bowels beforehand. But for now, the world's fair is beckoning and I mean to see it while I still have the sap."

"You ain't a-gone to electrify Lilly is ye?" Idee cried out, as she finally deciphered the conversation between Mr. Tillman and Mr. Tesla.

Tesla looked up with indulgent surprise.

"I ain't a-gone to stand fer it!" she declared. "There ain't no call! What we did afore was play actin'. Lilly ain't gots the strength. She's all poorly and you'uns'll zap the life right outin her!"

"Madame, I assure you..."

Sam loudly cleared his throat. "Mr. Tillman, I was meaning to request: Can you spare your matron for a morning's diversion, or is she condemned to another day in this cave?"

"What's that?" Idee asked, confounded as Sam gave her the most genteel of bows.

Sunner aided the misdirection, "Mr. Clemens wants you to accompany him," he told her and steered her away from the table and Tesla.

"Laws, ha' mercy," she flustered. "I can speak fer my ownself iffin' he be askin'."

"Forgive me, Madame." Sam said. "My request was improper and addressed to the wrong party. Mrs. McIntyre, will you do me the honor of allowing me to be the ornament on your arm as you display that fine new frock on the promenade?"

Idee blinked and looked helplessly at Sunner.

"Go on, Idee. Mr. Clemens just wants to show you the fair."

"I seen it."

"But I have not." Sam said. "Not much of it, leastways. Come now Idee, even you can agree that the finest supper has less savor if there is none to take it with?"

"I reckon."

"You would not have me endure the pleasures of the fair alone? I need someone to help carry the burden of all those amazements."

"But what if I'm needed here?"

"Ain't you jist longin' for a day o' leisure?" he matched her accent. "Ain't thar summat you been keenin' to cast yer eyes upon?"

Idee begrudged a confession. "I shore'd be keen to see the stock. They's sheeps in the pavilions this month. That'd be something fine to tell Magnus when he comes home; 'Bout them fancy stockyards and all them sheeps from cross't the world. I hear'd they got sheeps with four horns atop they heads! Can ye 'magine that? Four! Why theys prolly got goats as well, and who knows what all kinds and numbers of horns *they* got. Do you reckon we could enter Pi in the goat contest?"

"*No,*" Sunner and Tesla said in unison.

"No, I reckon thas not seemly, bein' as she ain't been borned yet, bein' from the future n'all."

"No division for that," Sam Clemens agreed. "And no competition, which is a pity as such a contest would be well attended if properly advertised."

"Still, I should like to admire the ever-day goats, just the same."

"Well then, that is where we shall go. But mind you I should like to see the entire grounds and that is a mile or more of walking. But never fear, we shall take the elevated train as long as you do not mind a stowaway. This pussy will not permit me to wonder off without her direct supervision." He exchanged his tobacco pouch for the kitten in the crook of his arm, dropping her deep in his jacket pocket where it seemed content to settle in, barely making a lump.

"The train will pass the wind-o'lasses!" Idee realized.

"Won't that be a fine thing?" he agreed. "Acres of whirligigs and windmills flailing the air with their pretty painted sails for no other purpose than to delight the eye. It will be a gay sight to behold, and I will be in sorry circumstances if I return to Olivia and the girls without postcards of that at least. You can help me find some." He steered Idee to the door with a wink at Sunner.

Just then the boot leapt from Tesla's hands, arced to the floor and skidded across to Sam's feet where he stood holding open the door.

"Bless me," Idee gasped. "I clean fergitted Lilly."

Sam frowned and said in tones deeply chiaroscuro'd, "Maybe she is affirming that you should go," and he eased backward away from the boot and into the passageway, keeping a suspicious eye on it should it decide to chase him from the building altogether.

"Or she pines to go along," Idee speculated. "She creeps about the fair at night but she ain't never see'd it proper."

Sergei's alarm seeped coldly from Sunner's scalp to his toes.

"Lilly, please. We are so close now. I wish you wouldn't..." He let his words fail as he saw her chair shove backward from the table and was immediately sorry for the worry in his voice, but it couldn't be helped. Nothing exaggerated the vast inventory of threats to her life, as did his comparative longevity. Only time would tell if the antidote to aging had passed to his new younger incarnation as Sunner, but even if not, Lilly's life was a sputtering flame on a short candle compared to his and every gentle breeze gave him the terror of losing her. His heart wanted to bolt from his chest even as she bolted from her chair.

∞

For her part, Lilly meant neither to encourage Idee to go, nor to ask to go along. When Sam opened the door, she had seen a figure dart away. Someone had been lurking and listening just outside and Lilly leapt from her chair and sprang across the room to give chase despite running on the dregs of energy. Within two paces she felt she'd left her brains behind. Blackness contracted her eyesight and made her legs stupid. She fell against the doorjamb, causing Sam to jump back at the *whump*. She cursed the new bruise on her shoulder, but at least the pain bullied her out of a faint.

In the pinholes of her vision she saw the light shift as the main entry door at the bottom of the stairs flung open to expel their spy, giving her reason to rally and wobble after him. There had been nothing threatening in the eavesdropper's manner, but he left a contrail of bad juju in his wake, jamming the gears in her solar plexus. Lilly scrambled across the mezzanine, down the grand staircase, and stumbled out into air so hot and bright it shot bolts through the blackness gathering in her head. It was as good as a slap. She worked her drunken legs and shambled through the alcove entryway out to the middle of the road, looking both ways. Turning her head too fast, the curtains of dizziness at the edge of her vision stirred and threatened to close again.

The way was thick with running men: cheapskates that had just hopped off the slowly passing freight cars to avoid the ticket gates. They were hoofing it to get lost in the paying crowd before the Columbian guards caught up. Good timing for the spy. Bad timing for her. All their heads bobbed together like a choppy sea and she could not pick out the one she wanted. When she realized he was gone, she lost purpose and focus. Lilly barely made it off the street. She wobbled back to the cold storage entryway and slid down the block that served the base of the statue of Columbus — one of many at the fair. This one stood about 12 feet high and was garishly painted. In one hand he held a globe, in the other, of all things, a white dove with its wings unfurling, as though it was about to take flight, as if Columbus was a kind of Noah and the new world was his Mount Ararat.

She smiled up at the white dove. It seemed an old friend although her thinking was too befuddled to remember why. It had pleased her when they moved into this building, and even Sunner had stood still to admire it and said it was a good omen. Now, the dove went out of focus and Lilly crumpled at the statue's base and hung her head between her knees to try to catch her breath. Her heart slammed in her ears, and she began to shake so violently she was unable give any sign or answer as the air was groped and her name was called by voices that she loved and yearned to answer. When the next faint came, she yielded.

CHAPTER FIFTEEN

"An artist's first job is to change the viewer's perspective."
—The Artist
A retrospective of 4D works from the Wardenclyffe Foundation

∞

Midway Plaisance

Lauder couldn't shake the feeling that he was being followed even though furtive glances over his shoulder didn't bear that out. He was relieved that providence delivered a hoard of gatecrashers streaming across the avenue in front of the Cold Storage building just when he pushed out into the heat of the day. He was momentarily blinded by the sunlight banking off of the white buildings. Blinking the daggers from his eyes, he stumbled ahead into the crowded lane and let the current carry him. They were headed to the Midway, of course, and he went along, head down, the back of his neck exposed and prickling. It wasn't just eyes on him he worried about. He imagined hands catching his collar and dragging him back, or cold fingers closing around his neck. He had no truck with weapons, but he wondered if you could sense the muzzle of a gun trained on your back. He thought mayhaps you could.

He stayed in the middle of the crowd not daring to raise his face until he felt the throng around him thin as the attractions wicked them off one by one. He found himself standing at last before Hawaii in-the-round, a circular building painted inside and out with panoramas of the islands. He heard a faint rumble and knew the volcano was erupting. Inside, the patrons were treated to red lights flicking behind streamers of cheese-cloth and to thunder from sheets of aluminum shaken by stagehands. He knew this like he knew everything about the fair. He made it his business to know. He had to be ready for wherever it was God delivered the Geezer into his hands — even though The Murderer wasn't a geezer anymore. Young or old, Lauder meant to have the advantage, whatever transpired. He knew every square inch of the grounds. Knew every build-ing, every exit, every hidden service door and had keys to many of them.

As he expected, and just when he knew they would, he heard the faint squeals of laughter as the spectators inside were pelted with wet sponges. Even that might be a diversion he could use one day. One never knew. When the call came, he'd be ready. God would find him a fit vessel.

Lauder recovered from his flight and eased back into well-worn miseries as he looked around. Watching the crowd, he felt a tug of compassion. These were his people, but he could not afford to become one of them. He was a remote guardian, watching and feeling how precious and precarious their world was. Such a perilous loneliness! He loved them, as he felt Christ must have loved mankind on his sojourn in the flesh. *Mankind* was the word: Man *was* kind, for the most part and that was the sorrow of it. Mankind did not deserve what was coming to him. When the doorway to that false paradise was opened, it would bleed out the world and its *kind* inhabi-tants one by one.

Lauder wept. He made a single gasping sob and then swallowed it. There was so much at stake. So much to be lost. So much to be *done.* Lauder prayed fervently he had the strength to do it. To fulfill his responsibilities, Lauder could not be kind. He would have to be, as the scriptures said, *In the world, not of it.* But he also wanted desperately to melt into the crowd and disappear. Live and let live, and let this ugly busi-ness be. Even though years of suffering the privations of this age had hardened him and strengthened him against bending to that temptation, he might have. He might have just walked away and let the world swallow him if what he had just seen in the cold storage building had not cemented his resolve. The Murderer of the World was busy. Lauder saw in the unused ice-skating rink and hanging by a chain, a cage like those he was very familiar with in his work with Kennelly and Brown. It was a killing cage; wired to an apparatus he could have operated himself. Except this cage wasn't for dispatching dogs. It was much larger. It had the handy dimensions to accommodate a person or two. The Geezer had fashioned himself a shunt already.

Lauder had gone cold at the sight. The murders had begun, then. Perhaps he had known that already. Lauder read the papers. He knew of the disappeared. He thought of the missing young ladies, whose families wrote heart-wrenching entreaties, but with little hope. After vanishing at the fair, their daughters were unlikely to be heard from again. It was the same in every age. A bitter remorse flared in his breast. He should have acted sooner. He should have done it already. How many lives were lost because he hesitated, because he was waiting for 'the right moment'?

Maybe the right moment wouldn't come. Maybe he would have to seize any moment that availed itself and *make* it right.

Lauder remembered the pamphlets he himself handed out. "Beware the electrocutioner's current," it warned. The Chief Elder Enge was indeed the grand executioner, but the electric chair alone had not drawn him out. And why should it? The Geezer could easily cobble together his own, and apparently he had. His little cottage industry of death was already set up and open for business. Lauder was heartsick. That geezer, the Chief Elder Enge, was already polluting the innocence of this age. *And he was not alone.* His cancer had spread and Lauder's simple objective to eliminate him directly was no longer sufficient. They were all in cahoots: Tesla. The old woman. The Gypsies. The decrepit imp named Sam. They were all in this together and Lauder felt the press of his responsibility grow. He could leave none of them alive. They were too dangerous.

All of them, then.

Lauder groaned within himself as the weight of this settled around him. The Murderer of the World still walked because ending a life wasn't as easy as Lauder had once thought. Life was resilient. Even one that needed ending, that *wanted* ending. Take those poor tortured bastards strapped to the electric chair; Though burned from the inside out, they persisted to live for many tortured minutes. –And *that* was with the combined efforts of many men. Lauder was alone. Well, alone in his terrible responsibility, while particularly *not* alone in this crush of humanity. Assassination required a degree of privacy, and there was precious little of it at the fair. Half of the population of the United States was converging on this one spot in the space of half a year. Getting alone with any of the Murderer's compatriots would be a fluke. Getting alone with all of them would be a miracle. But he was on good terms with the maker of miracles, wasn't he?

Lauder thought for the thousandth time, that he had to get rid of them all in a manner that would allow him to escape. That was critical. The last word on him would *not* be a paragraph buried in the back page of the paper, skimmed by eyes too jaded to care anymore about just one more bloke snuffed in the electric chair. Not if he could help it. Sacrificing himself might ultimately be necessary, but exacting justice on the World Murderer *here* was only one-third of the job. *He echoed*, Nidhi had told him. The Murderer was not only here, but his echo also traveled to the beginning of the 21st century. Furthermore, there was also his original incarnation to be dealt with. There was three of him: Sunner Tillman, the original. Sergei Eldridge, the imposter, and the Chief Elder Enge, as was the title he held as the gatekeeper of hell. The unholy trinity.

Lauder peeled back the glove on his right hand and looked at the three tattoos there. There were no coincidences. A life for a life, three times over.

Lauder's work had to be covert, it had to be successful, and he had to get away with it because he still had to live on *and on* to finish the job. Just the thought of it made him weak with loneliness and despair, but he set it aside with the facility of long practice, and firmed his chin. He didn't have time for self-indulgence. He had to plan. To accomplish what he needed to do in relative privacy, he needed a diversion. A big one.

There was a colossal mechanical groan and a big sweeping motion descended on him. Alarm pulled him out of his troubled contemplation and instinctively he raised his hands above his head and ducked. So did the people around him and then there was a shared twitter of laughter and relief. It was just the Ferris wheel advancing to take on more passengers. Standing midway along the Midway Plaisance, Lauder gaped up at the Ferris wheel as though seeing it for the first time. A plan began to gel.

CHAPTER SIXTEEN

"Any emotion, if it is sincere, is involuntary."
—*Mark Twain*
Wardenclyffe Foundation Archives

∞

Hercules Ice Skating Rink

"There she is," Esmeralda said, and pointed to the ground at the base of the Statue of Columbus. Sunner shuffled forward like a blind man and dowsed around with his hands until he felt the repelling force that marked Lilly's proximity. It had taken half the day before they located the Gypsy seer and set her on the track to finding Lilly. Esmeralda's success was almost immediate but Sunner's elation crashed when he realized Lilly hadn't gotten more than a few paces from the door and had not had the strength to return again. She made no sign she heard his urgings.

"Here," Sunner confirmed and Vladimir dropped the sheet they'd brought over her and together they prodded the resistant air and slippery boundaries of her form until they were reasonably satisfied they'd caught her up. Sunner gingerly lifted her slight weight. Sam and Idee stood out of the way, silently questing for some sign she was alive.

"Jesus, she weighs nothing at all," Sunner lamented. "Is she breathing? Can you tell?"

Esmeralda had both hands clamped over her mouth afraid of the truth that might escape. She was shaking her head.

"Very bad. Very bad," she murmured. "She is so weak. She is so hungry and thirsty."

Sunner carried Lilly back up to the rink, with Vladimir's assistance on the stairs. Esmeralda, Idee and Sam walked somberly behind and would not meet one another's eyes.

Tesla glanced up at them when they entered, and made the right conclusions from the limp form in Sunner's arms. Without a word, he resumed working with grim determination.

"I had no idea she was so..." Sunner faltered, couldn't continue, and dropped back within himself to let Sergei's anger bubble up to sustain him.

"Goddamn it, Lill! You should have told me. *Goddamn it!*" It was all Sergei could do to restrain accusing looks at Esmeralda, who must have known the condition Lilly was in, but had instead agreed to keep him in the dark.

"How do you feed a ghost?" Vladimir asked Esmeralda who was busy unpacking the fresh milk from Pi she'd brought along in jars wrapped in her shawl. Pi was at the moment tied under their wagon, because a Gypsy camp is as safe as houses. No one steals from a Gypsy and plans to live. Everybody knew that. But with Lilly unconscious, they now realized they needed the goat here. They couldn't interphase with Lilly without her.

Sunner held the sheeted bundle in his arms and tipped a glass where her mouth ought to be. He succeeded in spilling the milk with no sign Lilly had taken any. He wanted to shake her to get a response. He wanted to put his mouth to hers and breathe. He wanted to shriek and howl and even resort to prayer.

"I need a plastic ... no: I need *rubber* tubing. Can we get that? Do they have that now? Lilly *please...*" he said. His voice was forlorn and weak and confused. It was Sergei's voice, lost, time fuddled and flirting with dementia. In spite of his better judgment, he took a deep breath and probed beneath for her mouth, and immediately keeled over. Vladimir leapt forward to catch Sunner. Instead, the gypsy dropped like a sack of sand next to his friend.

Sunner came-to with Tesla kneeling over him, screwing corked shoes onto his feet.

"I told you insulation is required," Tesla said. Now, if you will please stop wasting time, let us put Lilly into the Faraday cage. I have installed the commutator and we cannot delay."

Sunner saw Esmeralda was helping Vladimir to his feet, who swayed and grinned and then sagged against his wife. The bundled sheet lay crumpled between them. *Had they cushioned her fall?*

"Pull yourself together." Tesla commanded. "There is work to be done."

Sunner stammered the objections that thundered from his heart, but he rose and managed to do as he was told, lifting the edges of Lilly's sheet with Tesla taking the other side. The Serbian had no difficulty at all balancing on the cork platforms on his own shoes. He was used to working that way, while Sunner wobbled like a child in his mother's high heels.

"Generally a Faraday cage permits electrical fields to flow harmlessly over those inside," Tesla said, not to patronize him but to soothe him back into an objective frame of mind, "In this case I shall apply a direct current to the cage itself, and to Lilly within it, gradually upping the frequency until we achieve a harmonic resonance ..."

They eased the bundle into the cage set in the center of the room with wires trailing from it. Sunner was reluctant to step back, but Tesla pulled him firmly away while continuing his conversation like he was lecturing students in a hall.

"Next we shall introduce a direct current and entrain her to our magnetic field. I was reminded when I saw Mr. Brown's assistant, that Lauder fellow, that he had used a similar vehicle, but to a very different end. However, the resonance he supplied was ... inharmonious." Tesla did not to elaborate on how Lauder's cage was used to electrocute dogs.

He and Sunner had been over this many times as they worked out the details the past few days. They'd struck the premise that since they could not attach electrodes directly to Lilly, she would need to be contained. Sunner knew this as well as he did. Tesla's words were gentle reminders: scaffolding to prop up his mind and frame his resolve that the time was now. Now or never.

Sunner was grateful to yield to Tesla's confidence, as he'd scraped the barrel of his own and could not focus on anything more important than the inert bundle in the sheet. He just stood by dumbly when Tesla poured a pitcher of water over her, to plaster the sheet against her and make a puddle on the floor of the cage, assuring contact.

Idee had the sense to hold her tongue.

"Step back if you please, and mind the wires, all of you." Tesla closed a circuit switch with no drama whatsoever and turned to his meter and dials. "Please inform me when she stirs." *When*, he said. Not *if*. Sunner measured out his gratitude while Tesla lightly finessed the controls.

There was no sound at all, and the only movement was the needle on the dial.

Sunner swayed with fatigue under his laboring heart, and Vladimir and Esmeralda propped one another up, while Sam twiddled the kitten clinging to his shoulder and chewed his cigar for comfort. Idee was a statue. Accustomed to bracing herself against misfortune, she braced herself now and dared not to hope, but only to endure.

"Great Scott!" Sam Clemens cried.

In a fold of the sheet and as still as a cut flower stem, the curve of Lilly's arm took shape. The flesh didn't solidify as much as it emerged from the darkness, as if it were the product of one's eyes adjusting to the dark of a moonless night, gradually perceiving something that had been there all along.

Tesla's hands took flight and hovered above the dial as he too stared with intense and un-distracted interest at Lilly emerging. He trusted his fingers to know, *just know*, when the dial should be caressed again. His fingers lit and arose and lit again with no more force than a dragonfly might exert alighting on a blossom.

Sunner and Sergei were at truce and of one mind, and all of it resisting the evidence of how very still Lilly was. "Please," he whispered, to any ear that might hear.

"Good God, Nicky," Sam muttered. "This is interminable."

"All in due course," Tesla answered. "Almost there."

Sunner moved as close to the cage as he could and squatted next to it.

"Lilly. *Come on*, Lilly. Can you hear me?"

"Caution, Mr. Tillman."

"I know!" he snapped. And then raked back his hair and clasped his useless hands behind his head and folded down like he was waiting for the bombs to drop, balanced precariously on those damned cork-soled shoes. "*Wake up.*" His voice was thick and muffled, and Esmeralda had to turn away and hide her face in the crook of Vladimir's neck. If she harbored any lingering doubts about Sergei's sincerity, the last of them evaporated here and now.

Lilly did not stir.

"I think..." Tesla said as he opened the jaw-switch connector, "that the field is stable. I am switching off, but do not..."

Sunner didn't wait. He sprang up and climbed into the cage, lifting and cradling Lilly in his arms. He peeled back the wet sheet and peered into her face. *He saw her.* Her eyes were closed as if asleep and *not* fixed and unseeing in death. Her lips were pale but not blue. He tentatively drew his forefinger across them, and was not affected by it other than to suffer a cascade of relief to find them soft and yielding. He readjusted his hands and pressed into her neck and felt her pulse after some trouble. There it was, but no time to celebrate.

Esmeralda was at hand, pressing the cup of milk into his hands again. This time he propped Lilly on his lap and tilted the milk between her lips. Some trickled down her chin, but he saw her throat contract. She swallowed in reflex. And then again and again. Still unconscious, but her body knew what was required.

"Hear, now. It's too chilly in here for her to be wet like that," Idee said. "You men-folk step out'n here and let Essie an' me peel 'er down and swaddle her up." She pointed to the blankets on the cot shared in turn by Sunner and Tesla as they'd worked nearly around the clock. "Jist carry her over yonder."

Sunner hitched to the edge of the Faraday cage and centered himself over his shoes before shifting his weight to stand with Lilly in his arms. Idee hurried close. "Ain't she a purdy thing, though?" she crooned and reached out to smooth back her damp hair.

The hill-woman yipped and dropped onto the floor. Sunner crumpled next to her, and Lilly seemed to just evaporate.

"Get back!" Tesla shouted and whipped a dry blanket from the cot and used it as insulation to rewrap Lilly and grunted to lift her up without touching the floor in an awkward quick scoop. He staggered but kept his feet and managed to lay her back in the cage. Vladimir didn't need to be told to drag Sunner clear and Esmeralda was doing the same with Idee, but with a great deal of difficulty.

Tesla was back at the controls, grimly recalibrating, leaving the gypsies to pat the hands and faces of the unconscious to revive them. "Everyone clear?" he asked, and when there were no complaints, he closed the switch again.

This time Tesla had to fly by his instruments because Lilly was entirely obscured by the blanket.

When Sunner got his head back, he needed no further lectures, but paced around the cage, cursing himself. No one else was permitted in proximity without insulated shoes. In that there was no dissent. When the switch was closed, Sunner froze and waited for Tesla's instructions and followed them precisely. He eased into the cage and unwrapped Lilly to see that she was in the same state as before.

"We won't take her out," Tesla said. He alone passed another blanket in with great care. "Dry her off, and warm her," he said, "To prevent her from grounding again, we must keep her in the cage. She is too unstable."

Sunner pared back the wet sheet and began removing her clothes. Sam and Vladimir turned their backs but did not leave even though Idee clucked with disapproval. Tesla attended closely to his instruments, but glanced up periodically as discretely as he could, not entirely trusting Sunner was past care-lessness in his emotional state.

Sunner bathed Lilly in his sighs whispered over her bones as he dried her and threw the wet linens clear from the cage. He rubbed her skin vigorously with the dry blankets to add the warmth of friction. He opened his vest and unbuttoned his shirt and pulled her onto his lap. With her back against his chest, he crossed her arms beneath one of his own and with the other, tucked the blankets around them both to trap the warmth. As he clung to her, he tried not to crush her with his desperation as he trembled with despair and hope and the resonance of the cage.

This time the milk was handed to Tesla, who donned rubber gloves before handing it across to Sunner. He had some success getting Lilly to swallow more, with his thumb in her mouth to hold down her tongue.

"Her teeth are loose," he choked, and put down the glass, as he felt he had no more strength to hold it anymore.

"How are you feeling?" Tesla asked sharply.

"Woozy."

"I beg your pardon?"

"I feel like shit. But don't tell me to get out. I won't do it."

"You are uncalibrated. I need to repeat the process with you inside."

"It won't be too much for Lilly?"

"To the contrary."

"Do it then."

"Grab hold of the cage. You need good contact."

Sunner did as he was told and closed his eyes. He heard the switch close and felt a tingling along his arm, like it had fallen asleep. The feeling erupted everywhere at once.

"*Huh*," he said.

"Hurts?"

"No."

"Tell me if it hurts."

"Will do."

Sam Clemens began fumbling with a match. Simply chewing his cigar had lost its effect.

"Not here, Mr. Clemens," Tesla said without looking up, and the room fell silent again.

Sunner became so still that after a moment, Tesla was worried.

"Still with us?" he asked.

"A-okay."

"You might give some indication," Tesla complained. "Keep talking. Sing a song..."

"Ah." Sunner paused in thought and then cleared his throat and began to softly sing:

The water is wide
I can't cross o're
And neither have
I wings to fly...

It was an old English ballad, and Sam knew it and re-lieved for something to do, joined in with a surprising baritone that boomed off the walls of the vault.

Build me a boat
That can carry two
And both shall row
My love and I

Idee knew it as well and came in on the next line with a high warbling harmony. Esmeralda added her alto vibrato and Vladimir matched Sunner's melody with strength.

There is a ship
And she sails the sea
She's loaded deep
As deep can be
But not so deep
As the love I'm in
I know not how
I sink or swim

Oh love is handsome
And love is fine
The sweetest flower
When first is new

Tesla did not sing, but felt his spirits lifted and fortified, and was somewhat surprised to observe the resonance of the voices matched those frequencies displayed on his dial. The observation tingled his skin as keenly as Sunner was feeling in the cage, and he marked it for future contemplation.

...But love grows old
and waxes cold
and fades away
like summer dew.

Build me a boat
That can carry two
And both shall row
My love and I

When the song ended and the room shushed the last echo, and all was still except for the cage which swayed like an Esquimaux cradle to Sunner's gentle rocking, there was the softest slurred murmur from amongst the nest of blankets.

"S'nice," Lilly sighed. "Sing it again."

They did.

And this time Tesla joined them.

CHAPTER SEVENTEEN

"The importance of the fair can't be overstated. Let me give you just one example: Frank Baum. Frank takes a ride in the captive balloon over the White City and he comes back down pregnant with the idea of the Emerald City. Soon thereafter he wrote The Wonderful Wizard of Oz; whereby he inoculated the childhood imagination of the first generation of Science Fiction writers who would in turn infect the imaginations of a critical mass of geeks, if you will. Nikola Tesla's importance is critical, but if you want an event horizon, my money is on Frank. If we come this way again we'll need to keep an eye on Frank."
—*The Chairman's Notes*
Wardenclyffe Foundation Archives

∞

Above the Hercules Ice Skating Rink

Lauder shivered in the narrow attic above the skating rink where he knelt on a mat of burlap laid over the thick insulation of straw that covered the blocks of manufactured ice. In one yard-wide section, he had wallowed the ice and straw away from the floor, and with a hand-cranked drill had made a hole between his floor and the ceiling above the dry rink.

Now he sat, his ear to the end of a large ear trumpet. It served well enough to pull up the sounds from the next floor, except he felt like a 2-D cartoon character, hunched with his ear to his comically low-tech listening device. But it sufficed.

He was shivering, not because of the cold, but because of what he heard. The little gang of Murderers was preparing to disperse, and not as in their previous plans where all would leave on a train to Tesla's lab in New York. That plan had delayed their departure in order to have an entire car to themselves and their equipment, but none were currently available for hire. Now their plans had changed, although there was some argument about it. Now they were heading to various destinations that needed no more preparation than to purchase the tickets to ride.

The old imp called Sam said he would return by steamer to Europe, to rejoin his family. The Gypsies would travel in their own caravan by road. The Murderer of the World was headed back to Arkansas. His traveling companion would be the old woman with the impossible accent. The young woman, the one Lauder thought of as 'the magician's assistant' and who had only recently joined the inner circle, was unhappy about this, and resorted to scripture to make her case, but she was to accompany Tesla to continue her treatments. Lauder hadn't seen her before, except in shadow on the paper sail in the 'Sergei the Amazing' sideshow, and he had to infer her identity from context. He was surprised to learn she was an invalid, and her name was Lilly, like the flower, and that made him sorry. Killing the young woman with the delicate name and frail condition would be harder and seemed *more wrong* somehow, than killing the others. He wasn't sure why. Maybe the sensibilities of the age were rubbing off on him.

From his earpiece he learned that in Arkansas there was a farm, and on that farm was a *hole within a hole*. Lauder had to assemble the puzzle from the scraps that he heard over the past few days, but by and by it came to him that they believed the Hadron Cell, the black hole, the one that powered the QET, had been lost down an actual hole in the ground. Down a latrine, of all things, in what would eventually become the keep of the Chief Elder Enge. Tesla and the former Geezer discussed this with voices rising in pitch as they speculated back and forth and with growing excitement that the hole-in-the-hole had been a factor when Sergei misfired an apparatus in a barn built over it years later, in the 21st century. The Murderer meant to return to find it and use it to return to the 22nd.

This worried Lauder until he gave it some thought. If it was still there 100 years hence, causing young Sunner some troubles, then Sergei, as he called himself in his current deceit, *had not* and *would not* find it. Lauder had several years under his belt contemplating the snarls of cause and effect. Finding the Hadron Cell *could not* happen because it *had not happened*. End of story. It was a paradox, and the Murderer would fail in his quest. Paradoxes were an artifact of a single time-line, and Lauder intended to keep the universe linear, just like he hoped like hell he was the reason the Murderer would fail. If splitting the universe into alternate possibilities was prevented, then the Murder would be subject to his own paradox.

As for Tesla, he was planning to return with the female assistant to his lab and workshop in New York, set up some equipment, and then head on to Niagara. Sergei had astounded both Tesla and the eavesdropping Lauder by foretelling the inventor would win the commission to harness the great waterfall with his turbines, and they would still be in good operation in his own day and age. This had both amazed and dispirited Tesla, and he said so. It seemed a shame to him that 100 years would not improve on his design.

For some reason this made Sergei laugh. Yet he was adamant that Tesla should continue his work. *It was terribly important*, he was told. Besides powering the Eastern Seaboard, his innovations would be the underpinnings of many essential future technologies, at least as far into the future as Sergei knew about. Tesla argued that perhaps it was *because of*, not *in spite of* his association with Sergei that he would be able to accomplish this. The Chief Elder Enge denied it strenuously, but Tesla only demurred when he was assured the Murderer would return just as soon as he found his Hadron Cell. After all, they had a time machine to build.

Lauder lost the thread of the conversation then. In his former life, he had never heard of Tesla until he found the book about him in the Murderer's keep. That wasn't surprising. Histories weren't something you *learned*; they were something you *googed*, and only then if it was relevant to a pressing concern. Lauder was neither a historian, nor an engineer. He wasn't even a wire-punk game-head, so why should he have ever pinged Tesla? But Tesla *was* of historic importance, and after this brief interlude, this brush with nefarious destiny, Tesla might go on his way without murdering anybody at all. Maybe he was just an innocent who allowed his talents to be briefly hijacked by the Chief Elder Enge. He might be the first, historically speaking, but he sure as hell wouldn't be the last.

Lauder could rationalize that the rest of the party was insignificant, and wouldn't be missed. At least that would be true if he could stop them before they did any real damage. The two geezers were nearing the ends of their natural lives anyway. Given the current state of medical science, the days of the invalid Lilly were also numbered. And the Gypsies? Gypsies barely existed on the fringes as it was, but Tesla was a different story. If Lauder took Tesla out, it might have ripple effects. More than that, it might be enough to shunt off another branch of reality just as effectively as if the World Murderer had done it, except in this case, Lauder would be the one holding the bag.

Is it possible that in eliminating Tesla, Lauder would be the first to rip the world?

The horror of that thought caused Lauder to collapse back in the straw.

He lay prone on his back as though struck dead: paralyzed by the complexities and permutations of disaster that paraded through his skull. The angels screamed in his head as they always did when his unconscious thoughts touched on his off-line implant, seeking answers that weren't there. They were too loud to make sense of. The roar had no meaning; it contained no guidance in it at all. The sounds in his head were just static.

He just lay there, staring at a sliver of daylight way up in the tower that telescoped above him nearly a hundred feet. *There.* His attention was caught by light leaking in where the roof had pulled away from the chimney. The light seemed to vibrate with the steady *whoosh* of heat rising from the coal furnace on the ground floor — the furnace that ran the power plant that operated the refrigeration units.

At that moment, you could say Lauder *saw the light.*

His other diversion was already in place: Lauder had rigged the Ferris wheel. He only had to trigger it. It was a grand plan undertaken swiftly by the grace of God and a few well-paid laborers who believed they were doing repairs. All work at the fair was done at night, so as not to detract from the visitor's experience during the day, so there was nothing unusual about a hurried excavation on the grounds under the cover of darkness. So much was always going on, who could keep track of it all?

Lauder had done it on faith and had not known until this moment what the diversion was *for*; or what he needed a diversion *from*. But now, as he stared up at the chimney where it was parting from the roof, he did.

CHAPTER EIGHTEEN

"People used to worry about a singularity of technology: When bio-life gives way to inorganic life. 'The rise of the machines!' 'The-end-of-the-world!' But in fact, the singularity was when everyone finally got what they wanted most: Immortality."
—*The Chairman's Notes*
Wardenclyffe Foundation Archives

∞

The Palace of Fine Arts

Sunner placed one foot ahead of the other with painstaking care. It was a hot Indian summer day and his hands were damp in their gloves. He checked them often against his cheek to be certain the wet did not go through, even though he was insulated in his cork-soled shoes. Luckily, the bent-willow wheelchair pushed easily over the way pressed smooth by a million footfalls, and the burden was light. He looked down on Lilly's head, her hair escaping from under the silk scarf. It began as a veil, but as soon as they moved out of Tesla's sight she raised it and grinned up at Sunner and teased one glove off with her teeth. She crossed her right hand over her left shoulder and slipped her fingers under the lip of his glove to tickle his wrist, skin to skin.

There was no arguing with her. He leaned over and kissed the crown of her head, pressing his mouth hard against the solidity of her scalp until he felt the resistance of her spine. His nose filled with the bouquet of her hair and his lips tasted salt.

There was no arguing with *him* either.

Tomorrow was "Chicago Day," when the gates would be thrown open and admission was free, and so today the crowd was lighter than it had been since their arrival two months ago. This was their farewell tour; tomorrow they would depart the fair for good, and temporarily part company one last time. She would go with Tesla to New York, and Sunner would go to Arkansas, to sift through the whole farm if necessary until the Hadron Cell was found. He hoped it wouldn't take long. He *assured her* it wouldn't take long, and he would return to her as quickly as he could. They would reunite in New York, at Tesla's lab, and from there, the two of them would continue on together. 'On' being whenever they wished. With the Serbian's help he meant to make it back, *all the way back* to 2123 or thereabouts. Not the long way, but by a shortcut of his and Tesla's making. Lilly was frail, and healthcare in the current age was dicey, to say the least. She would recover best in the 22nd century, and once recovered, they would 'take the cure' as it was described in the current vernacular, and her body, like his, would age no more. This was the ultimate cure: *S heart L, forever.*

But today was theirs.

He walked slowly, sharing the wonders of the fair that up until now had only been the backdrop to their race against time. Tomorrow they would board separate trains, but today they could finally give the fair the attention it deserved. For now, they were present and together, and they spent the time marveling at the ingenuity of a people who had done so much with so little.

"We sell ourselves short," Sergei observed.

Sunner just kept saying, "Damn!"

Like 19th century tourists, they gawked up at the colossal facades that towered alongside broad Venetian canals. The lagoons were a chaos of boats under sail, or rowed, or sculled by gondoliers. There were even little barges propelled by battery power, threading back and forth between the columns of the immense Peristyle. Sailboats glided through and into the Great Lake, swinging north to compare themselves to the Viking longboat or to the replica of the Santa Maria.

In the White City itself, every corner, pinnacle and capstone teamed with a riot of whitewashed statuary, mannered and poised and winged to such heroic excesses it tipped the scales to the ludicrous.

"Look at *that* one!" Lilly cried for the umpteeth time, pointing at statue that depicted a tangle of nymphs climbing Poseidon like a tree.

Sunner laughed, and said his requisite "Damn!" giving the handles of the chair a little shake to show he really meant it. Both of them grinned so much their faces ached. At the center of this hurricane of affectation was golden Columbia herself, topping out at 150 feet on her pedestal island in the center of the main lagoon. She held aloft her torch with a stoic *up-yours* to the Statue of Liberty. She was not pretty or graceful, but it didn't matter. She was *big.*

Less than two years ago all of this was a wilderness marshland, deep with fetid mud and tangled reeds and hillocks too shifty to bear the foundations of a small house, much less a city. This was the tubercular bog Chicago had been built to the north of to avoid. It was optimistically named Jackson Park. Daniel Burnham looked on this unholy real estate and by the dictates of his vision unleashed a cavalry of teamsters with their wagons and mules, and an army of laborers with shovels and trowels. With blueprints from a congress of architects, landscapers and *escapists,* Americans plotted the new Jerusalem and shouted across both oceans, "Look what we can do!"

The buildings and sculptures were mostly plaster and chaff pressed onto slats over armatures and held together with paint. It was a papier-mâché city: a sham, but the grandest ever. At risk from rain and fire, each night it was triaged with shims and spackle and wishful thinking. It was a monument to self-delusion; an absolutely appropriate tribute to the misdirection of Columbus. Here was the germ for the Emerald City and Disney World. Here was the American dream of empty promises that would bother the nation's restless sleep forever after.

This, *this* is what the emigrants had come here expecting, and it was artifice and deceit.

But it was also wonderful.

Lilly and Sunner took it in with no concern more pressing than where they should take their lunch. Lilly held on her lap a small hamper filled with wine, bread, oranges, coleslaw, sweet-potato cakes and not a drop of milk. Sunner pushed on until he found a patch of lawn not yet bare from the wear of foot traffic, where they could enjoy their picnic.

He used his thumbnails to peel electrocuted oranges and pressed them slice after slice into Lilly's mouth. He kept on until his fingers were sticky and his cuticles turned yellow, and still she couldn't get enough of them, just as he couldn't get enough of watching her eat them. Her lips parted and her teeth mashed down on the squirting pulp and he blotted her orange-juice lips with a kiss. Citrus was her ambrosia, the nectar of her resurrection, and thankfully it was plentiful here at the fair. Her breath was sweet and orangey, no longer rank with the ketosis of scurvy. He could run his fingers through her hair now without strands pulling free. When he probed her teeth with his tongue they were firmly rooted – this, he re-confirmed as often as she would allow.

Lilly retained the habit of rustling and tapping as she had before. Her private sign language constantly signaled, *I am here, I am here.* His eyes fixed on her fingers; their dance as slight as summer heat rising to lift and rustle leaves, as subtle and constant as anemone fingering the tides. It did not cease to amaze him. *She was here! She was here!*

They lunched on the lawn overlooking the wilderness pond and the Wooded Island beyond. They would not risk a boat. Bobbing across the water was about as wise as bathing with a plugged-in toaster, given their precariously magnetized state. But it wasn't far, and from here they could admire the Japanese village and the paper lanterns strung from tree to tree along a path where other lovers strolled and the occasional big-wheeled bicycle wobbled along.

A faint tune crossed the water, sawed on a Javanese lute, but the music they listened to most intently was the deep enveloping silence of a world mostly ignorant of machines. It was an undercurrent of silence profound against the background of the clamoring fair.

This and the wine pacified them to a drowsiness so sublime that Sunner could only resist by remaining on his feet. Lilly murmured to him to rest on the grass as her own head nodded and her eyes grew heavy. But he would not forfeit the luxury of enjoying her touch by 'walking on the earth like mortal men' as Tesla had warned. Hanging in the electrified cage was only a little uncomfortable and a small price to pay, but the cage and equipment were being packed away at this very moment, and grounding put a barrier between them he was not willing to endure. So, he was careful to touch nothing but her. He paced slow circles around her as she napped, keeping close watch until her sleep threatened to topple her from her chair. When he kissed her awake it was with an electric elation that had nothing to do with Tesla or his devices.

"Let's go to the art gallery," he told her when her eyes focused and she smiled up at him. Sunner thought, and he was right, that Lilly could do with a dose of art. *Real art.* Not the artifice all around them. A tribute in a way, to what had brought them together.

He wheeled her past the botanical gardens that rioted up to the glass walls of the domed Horticulture Building, over another lagoon bridge and past the fisheries, to the Palace of Fine Arts. Sunner pushed her right up to the broad limestone steps that rose from the water, where the gondolas disembarked from the north pond.

"No handicap ramp, I betcha," Lilly said.

A passerby, a gentleman, a *Good Samaritan*, reached out his hands toward the chair and said, "Allow me..." Lilly and Sunner both shouted *"No!"*

The man stumbled back when Sunner hissed the dreaded word: *"Leprosy!"*

Lilly smiled apologetically and waved. She held her hand like a claw within the glove and acted as if it was a great effort.

Their Samaritan made a hasty about-face and hurried away, his face white and greasy with a sudden sweat. The few people on the stairs within earshot parted like the Red Sea.

"Leprosy? Really?" Lilly said through her clenched smile. "Now they won't let us inside."

"Sure they will. Who'll stop us?" And he turned her about and began pulling her step-by-step up the long flight of stairs.

She tapped her cork-soled-shoes to make a point. "I could walk you know."

"I know."

"But you won't let me."

"Nope."

"'Kay. Enjoy your heroics."

"*Am*," he puffed.

When they got to the top and he turned her around, she said, "Déjà vu"

"You recognize it?" he said in a way that made it clear he was pleased.

"I think. Maybe."

"The Chicago Museum of Science and Industry," he said with a little reverence. "*Someday.* That's stony-stone you are looking at. The real McCoy, So it's still here. Or *there.* You know what I mean."

I do. Her hands fluttered in acknowledgment.

The Palace of Art was big, but the false edifices of the fair still dwarfed it. This was a grand manner house in the district of castles. Nevertheless, it would survive every other building of the fair.

He pushed her inside, and as he predicted, no one moved to stop them. In the massive main hall, the Columbian guard shared the floor with a brigade of international security agents, presiding over their national treasures with sidearms in plain view. It was evident why only a stone fortress would do. It was secure. It was fireproof, and it didn't leak. The fact that it was built on the same schedule as the temporary buildings was another thing to add to the Columbian Exhibition's list of many wonders.

Every square foot of wall-space contained paintings from the top of the 20-foot ceilings down to the marble floor with barely inches to spare between them.

"Holy cats," Lilly said. "Sensory overload."

"Think there'll be a *Pia Stiller* in here?" he teased.

"Just as soon as I paint one. Lordy, I don't know where to begin. I think my eyes might bleed from friction."

He pushed her to the center of the first side room where they parked so Lilly could drink her fill. It was oranges for her soul.

Anytime anyone got too close he said the magic word: *Leprosy*. It cleared each room and even the guards edged to the doorways and didn't breathe their air.

The French exhibition filled three halls. Italy was represented in two. The Americans defended a superior territory of four whole rooms, but then, this was their fair, wasn't it? Non-Western art was lumped together in one of two annexes, but like everyone else they made use of every surface, partition and pedestal, and in some cases works were attached to the ceiling.

"You know what's missing?" Lilly said as they passed under the arch separating France from the United States. "Matisse. Renoir. Monet. Toulouse-Lautrec, Gauguin, Van Gogh. Degas, Cezanne. All the great painters of this age, *excluded*. Isn't that something?"

"Not really," he said.

"Is that so?"

"I expect it is always like that. The appreciation of greatness takes perspective. It is the same with science."

"Art and science are two different things entirely."

"Are they?" he asked, and let the question hang.

"Who *do* you recognize?" He gestured to the wall.

Lilly scanned from horizon to horizon and could not name a one, *not one,* while somewhere Donald Harington spun in his grave. Or would, after he was born, schooled her in art history, and died. No wait, that wasn't quite right. She had seen a Rosa Bonheur, and a Mary Cassatt. So *two*, anyway, but not here. She saw their paintings one night while pillaging in the

Women's Pavilion. Their work had been segregated by their sex, and yet they would surpass in fame all those they had been sequestered from.

"What will be said about this collection?" he pressed.

Lilly looked sorry, putting on an exaggerated accent to say: "Pedantic. Uninspired. Death-throes of romanticism. Juried by populist Cretans..."

"And you?"

"Right here. Right now... in this time and place..." she had to gather herself to admit it: "They are just about perfect."

"Yeah, It is the same with science," he agreed. "I've seen it. Well, *Sergei* has. You're *living* it. We're all fashion-sheep. One thread is dropped when the next is picked up. One train of thought at a time, running past abandoned freight on parallel tracks that just sit there because their engines have been disengaged. Each generation believes itself to be the one to finally turn on the lights, while they turn off the lights behind them.

"But not Tesla. He didn't give a shit when I told him what *'we now know'*. I mean, he listened, but he didn't let it get in the way. That's his mad science: the genius and miracle of how he thinks. I'm willing to bet he *doesn't* put his pants on one leg at a time. His ability to just see what is there is only half of it. It takes balls to act on what no one else believes is true. It's a kind of insanity, don't you think? Or, maybe he's just a crazy S.O.B. who happens to be right. I can tell you one thing, he is unequaled in time and what he sees is dead simple. I missed it. I was too focused on *what I knew* while he just cut to the chase.

"I couldn't have saved you, Lilly. No way. Not by myself. Not even two of me. Tesla though, he saw what was needed. He didn't dick around with theory, either. He just did it."

They stood side by side and thought about that until Lilly shoved it off her lap like a cat that had gotten too heavy with too many claws.

"All these pretty pictures," she said. "Left behind. It's sad."

"I guess that depends on your perspective." He pushed her forward, close to the wall and squatted down next to her, careful not to touch the floor. "*Look*," he said. "At this one. Just look."

They focused together at a pretty little landscape hung before their noses. The view was from a hedgerow across a golden field of wheat to a quiet Dutch farmhouse dosing under its thatches. In the middle ground a single milk cow grazed. Beyond, a ribbon of water and a congregation of trees at the horizon under a cloudless sky. A wholly unremarkable painting, but very nicely done.

Lilly felt rather than saw Sunner's posture shift in that way that she had come to know as Sergei surfacing and he spoke to her in a reverent whisper.

"In every act, universes are spawned. They spin off infinite fractals of possibility, and each of those spin *inward,* in infinite divisions and nuances and shades of options. This painting holds *worlds*. In and of itself, it is the center of everything. Upon each brushstroke, Shiva's foot falls in the eternal dance. And the same can be said for us: Here we are, in a juxtaposition of miracles. You and I and *all of this,* in the same space at the same time. Right here and right now, this painting is all of creation and the artist of this moment is God."

"Beautifully said," she breathed.

"It may well be, but I meant it literally. Did you hear what I said? *Now look*." He wheeled her back a few paces, and stood by her side. Taking her hand, he covered it with his other and waited. "What do you see?"

Lilly's eyes flitted from painting to painting. As an artist she knew every painting held its secret doorway where the viewer's eyes could enter, but the room was too crowded with possibilities and a queasy claustrophobia coursed through her veins. Sunner felt her hand begin to sweat in his own.

"It's okay," he whispered. "Just keep looking."

She went back to the Dutch landscape, and found it. Her gaze fell through the canvas. The picture itself became a window and it opened out deeper and deeper in a way not described by an illusion of perspective and scale. Lilly felt herself falling toward it, into it. Sunner held firmly to her hand.

Lilly pulled her eyes out, looked from painting to painting, each of them opening up like holes in the walls and all of them endless, cascading into forever. She squeezed his hand hard.

"And there you have the eyes of God," he said.

"What just happened?"

"An idea took hold. It's no small thing."

But Lilly's face wasn't full of wonder. "I think I'm going to be sick," she said miserably.

"Good," he said. "That will ground you in a little reality. Nothing like a good barf to clear your head."

Sunner called out loudly, "The lady requires a basin!" He grinned at Lilly. "*Really,* after all we've been through?"

"Oh God," she moaned.

"Put your head down." He massaged her shoulders while she pulled her hair back.

"If everything ... everything ... *every-damn-thing* is possible, then it's *inevitable.* It's one big ironclad *thing* in the end, isn't it?" Lilly was shaking. "I'm crazy, aren't I? I'm already crazy. I'm not at the fair; I'm in a nice padded cell somewhere, right? Please tell me we aren't all Calvinists after all."

"What you think you see isn't a straight line," Sunner told her. "It's the shadow of the edge of..."

"Spare me! What difference does that make? It's open at my feet. I'm going to fall in."

"One of you will," he agreed. "One of you won't. You decide. This time, today, which one will you be?"

"It's all there."

"*Yes,*" he said with relish.

"It's all vanity."

"Try: '*It's all relative.*'

"What if I just sit here?"

"Don't check out on me, Lill."

"What if I just stop?" Lilly rocked in her chair while he waited. Moments ticked by to the echoed murmurs throughout the building along with the hushed footfalls and rustling peculiar to art museums and cathedrals. Finally she concluded: "It doesn't stop, does it?"

"No," he said.

"Not ever."

"No."

"No matter what."

"Don't be too hard on yourself. It comes from *thinking.* Mathematicians, physicists, philosophers ... the loony bin is full of them. I'd have been disappointed, frankly, if you had shrugged it off."

"If everything is inevitable, what can I do that matters?"

"Look at it this way: Not only is everything possible, every possibility exists. You *can* get there from here, if you are clever enough to find the way. Isn't that liberating?"

Lilly didn't look liberated.

He folded her hand in his until it was a fist, then he squeezed it until it hurt just a little. Just enough to focus her attention. Her eyes turned to him in surprise. He let up, gently laced his fingers with hers and said, "It is *your* truth, Lilly. It's what you make of it. Look at us. Look at *us*. Is it less of a miracle that we are together *here,* where there are infinite realities where we are *not*? That we are together *right now* in this conscious aspect is, by all reckoning, practically impossible. That sounds like a miracle to me. By that accounting, every moment is a miraculous juxtaposition. It happens just this once. Because one thing infinity is not, *it is not redundant...*" he paused, "Or maybe it is. Maybe it *has to be*. Hell, I don't know." It was now Sunner that laughed and let go of her hand to yank his hair and shake the imps out of his ears.

"Infinity will make you nuts," he agreed, "but which is worse: thinking you have one shot at something and everything else falls away into nothing? The void you are used to on either side of your linear life view is still an *infinite* void. You are used to it, that's all. I'm just saying there is no void. *Still infinite*. Just not a *void*. Why are you more comfortable with 'nothing' than with 'everything'?"

A pail slid across the floor within reach, and a janitor stood unhappily with his mop a few feet away.

Lilly looked at it dismally. "Isn't 'nothing' one of the infinite possibilities?"

"Pretty good for 'just an artist.'" He laughed. "The math ain't pretty, that's for sure."

"I'm not going to need this." She nudged the pail away with her cork-clad toe. "Sorry I overreacted. It finally caught up with me, that's all. Just a bit of motion-sick on the ole' crazy train."

"That's the advantage of pairing up. You get to take turns freaking out."

"Thanks."

"You saw me through mine, back in Arkansas. Time to return the favor."

"I get the feeling it doesn't get better."

"Nope," he agreed. "You just get used to it."

"Swell."

Sunner decided she needed a change of scenery and wheeled her into the next room.

"Now there's something," he said.

Lilly was wheeled into position in front of a large oil painting. The landscape was placed too low, too close to a corner, but it dominated the room in spite of both these handicaps. On the canvas, a fiery haze parted to reveal ramparts of crumbling ruins and toppled statuary. In its darkest-dark recesses, ghostly figures emerged and retreated as smoke on the periphery of her vision. Leaning forward, Lilly couldn't see the figurtes at all if she looked directly at them. It was a mirage in paint. In the foreground, there was a broken Grecian pedestal with a crumbling basin such as might still be on the lawn of Olympus. Above it a white dove fluttered down on wings that troubled the atmosphere in the midst of a transfiguration between dream and memory.

"I like that one." Sunner leaned in to read the card:

"*Ruins at Columbia...*" He stopped there. He didn't read the artist's name aloud.

"*Holy shit,*" Lilly whispered.

He skipped to the next line and agreed. "Oh shit, indeed."

"Don't say it," Lilly shut her eyes against what she'd already involuntarily read.

She *wanted* the painting to be the one by Edwin Dickenson of the Hudson River School. She'd seen it before, or one similar to this. She closed her eyes to pull the facts from the card catalog in her memory. She visualized the over-varnished pine drawers that would someday be retained in the University of Arkansas Fine Arts department library just on aesthetic principles. They afforded a tactile knowledge and she preferred them over the computers as many art students did. It was a point of pride to use the old card catalogue. Just now she needed very badly to hold on to tangible facts. Her fingers groped for want of index cards, dog-eared, notched and worn to velvet edges. She imagined, *remembered,* a tiny landscape of uneven letters from a sticky-keyed typewriter. She grieved there was nothing here to back her up. Her senses reeled looking for the right input. She wanted the scent of floor wax, Xerox ink on hot sheets of paper, book mold, the funk of patchouli oil and cannabis, highlighter pens and dust. She got none of it. The painting was not by Dickinson, who wouldn't paint like this for another fifty years. It was by *Pia Stiller.* But Lilly *was* Pia Stiller. So said the accidental signature on *The Devil's Portrait* that she had painted in Idee's cabin that it might, in time, fall into Sergei's hands and lead him to her, as it had. She read the placard aloud.

"Oil on canvas by Pia Stiller. On loan from the Wardenclyffe Foundation Collection." Sunner finished for her. "Who gets to freak out next? I've lost track. Is it my turn?"

They were treading chin deep in creepiness. More than déjà vu, they knew exactly when this sort of thing had happened before. That one very specific moment they'd spent side by side in incredulity under the Decatur Municipal Building back in the summer of 2010, when they were still in their own time and place.

"It's not possible. I could never paint like that."

"*Never* is a long time," he whispered.

Lilly turned and said, "*Sergei?*"

Only his eyes shifted, but Sergei the elder looked at her and waited.

"When Sunner and I first went looking for *The Devil's Portrait* and found the note and the pig's ear behind the keystone instead, were you the one who put them there?"

"I don't ... *Oh.*" He registered the memory Sunner presented to him with the ticking of his eyes. "No. I did not," he said gravely.

"You didn't," she repeated.

"No."

"Then you're not the one screwing with us, are you?"

"No. Of course not. At least, *probably* not."

"Do you know who...?"

"No."

"We're still being played, aren't we?"

"Maybe."

Lilly's hands fluttered in frustration. Sergei caught them up in hands that were equally his and Sunner's.

"Sweetheart, in all the world in all of time, from every dimension branching forevermore above us, do you imagine we will be the only ones dipping into the dime-stream? Or that we'd be the only ones clever enough to figure out how? And out of that probable and considerable population, why would we be the *only ones* curious enough to visit the fair? Hell, who's to say half the people we saw strolling the promenade today weren't time travelers? I would venture to guess quite a lot of them, and no doubt there is a prankster or two in their number."

But he wasn't thinking of practical jokers, he was thinking of a man with three bars tattooed on the back of his hand. He thought of the 'someone' Lilly had chased from the rink when she was still out-of-phase and they'd nearly lost her. This turned his stomach, though he made a decent effort to hide it, and was almost successful.

"It's a long way to come just to ride the Ferris wheel," she said stubbornly.

"The fair is the *Eighth Wonder of the World*," he pointed out.

"It's not just the fair. It's *us*. This is directed at *us*."

"Hey, as far as I know, we're the first to pull it off. Maybe we're celebrities? Anyone ask for your autograph?"

Lilly frowned. "No, they haven't, and I'm pretty sure I wouldn't travel to 1968 just to bug Neil Armstrong for a souvenir, let alone play practical jokes on him," she said. "Seriously, Sunner. Someone is messing with us for a reason."

He considered it. "For all we know," he said, "*we* are messing with us. What's to keep us from coming back again and again? Maybe this is our preferred vacation spot and maybe this," he gestured at the painting, "is just a little present to ourselves: Our version of carving our initials into a tree."

"It bugs you too," Lilly said. "I can tell."

He shrugged it off the best he could. "The possibilities are endless. Speculations are just a parlor game. When everything is inevitable, all that's left to do is observe and say '*yes*' to it."

Lilly looked at the painting, no more satisfied now than before. "Would the real Pia Stiller please stand up," she said miserably. "Just once I'd like a little solid reality I could sink my teeth into."

"You know what I want?" Sunner asked. He'd just decided they had enough mind-tripping for one afternoon so he took hold of the handles at the back of her chair and spun her away from the painting.

"What do you want?" she took his bait.

"I want to ride the Ferris wheel."

CHAPTER NINETEEN

"Virtually every American refugee can boast an ancestor that attended the fair whether they know it or not. It stamped the collective memory of what greatness should be. For better or worse, it was the blueprint of the modern mind, and the modern mind is insatiable. It wanted more. Always more. And soon, very soon, it became fixated on the idea that there was not enough to be had.

That idea nearly undid the world. — But of course that was back when people believed that there was only the one world and resources were limited."

    —*The Chairman's Notes*
    Wardenclyffe Foundation Archives

∞

Ferris's Great Wheel

"You're sure about this?" Sunner asked. Now that they were approaching the Ferris wheel, he was having second thoughts. It wasn't safe for them to press in with a crowd and if Lilly touched or was touched by something that grounded her, she'd be gone again.

"Oh hell yes!" she laughed up at him. "This isn't *a* Ferris wheel, it's *the* Ferris wheel. C'mon 'fraidy-man. Where's your sense of adventure?"

"Really, we can come back and do this all over again once you are stable."

She knew he didn't mean 'this time around,' because the fair was closing soon. He meant on a different time-stream. — Or, *dime*-stream as he called it to indicate a different dimension.

"Do you see us anywhere?" she looked about with a distinct air of sarcasm. "Nope. Sorry. It looks like today is the day, Sunshine."

At least the line was thin and moved fast. Not only was attendance light on the day before Chicago Day, but also riding the wheel took the princely sum of one whole dollar. Most of the crowd around the wheel were onlookers without the sand or the scratch to step aboard.

Lilly and Sunner were accustomed to the immense wheel that dominated the skyline and blazed with thousands of lights each night, but standing under it imparted a unique vertigo as they watched the tremendous mass descend over them from 260 feet above. This was not a carnival wheel. This was the greatest feat of structural engineering since the pyramids. Or so the brochure said.

The brochure got no argument from Lilly and Sunner. Eight towers supported the largest single piece of steel produced thus far and from this shaft dual wheels were suspended. Despite the massive supports, each one had spokes so slender they seemed no more substantial than a wire bicycle wheel. Trussed between them were 36 ornate train carriages decked out in full-on gilded age frippery and frosted with lights.

"Another *first*, if you are keeping track," Sunner marveled.

"Why start small?" Lilly said. She imagined the wheel might compare to the London Eye, but she'd only seen that in pictures from a distance, so she wasn't sure. If there was anything to argue against the superiority of her own time, this was it. It was thoroughly thrilling, even to a woman of the 21st century and to a man of the 22nd.

When they got to the top of the switch-back two-story loading ramp, the operator told them the wheelchair could not come aboard. Not because it could not, because it would not be permitted. Frail passengers were discouraged, as the thrills of the wheel were taxing to the constitution.

"I will walk," Lilly said and stood on her cork shoes.

"Gloves..." Sunner advised, and she pulled them on and graciously declined the helping hand offered by the Pullman Porter, there to comfort and supervise passengers as they might expect in a first class train carriage. Instead, Lilly took Sunner's arm in a ladylike fashion. She rewarded the man a conciliatory smile, just to show there were no hard feelings. He tipped his hat to her and grinned. He was proud in his uniform and stepped aside to let them pass into the car. Inside were narrow benches around the edge but most passengers were expected to stand. Thankfully they were not at capacity. They kept the cars light today. It was easygoing. There were 18 people boarded where there was room enough for 60.

They stood in the far corner.

"Welcome aboard ladies and gentlemen," the car-man said. "I am locking the door for your safety. However," he said coyly, "if any become excitable or unmannerly, I may unlock it again."

Nervous laughter was shared around the car.

"The ladies are advised to sit, if they will. All others may take hold of the straps for security. Expect the car to sway a bit, although I assure you even if you were to pace from side to side in one accord, you would exact no more danger to your fellow passengers then in the gentle rocking of a baby's cradle."

Lilly did not sit. Sunner did not take hold of a strap. Instead, he stood in barricade, triangulating her in the corner with his feet braced and his hands on her waist to steady her should the car lurch, to keep her from grabbing the handrails, even though their gloved hands likely gave them enough protection.

They grinned at each other.

The great chain rattled in its sprocket and the car lifted off. The passengers gasped and twittered even though the lift was slow and short lived as it paused to refresh the passengers on the car below.

Lilly giggled. "I'm giddy. Positively giddy. You'd think I'd never been on one before!"

"We should have waited for Sam and Idee."

"We'll do it again." Lilly agreed. "But you won't get Idee on this, not without a blindfold and a few glasses of whiskey."

"Don't be so sure."

The car lifted to the next stage. As they progressed, each new level brought exclamations over what was now seen that wasn't seen before. Just a quarter of the way up, and they could see out over all of the fair. Seen all at once and laid out below them like this, it seemed even larger and more magnificent than gazing up at one building at a time. At three-fourths of the way up, they shared the horizon with the roof of the Manufacturers Building, Golden Columbia and the Peristyle water gate through which boats sailed out into Lake Michigan.

"Tarnation!" Lilly laughed. "I can see my house from here."

They looked down over the Midway, past the wall to 67th Street where Buffalo Bill Cody's arena was at the end of the crazy-quilt tent city. They could not see their own tent, nor the magician's stage (now closed for business), because it abutted the other side of the wall, but they could see Vladimir and Esmeralda's caravan parked under one of the few trees in the campground. They were also closed for business, so there was no line of shills waiting to have their palms read by Esmeralda or the shape of their skull palpated by Vladimir.

Vladimir would be in the Cold Storage building along with Tesla, Sam, and Idee, packing up the last of the equipment to be loaded on the freight car. Esmeralda was probably in the caravan, securing their gear as well. Before Lilly's recovery, the Gypsies had planned to go in the freight car with the rest of the party, and had arranged for their wagon to be hauled by roustabouts to the Wild West Show's winter quarters. They were to reclaim it when the show resumed and passed through New York next spring. The show was always in want of winter accommodations, and they were glad to have it. But now that Esmeralda was no longer needed to communicate with Lilly, they would drive their own wagon to New

York, which required a different set of preparations, including stocking the larder.

It was also Esmeralda's turn to mind the goat, a chore none of them minded much. The goat was no longer critical, but she was essential: Pi was and would always be their cherished mascot and an honorary member of their extended family. Lilly couldn't see Pi from the wheel, but she imagined her contentedly chewing her cud under the wagon with Spitfire asleep nearby.

"I think maybe you should sit, sir," the car-man softly drawled.

Sunner and Lilly were pulled away from the scenery to look down the other end of the car. The car-man was addressing a passenger who did not look well at all. In fact, he was so distressed the panama hat he held had started to fray from the incessant working of his worried hands. He was pale but the front of his trousers was dark where he'd peed himself. He ignored the car-man's entreaty, and his eyes darted around wildly, looking for some way to escape.

"Oh, no," Sunner said just quietly enough for Lilly to hear. She felt his hands tighten around her waist.

"What is your name, mister?" the car-man asked. He only got a whimper in response. "Here ... let me help you to a seat," he suggested, but the seats were closer to the window and the expanse of air beyond.

"Lemme off," the man managed.

"If you please sir, you are going to sit right down where you are and close your eyes a bit. We will be on the ground in no time."

"Lemme off!" he barked and violently shrugged off the porter's hands which had taken firm hold of his arms to lower him to the floor. "Stop this carriage and let me off!"

"See here now! Compose yourself. You are frightening the ladies. There is no call for that now. Look, we have crested the top, and there is no more to it than that."

The Ferris wheel was full with fresh cargo, so the wheel began an uninterrupted descent, and the rest of the passengers turned away again, so as not to miss the view. Because of its mass, the wheel turned slowly and there was none of the pit-in-your-stomach drop Lilly was expecting. It was as smooth and easy as a slow elevator. The crisis seemed to pass. The man began to cry with relief for each foot closer to the ground, but neither was the wheel slowing to let them off.

Sunner anticipated trouble and caught the eye of the porter. "Kindly signal the operator," he said. It was not a request, but the car-man shrugged behind the distressed passenger's back. He made it clear there was no way to request the wheel be stopped.

"Well, that's a clear design flaw," Sunner grumbled. The glass windows were open to admit a cool breeze, but the casements were covered with a mesh wire, and beyond that, they were barred. It would not so much as permit a hanky to be waved in distress.

As they came to the lowest point of the undercarriage, it became apparent they weren't slowing, and the man howled and flung himself at the door, hitting it so hard the glass splintered and fell in shards inside the carriage when the mesh prevented it from falling out.

"*Great.*" Lilly said.

The porter was thrown aside and the crazed man rushed the other side of the car where Lilly and Sunner were. They backed away cautiously as he attacked one window and then the next. In one place he broke through the mesh but the bars held. When that failed he ran like a bull again at the door, bending the thin sheet metal panels. Several more rushes like that and he'd be through, if he didn't tear the car apart first. The car was rocking more than the porter had suggested was possible.

"Gentlemen, I require assistance," the black man pleaded.

Four men stepped forward, while Sunner pointedly looked away and cursed under his breath. Lilly patted his arm. Their Faraday cage was packed now for certain. If he were touched he'd be out of sync until they could re-tool in New York.

The four men and the porter converged on the maniac, but his panic gave him strength and he toppled them into a heap, even though the women called encouragement and pointed out how they might take hold and subdue him. Two men nursed bloody noses. Another was gasping because the wind was knocked out of him.

They were coming to the second crest and it finally occurred to the man that the car-man had keys to the door. He jumped on him, clawing at his uniform jacket to get at them. "Keys! Keys! Keys!" he begged and demanded.

Sunner cursed loudly and gave Lilly an apologetic look. This was untenable. He would have to conscript with the rest of the car's men to settle this.

Except that Lilly stepped forward first. She unhooked her skirt and pulled it off so she was standing in her gartered stockings and short pantaloons. Even the crazed passenger paused in astonishment. She gave him a tender smile and crooning as if to a small child, dropped her skirt over his head, and wrapped her arms around him and pulled him over into her embrace. She managed all this deftly balanced on her shoes, and not in contact with him at all. She rocked and sang a lullaby, each pause filled with her *shush-shush-shush.* He didn't even whimper, he was silent under her skirt and in her arms and altogether pacified.

They pushed over the crest and stopped.

"See there?" Lilly said. "They are starting to let passengers off. Our turn will come soon, don't you worry now, baby. Don't you worry anymore." She changed her tune to *Mockingbird*, which she hoped was cheerful as well as distracting.

Time dragged on. They did not advance down to the next stage. She reached the end of the song and started over, glancing up at Sunner but he was riveted to the window.

His posture telegraphed an alarm to her that the panicked man had not, and along with it, there was a change. Lilly couldn't put her finger on it at first; it was like a drop in the barometric pressure. A shift in the wind. A loss. An opening up. And then she had it. The fair had hushed.

One by one the other passengers turned their attention away from the spectacle in their car to the one out. Lilly began to sing louder, to drown out the whispers, while she waited for Sunner to give her some sign as to what was happening.

The power's gone off. He mouthed to her.

Lilly gave him an appalled shrug. What difference did that make? The wheel was powered by steam. They'd camped near its power plant outside the wall, when they'd stayed in the tent behind the magician stage. It was where the coal fires were stoked like a locomotive and steam was piped underground to the works of the wheel.

That the power had failed at the same time the steamworks for the wheel had stopped was just a coincidence.

Wasn't it?

She bathed her face in question marks and he showed her his palms were empty, and shook his head. He was firmly in the camp that this was no inconsequential coincidence, and was actively recruiting her to join him. His 'anything is possible' philosophy was no comfort at the moment.

She kept singing.

CHAPTER TWENTY

"Life is and will ever remain an equation incapable of solution, but it contains certain known factors."
—*Nikola Tesla*
Wardenclyffe Foundation Archives

∞

The Power Station

Nikola Tesla took another handful of straw and tamped it around the muslin bag that contained his resonator. It was in the center of a large wooden crate, one of the last to be packed. Vladimir was loudly nailing a smaller crate shut, while Idee and Sam fussed over the hamper and debated how much food Lilly would need for her journey, and how much could be packed as freight. Altogether there was enough for a fortnight. They opted to tote all the perishables, and pack the preserves, fruitcakes and most of the longer-lasting citrus. If reassembly of Tesla's resonator took longer, Lilly would be back on a diet of goat's milk and yogurt again, at least for a while.

That's when the lights went out.

It was suddenly and utterly dark in the skating rink. All the windows to the arched promenade around the exterior had been boarded up to help conserve the cool temperature inside the building after the rink closed. Now it fully resembled the cave Sam complained it was. Cool, dank and dark. They stood and joined the fair in a moment of silence.

Tesla broke it by muttering something in Serbian and Vladimir snuffed in companionable appreciation of the colorful phrase.

"Are we just agoin' t'sit here in the dark?" Idee said in disgust.

"That is the way of civilization, Madame," Sam Clemens' voice echoed in the empty rink. "There is only so much room in the brain. Each new comfort unseats the skills that predicated it. It may be months before our bones are found. First mankind must reinvent fire..."

Tesla found and opened the door to a weak light coming up from the cavernous entryway. "... or the brightest among us will open a door," Sam concluded.

Tesla walked out onto the balcony mezzanine and gazed down at the grand staircase. All the fixtures were dark.

They all shuffled after Tesla and stood at the top of the stairway. Above them the 100-foot chimney was roaring in the wooden tower as the furnace was fully stoked to run the refrigeration units full bore against the late summer heat. The lights in the building, however, were wired into the primary power supply of the fair: to the Westinghouse Generators, the ones Tesla had designed and upon whose success depended the final outcome of the Niagara Falls contract. If they failed the fair, General Electric would likely be awarded the honor of harnessing the falls. Who knew if their late-in-the-game AC generators were up to the task? If not, what would power the engines of the industrial revolution? Tesla saw the crippling of the industry as clearly as if he had seen the future. Which, in a way he had, and long before Sergei had come to confirm it. Perhaps in his coming and in the telling of it, the future had shifted. Niagara was not in the bag. Of that Tesla was sure.

Tesla spat another Serbian explicative that caused even Vladimir to place his hand over his mouth. Tesla didn't pause for an apology but sprinted down the stairs and was last seen emblazoned against the rectangle of sunlight before the door banged closed behind him.

Those left behind stood silent and watched the building administrators and guests that came to gawk at manufactured ice evacuate the windowless building. They had a brief discussion up on the mezzanine, took a vote and decided it was better to wait indoors in the cool than out in the sweltering afternoon, even if it was dark.

"Ain't theys a lantern nowheres?" Idee complained.

Vladimir satisfied her by going down and propping open the doors at the bottom of the grand staircase to let in some daylight. It was enough that the three of them could resume their packing in the dim light that reflected off the polished floor at the bottom of the stair.

∞

The Power Plant was not far from the Cold Storage building; It was located in the Machinery Hall just across the train yard, where the station was the terminus for 10 parallel tracks and the trains were always in motion. For convenience, most services like cold storage were on the south end of the grounds, where they were also in good proximity to the tenements, giving easy access for the fair's laborers, maintenance workers, garbage collectors, re-stockers and those who raked the gravel pathways smooth again each night.

The Power Plant was no different, and like many of the fair's utilities, it was also an exhibit. It was the spring that wound the clock of the future and it was the primary destination of the engineers and the captains of industry who came to gawk and hammer their visions on the anvil of what they saw. They marveled at the turbines the way others were mesmerized by the Statue of Liberty carved from a giant block of chocolate, or by the aquariums with living octopi, or at the moving sidewalk which would carry you a mile on benches out to the end of the pier and back – at least when it was working (which wasn't often).

But to reach the Machinery building Tesla went the long way around, all the way up to the Court of Honor and past the chocolatiers, and around to the front entrance to avoid the unpredictable trains. To make up the lost time, he covered the distance in a dead run. By the time he came panting up to the doors a small contingent of the Columbian guard had evacuated the building.

"Only Nikola Tesla is to be admitted, is that clear?" one of them shouted.

The Guardsmen parted as he pounded up to the entrance and the door was held open for him.

"Mind the entrance," Tesla said. "Absolutely no one else is to be admitted. Very dangerous, do you understand? This is under control." He pushed into the building, while one of the guards entered the power station behind him and bolted the door from the inside.

The turbines were not silent. They were cranking at full bore. Tesla paused at each one, seeing as much as he could in the dim light and was satisfied and puzzled at the same time. He pushed on to the switch room, where he expected technicians but there were none. The only person other than himself was the man that followed him in and locked the door. He kept pace with Tesla with his hat pulled low. Tesla was grandly preoccupied and never glanced at him once.

"Where is everyone?" Tesla demanded. "These machines were to be attended at all times,"

"Some trouble with the Ferris wheel, Mr. Tesla. Emergency operations. You know how it is." He kept his head down and appeared to be addressing his own feet.

The switch room was windowless and dark. Tesla pushed the door wide to admit as much window-light as possible, and tripped at the threshold. There was a low sandbag lying across it. A precaution against leaks, perhaps.

Tesla recovered at the threshold and stepped over and in, letting his eyes adjust. The jaw switches were closed, every one. He threw the first one, which switched on the lights in the room without a fuss. He could see the other switches clearly now. Nothing looked amiss with them other than the fact they were switched off. He reached to switch another one *on* but hesitated. There had to be a reason why someone had ticked them all off. An emergency shutdown? He looked back at the one he had just opened and now noted additional wires leading down; tacked to the wall and split at the baseboard to fork into tails that lay exposed on the floor. He frowned. It was deliberately dangerous, these exposed wires. He turned to warn the other man to stand back, and was astonished to see him standing at the doorway. With a bucket of water.

It was the Salvationist in a different uniform, but Tesla now saw him for who he was: that Lauder fellow, lately in Brown's employ: The executioner of dogs and calves and horses and one elephant. And men. Let us not forget men.

There was a wooden stool set precisely in the center of the room. Tesla leaped for it and pulled his feet up to the second rung as Lauder dashed his bucket across the floor and grabbed another and another until the water stood an inch deep over every square foot of the small room.

"It's a pity the Geezer couldn't have been here," Lauder said when he was through and Tesla was marooned. "I'd rather hoped for a game of musical chairs. Still. Not altogether unsatisfactory."

Tesla saw clearly he was dealing with a madman. He took the prudent course and sat quietly with the sloped posture of abject submission and kept his eyes averted, as one would do as not to antagonize a rabid animal. He automatically flexed his toes; His shoes bent too easily. He wasn't wearing his cork soled shoes today. *More's the pity.*

"Oh don't despair," Lauder said. "Perhaps you'll be rescued by and by. Although it may take a bit, as the authorities will be preoccupied with other matters today. I do hope you emptied your bladder recently. I shouldn't take a piss if I were you."

Lauder reached in to switch off the light, and closed the door. In the dark, Tesla heard a key turn in the latch. With the turbines thrumming in the hall outside, he knew his chances of being heard were nil.

He shifted on the stool very carefully, and hitched his weight in a couple of experimental bobs, but the stool was too precarious to risk hopping it across the floor. He wasn't going anywhere – and in fact, he *did* have to relieve himself. With a sigh of resignation, he carefully began unlacing his left shoe while the darkness played hob with his equilibrium.

∞

Lauder was breathing hard as he leaned against the west wall of the Cold Storage building to catch his breath. He had just retraced Tesla's run at the same urgent pace, yet he found that resting was not slowing his pulse at all. He mightily wished he could keep on running and just leave this terrible business behind him, but he refused himself the option. Instead he found the thin cable trailing down from the roof where he left it. From the top of the fifth floor it angled across empty space and up the side of the central tower to its very top. Earlier investigations showed that the crack of sky he had seen from the ice floor was because the chimney cap was not properly affixed and was pulling away, due to its hasty construction. From the catwalk inside he'd been able to remove it entirely. He also pulled free the flashing at the top of the exhaust pipe, effectively lowering the chimney a good two feet lower than the tower roof. He wasn't trying to catch the fumes; he wanted heat. He wanted sparks. He wanted a diverting display.

It was only twenty-two years since the great Chicago fire. You might suppose they'd have been more careful; For all their waterways and fire brigades standing at the ready, the White City was still constructed of whitewashed chaff. It was virtually a paper tinderbox baked dry in the summer sun, and the Cold Storage Palace was no different. All it needed was a match to set it off. Or a chimney fire. That would do just as well. *Yes indeedy.*

Lauder would have preferred to have waited until the prevailing winds shifted off the lake in the evening, to sweep the coming holocaust away from the rest of the White City. He hoped the gravel rail-bed and the wide loading docks around this building would buffer it enough. He found it easier to worry about the buildings than of the people within, but he earnestly wanted no innocents to die.

Tesla — and his role in history — was at least held safe for the time being, but the rest of the Murderer's company were still inside, packing up and fixing to leave. They were alone and they were together. It was now or never.

Lauder gave the cable a yank and then stood aside as it pulled free and snaked down to coil at his feet. At the top of the chimney, a board slid to bridge the gap. It was wrapped in linens soaked in lamp oil and its end extended into the attic walls with its straw and horsehair insulation. He stood for a long while until the first wisp of smoke signaled his success.

His next task was to bar the doors, God help him.

∞

Esmeralda frowned at the saltcellar in her hand. She had just lifted it off the shelf to put it in the crate with the other loose items on her pantry shelf so it wouldn't shift and fall to the floor when they hitched their cob to the wagon and set off down the long bumpy road to New York. But something was wrong. In her hand, the saltcellar began to shake. Something was most definitely wrong. She set it down hastily and regarded her trembling hands and then looked about her. There was a slight change in the air, a lessening of the compression of sound that she'd grown accustomed to since parking near the cacophonous fair, but that was not enough to account for her shakes. She straightened up and stepped off the back of the Gypsy wagon.

There was a dark tang on the air. Smoke, but of an unusual kind. It did not have the metallic edge of a coal fire and it was without the sweet richness of a campfire. The odd pungency redoubled her anxiety and she walked quickly around her wagon to ensure nothing of hers was burning. By the time she completed her circumnavigation, she was at a run and dead certain now from the churning in her gut that something of hers *was definitely* burning, but she had not found it yet.

Pi was roused when Esmeralda poked at her bedding under the wagon to make sure a stray spark from the campfire was not smoldering there. The goat lurched to her feet that she might ignore the woman with supreme indifference and stretched. Spitfire did not bother to get up. Idee's old dog couldn't be bothered to do much of anything anymore. He just raised his head and regarded the Gypsy with his good eye, then dropped his head again with a sigh.

Nothing there, but the feeling she had continued to rise, urgent and imminent.

Esmeralda lifted her eyes and they riveted to the dark plume arising from the distant tower of the Cold Storage building. She could only make out the letters HER of the words HERCULES ICE SKATING RINK. The rest were entirely blotted by smoke. The sound of clanging bells cut through the air about the same time as did her wail of despair.

∞

"Mr. Clemens, ye'd better stub out that thar cigar. You'uns know Mr. Tesla don't truck with no smokin' 'round his particulars."

"Madame, I am unlit," Sam told Granny Idee, and he shifted the cigar to the other side of his mouth. He was packing straw down around the edges of the last crate. "I'd be a fool of a scarecrow to strike a match over my own thatching."

"Well, summats a'burnin'," she insisted.

Sam removed his cigar, double-checked its end, and sniffed the air experimentally. "I do believe it is so," he agreed. "Vladimir, catch a whiff and tell us what you think."

Vladimir raised up from his haunches and frowned. While he tested the air, a hallow bang echoed through the empty rink and they were cast into darkness for the second time. The entry door he had propped open at the bottom of the staircase for light had slammed shut.

"Damnation, not again!" Sam grumbled. "How do you expect me to get this gear stowed in total dark?"

Except it wasn't totally dark. A steadily increasing flickering danced outside the rink's open door.

"Good. Some'uns done brung us a lantern," Idee said with satisfaction.

"That's no lantern." Vladimir said. They all three stood in dumb silence for a moment and watched the glow increase.

"Great Scott, we are afire!" Sam Clemens realized and he danced around the crate he'd been packing and found Granny Idee in the dark by telepathy and grabbed her by the arm. Vladimir found her other arm by similar mysterious means and together they rushed out of the rink and onto the mezzanine at the top of the grand staircase. Sam and Idee forgot their age and fled down the staircase nearly as fast as did Vladimir. The polished wood risers were dancing in halos of light around their feet in reflection of the fire above them. Sam dared to glance up over his shoulder. He did not do so again.

Reaching the bottom first, the Gypsy threw himself at the door and then bounced back with something like shock. He grasped the doorknobs and rattled them frantically. "Locked!" he cried to a disbelieving Sam and Idee. He threw his weight against the doors once again with all his might but only accomplished a bruised shoulder. The doors were large, heavy and decorative, meant to impress visitors on their way to the rink, and not meant to give way under pressure. Vladimir looked around wildly. There was no connecting hallway between the visitors' entrance and cold storage warehouse the rink was built over. The only other way out was that one service stairway at the back of the rink that led down to the cool vaults below. Vladimir shouted at them that they should turn around and climb the staircase again and exit the other way. He didn't need to shout; So far it was eerily quiet in the building. The heat and the noise were all going up and away from them, but he shouted anyway and it seemed right to do so. Together they struggled back up the stairs, Vladimir shoved both of them with his hands planted firmly on their backsides, and neither of them gave the slightest complaint.

The ceiling of smoke descended faster than they were climbing the stairs. Vladimir roared "Faster!" and put his head down and caught both of the oldsters with his shoulders and charged up the stairs like a bull. As they reached the rink doors, there was a deafening *whump* above them and accompanying heat threw them bodily through the rink entrance. Vladimir rolled on his back and kicked the doors shut behind them. They were in darkness again, but it was not yet the choking darkness of smoke.

The rink was raining. The manufactured ice stored on the floor above was melting — *had* melted, because the rain that fell was hot. The Gypsy helped Sam and Idee to their feet, grabbed a hand of both and dragged them along the wall that would lead them around to the back staircase eventually. They ran like scalded cats through pooling water and threw themselves down the back stairwell when they found it. Somehow they all managed to keep each other from tumbling in their frantic descent. Now that they were out of the dripping rink, the air was very bad and it roared above their heads. They proceeded coughing and blind, pulling loose clothing over their heads as they continued their controlled fall down the narrow stairs. The ground floor rose up to meet them and by the light of the fire they could see through slightly clearer air the loading docks beyond the storage vaults. They ran to the first sliding door. It wouldn't budge. They ran to the next. Same thing. Vladimir turned to see a crack of light diminishing along the edge of the last door and he dove for it, wedging his arm in the closing gap. Another hand from the other side met his and he was relieved, and then confused and then enraged because the hand began to wrestle with his and was pushing him back through the door.

"For Christ's sake, man!" Vladimir shouted. "Let us out of this inferno!"

The hand gripped his wrist with a savage strength and shoved Vladimir's entire arm back through the space. Though Vladimir had panic and the will to survive on his side, he still could not overcome the force that opposed him. He stared in shock as the hand flashed back out the gap and the doors slammed shut and a lock-bar rammed home. It moved blindingly fast, but not so fast that Vladimir did not see the three tattoos on the back of the hand.

"Are you the Murderer of the World?" the Gypsy cried. There was sudden silence on the other side of the door. The kind of silence of someone standing very still and listening. "You are the Murderer of the World!" Vladimir bellowed with rage and fear, and when there was no answer on the other side of the door he collapsed against it. "Sweet Jesus," he moaned and slid down to the floor, seeing at last the enormity of what Es had told him. "They put thoughts in your head as a wee lad — right into your head." Vladimir began to cry in pity and in helpless sorrow.

"God have mercy on us!" Granny Idee shrieked and she fell onto the door in a fit of coughing. It didn't stop her from pounding with her fists for as long as she could.

Sam Clemens pulled himself slowly erect and put his hand in his jacket pocket to caress the kitten crouched there. "There, there," he muttered. He was only momentarily stupefied at the situation he found himself in. He quietly determined there was not even a crack of daylight large enough to stuff the kitten through and so there was no hope for either of them. With long practice dealing with fate, he turned away from the temptations of regret and turned back toward the way they had come. He only had to go a few paces before he found what he was looking for.

Sam Clemens slowly sank to his knees, but not to pray. He bent low to light his cigar on a fallen ember.

CHAPTER TWENTYÖNE

*"What do you think happens when the fashion of 'more'
meets the philosophy of 'not enough'? And 'not enough' forever?"*
    — *The Chairman's Notes*
    Wardenclyffe Foundation Archives

∞

Above the Midway Plaisance

The riders of the Ferris wheel were among the first to see
the smoke, but none felt the dread of Sunner and Sergei as
their shared gaze followed the smoke down to its source at the
Cold Storage building.

The passengers in the car began passing the news of fire,
and practiced fears traced imaginary routes the flames might
take across rooftops to the Midway as they calculated if they
were to be held aloft in safety or roasted on a spit.

The clanging bells of fire-wagons sounded in the distance.

Sunner did not turn around, he did not show Lilly his
face. When he spoke, it hardly seemed his own voice, but it
was with supreme control and articulation: "Sir, is there not a
rope ladder or any other contrivance by which one may descend from this car?"

Lilly was astonished that he should ask, and ask in such a
way as to marshal everyone's attention. It brought on a renewed fit of shaking from the man she held pacified under her
skirt.

"We are as safe as safe can be if we just sit tight. The boys will get us going soon enough," the porter said. He was laboring as hard as Sunner in maintaining self-control, but the conviction had gone out of him.

The massive chain rattled in its sprocket and the wheel groaned and the car lurched a few feet downward on its course. The passengers were uncertain if that was a good or ill omen, as they were still suspended but now also freely swinging by the sudden inertia. Enduring a moment of chaos, they scrambled to brace themselves on sills or hanging straps or one another. Lilly's charge moaned in misery. She anchored against him, her calves and feet growing numb as she remained in a squat. Lilly figured it wouldn't be much longer before her thighs gave out and she'd fall on her ass and entertain her fellow passengers by disappearing.

"A little help here?" she asked, and the starch went out of Sunner. He rushed to assist her, pulling her to her feet and into his arms. She looked over his shoulder, but even from a standing position from the center of the car she didn't have the view to look down and see where the smoke was coming from.

"What is it?" she asked him.

Sunner's arms tightened around her and he whispered the terrible news in her ear. "It's us. The Cold Storage is on fire." He held her while the weight of that settled in. She stared for a long while at the smudge drifting lazily across the sky and when she'd had enough she let the circulation return to her heart and she looked at Sunner instead. He was gazing at her with such intensity she realized he was mapping her. Memorizing every detail of her the way a condemned man might relish his last meal. Even his hands traveled over her, adding the tactile memories in a desperate feast of touch. He did not believe, then, that she was long for this world. Not without the equipment that sustained her. First, she would lose resonance and drift out of phase. *Then ...*

The man under her skirt started whimpering again and she leaned forward to pat him through the fabric. "It's all right, I'm right here..." But she was speaking to Sunner.

The wheel eased forward another foot or two. The obstruction that had collapsed into the steam tunnel that drove the wheel had been found and cleared. The pressure that had been vented in the boiler was now allowed to build up another head of steam and some of it was already inching the pistons forward. It was all on track again, at least where the wheel was concerned.

Elsewhere, all hell was breaking loose.

Sunner eased Lilly closer to the window where they could face their fate together. The smoke that was but a moment ago a thin line was now at full boil. They watched the galloping horses converge from the fire stations on the grounds, pulling up pumper wagons. The firemen leaped from them and attached hoses to the water main that serviced the ice factory, while others raced ahead with the nozzle end. Stout fellows who sawed heartily away at the levers manned the pumps. Eventually an impotent stream dribbled from the end of the hose and then reached farther in a spasmodic arc that rose and fell, but gradually gained momentum. It seemed as inadequate as a garden hose to Sunner. He turned his attention to the activity on the building. It was aswarm with fireman already on the roof and setting their ladders against the tower in a race against the ones that took to the catwalk. A score of them scrambled to the top, dragging axes and hoses with them. Down below, a small brigade had cast ropes over the statue of Columbus and were dragging it out of the entryway that they might pull one of the wagons right into the alcove and closer to the flames inside. They seemed to be having trouble with the doors as one man worked at them with an axe.

It was heartening to see how fast they reacted. With a response as orchestrated as this, surely the building was also evacuated?

Was this the Wholly Roller's doing?

The thought jolted through both his psyches and he redoubled his dismay. With or without Lilly, he was not prepared to proceed in a world where Nikola Tesla and Mark Twain die together in a fire on his account. That world might not even resemble his own.

If wishes were fishes, we'd all cast nets. It was one of Idee's favorite sayings, and as it echoed in his head, another wave of grief crashed over him as he thought of their extended family. He numbered them, animals and people alike, and forgot how to breathe. He thought he kept this to himself, but he was wrong. Lilly felt it all, catalogued their losses in as much cherished detail as he had and sagged against him. Everything he had told Lilly so recently about the world containing infinitely wonderful possibilities turned to ashes.

Additional pumper wagons were trying to push through, but word about the fire spread and the population of the fair was clotting the roadways as they headed toward the smoke on foot for an unscheduled show. Rooftop walkways on all the buildings were filling up, and all eyes were trained south to see the fight.

On the Cold Storage building tower, some 20 firemen had made it to the catwalk above the columned portico three quarters of the way up. They dropped ropes to the roof where both ladders and hoses were tied to them, and they hauled them up, hand over hand. The spray from the first hose acquired was trained into the chimneystack, but it wasn't yet high enough to reach the decorative copula that housed it. By ladder they ascended to the next and final level, as each of the four sections of the tower were narrower than the proceeding ones. Visually at least, it looked as though each section might telescope down and nest together if the right mechanism was triggered.

Only five men and two hoses gained the final ledge. This time the range of the water was enough and the stream reached the flames issuing from the top. Around the fair a cheer went up to encourage them, as no one yet realized the fire was in the walls as well as in the chimney and had spread across the entire windowless floor below them.

The men on ladders focused all their efforts and attention on the top of the tower. Three stabilized the hoses from the narrow catwalk. A dozen more were starting up from the second section to join them. Far below, the roof of the main building began to ooze smoke. No one noticed at first.

As Lilly and Sunner watched, a bloom of fire erupted from the base of the tower and billowed up in a mushroom cloud around the tower itself, completely obscuring it. This was the moment that corrected everyone's estimation of the peril. There was a rushing tide of noise as several thousand onlookers gasped and then cried or cursed or screamed. The flames did not subside. It was not a passing gout, but a fully stoked and continuing conflagration that utterly engulfed the tower.

As the fire and onlookers roared together, a small figure on the catwalk leapt for a hose that had been secured to the tower above. He gained it and began a whipping slide down its length. He dropped below the fire line, but 20 feet above the roof the hose gave way and he fell with it and was lost to view. There was a renewed gasp and a cry from every rooftop. This did not deter four other men from leaping for the ropes, but the ropes burned through before they could manage to get far, and the men dropped with them.

On the top of the tower, three firemen remained. They huddled against the flames, embracing in prayer before they leapt. The smoke hid where they jumped and how they landed. But they jumped together, hands linked. To Sunner and Lilly, they were only specks in the distance, but their hearts plummeted with them.

Sunner looked away from the window. Lilly was likewise stricken but she couldn't take her eyes off the figures that tumbled through the air until they disappeared into the smoke. When it was done, she returned without a word to the acrophobic man and comforted him, because Sunner would not be comforted and she very badly needed to exert some positive good while she still could. Despite the cries and weeping of the other passengers, he seemed to pacify again at her insulated touch. Sunner was slow on the uptake, but eventually he followed her to help.

The wheel's chain finally took hold when its axle was turned by a fresh charge of steam, but they only dropped a few feet before it stopped to let passengers off the first car. No new passengers were allowed aboard, so it was fast unloading, relatively speaking. As they ratcheted down neither one of them returned to the window. Instead they commiserated in silence over their known losses: of the equipment that stabilized Lilly for this world and polarized her food. —And of their unknown losses, which were too dear and tragic to speak of.

Lilly for her part was stoic. The expression she wore was one she was accustomed to. Sunner realized it was the look he'd been spared seeing up until now. It was one of hopeless resignation. She looked closed off to the future, braced for only the next damned thing. The expression fit like a glove and the lines around her eyes deepened to accommodate it.

Sunner wanted to offer her the hope that had sustained him over the years but just now, he seemed to have misplaced it.

When at last their turn came and they touched down on the platform, she whipped the skirt off the frightened man's head but didn't pause to put it on, as she and Sunner hurried to be the first off the carriage. There was a smattering of startled laughter from those already on the ground. The surprise of seeing a woman in her short pantaloons and garters arrested the crowd and stoppered up their retreat. Their fellow passengers came to her rescue and positioned around her to silence the crowd with severe glares. Together, they all moved resolutely down the access ramp while affording her a little dignity and space to pull herself together. She did so with surprise and gratitude. Lilly wriggled into her skirt and fastened it at her waist, all while moving forward in the middle of her protective phalanx.

Once decent, the crowd parted and she and Sunner were off and running.

They didn't head down the Midway toward the Court of Honor that was the hub of the fair, but ran to the wall, to one of the many hidden entrances punched through. Because of the distractions, they eased through without paying a fee and pelted up the road that ran through the tent city and around the outside of the south service entrance. It let them get there in a fraction of the time while avoiding the pressing crowd from within.

But they had underestimated the crowd that pressed from without. There were many in Chicago who were willing to swap a day's wage to watch the White City burn, if it was to come to that. Spectators were pouring down from the city. The service gate was the closest to the fire and it was packed.

"How do we get in?" Lilly howled. Sunner held her back. They'd pressed their luck too hard already. They now had to be absolutely vigilant not to contact and ground with anyone. But this frantic realization was paused when there was a great collective cry that caused them to look again at the fire. They watched as the tower collapsed and a massive fireball rose up to take its place. They were struck dumb as each was reminded of a time in the distant future when the whole world would watch other burning towers fall. Neither one of them needed to put it into words. It was a shared memory and best done in silence.

"It's no use," he told her when the moment passed. "There is nothing we can do now."

"But what if they were in there? What if they're dead?"

"What if *you* were dead?" he demanded, and was immediately sorry.

Lilly looked at him with shock.

"I will go," he told her. "You go back to the Gypsy caravan and wait. It's where they will meet if ... *After...*" He shook his head savagely. "It's the only place left to go. That or Victoria House. I will check there if we don't find them here. Okay?"

She was staring at him.

"*Okay?*" He was desperate.

"Okay," she said quietly. "I should go check on Pi."

"Yes, you should." They both realized how true that was. "I'll walk you back."

"No you won't. You won't waste another minute," she told him.

That was it. That was the compromise.

Sunner took her by the shoulders, looked hard into her eyes and gave her a fateful kiss, long, deep and desperate. It promised nothing.

When everything is inevitable, all that's left to do is observe and say 'yes' to it. That's what he'd said just a couple hours earlier, but now he was shouting '*No!*' with all his might.

Leaving her standing there was one of the harder things he'd ever done.

CHAPTER TWENTY-TWÖ

"If I were ever assailed by doubt of ultimate success I would dismiss it by remembering the words of that great philosopher, Lord Kelvin, who after witnessing some of my experiments said to me with tears in his eyes: 'I am sure you will do it.'"
—*Nikola Tesla*
Wardenclyffe Foundation Archives

∞

The Conflagration

There was no question about entering the Cold Storage building. By the time Sunner got there it was totally engulfed. When the tower collapsed, it fell inward into the roof of the main chamber. Every doorway was a threshold to a wall of flames. The encasing walls enclosed a roaring furnace that kept the heat channeled up, rather than out, and the crowd pressed closer than was prudent until they were driven back, dancing from the falling embers, but there was hardly room to retreat. Sunner registered the dangerous press from behind and was alarmed to see that a surge from the perimeter of the crowd could push those closer in right into the fire. He steered clear.

There was another concern: The heat encouraged men to pull off their shirts. Bare skin glistening with sweat may as well have been electrified copper plate. Sunner could never get through without contacting and giving up – possibly forever – touching Lilly.

He hung back to where he could follow a broad arc outside the straining crowd until he was across from where the pumpers were. He fell back to the train yard and found a boxcar uncoupled on the side-track and climbed its ladder to gain a better vantage point. Several young men were atop it already, and he joined them. Even from the roof of the boxcar, it was hard to pick anyone out from the crowd, but he searched methodically, face to face, starting at the ambulances which were loaded and tying to depart through the crowd to the fair's infirmary which was as large and well equipped as any hospital in Chicago.

Save one, he could not tell if the ambulance cargo was uniformed or civilian. They were too badly burned, except for one man who shrieked, white bone shining from his uniformed thigh. It was the fireman who had leapt to the hose and rode it down. Sunner tore his eyes away from the terrible sight and scanned the crowd instead.

Then Sunner saw him: *Vladimir!* The Gypsy was one of the relief volunteers manning a pump. Sunner was sure he would not be doing so if the others were injured or unaccounted for. He could not entertain the idea that Vladimir would have exited the building without all of their company safe. Sunner saw only Vladimir, but relief warmed through him like a jigger of whiskey, and was reassured with every passing moment as he watched him at his labors; He was serious, intent, heroic and not at all incapacitated with grief as he put his back into sawing the pump.

More people were climbing up the ladder and the rooftop of the boxcar was getting crowded. Sunner saw his physical isolation was at risk. "Make way!" he cried, *"I'm a doctor!"* To his relief people moved back and he made it safely to the ground without touching anything except with his heavy gloves and the cork soles of his shoes. As he picked his way across the tracks, a shrill whistle caught his ear and he looked to see Idee and Sam huddled together. Idee had her fingers in her mouth. It was she who had signaled.

Sunner sprinted over to them so awash with joy his legs were rubbery, making him stagger like he was drunk. He only just managed to keep his head and not give in to the powerful urge to hug them.

As he drew close, Idee and Sam assaulted him with two questions: *Where was Lilly,* and, *Did he know where Nicky was?*

He swallowed his alarm that Tesla was unaccounted for long enough to assure them Lilly was safe at the caravan. Then he shut up to listen to the story about Tesla leaving them when the power went off, —something he had entirely forgotten about. At least Tesla hadn't been trapped in the fire! But, a glance around told him that the power was still off. If Nikola couldn't get the power restored, it would be very bad for them all. Not only did it put the Niagara contract in jeopardy, departing for New York tomorrow was imperative. With the resonance chamber lost, they had no time to waste retooling. But would Tesla agree to leave his turbines? It was critical to history that the fair was put to rights. —At least to the history Sunner and Sergei were accustomed to. But Lilly was on the opposing side of that equation.

So much now depended on which path they took.

When the premise offered no good solution, there was only one course of action: *Reject the premise.*

Sunner took off at a run. The path he took was across the train-yard along the fair's southern border to the Machinery Building, because trains be damned, that was the shortest route to keeping Lilly safe. But before he took off, Sam pulled him aside.

"Watch yourself, boy. There is mischief afoot. That fire was no accident. The doors were barred and we were trapped inside. I mean to tell you, and attend closely: someone meant to do us harm. By providence or prudence the smoke was seen in time and we were released." He carefully took Sunner by the lapel and looked him in the eye. "There is a bad character out there, and he has unfinished business. More than that, our Gypsy friend told me to tell you it was the man with the trident tattoo."

"I understand," Sunner said. But he didn't. Not yet. Not really.

CHAPTER TWENTY-THREE

"Sometimes all you can do is stand and watch. Because sometimes, just being a witness is enough."
— *The Chief Engineer*
Wardenclyffe Foundation Archives

∞

The Gypsy Caravan

Lilly walked alone through the tent city. It was hazardous being an unescorted lady as there was no shortage of gents who offered to escort her. *Gents who were up to no good.* Most of the illegal population was mesmerized by the fire and those who had not squeezed through the wall already had found vantage points along its top or up trees and telegraph poles. The true professionals however, saw the fire as a splendid diversion. She feared the pickpockets the most; should their snaky fingers manage to brush her skin she would be back in her former circumstances. So she stomped her feet, swung her arms and barked like the barking mad: "Get away! I'll bite you! I'll bite you!"

It had the desired effect. She was unmolested all the way to the Gypsy camp, where she was allowed passage under the implied protectorate of the seer. Under the shade of the camp's large elm, Vladimir and Esmeralda's caravan was still and deserted, as she was afraid it might be.

"Es?" she called. There was no answer. She could not blame her for abandoning her post once word of the fire had been shouted across the camp. Lilly would have done the same. At least Spitfire came out to greet her. Or tried to. He could barely hitch and stagger to his feet.

"Pi?" Lilly called, bending low to see under the wagon. "Pi, Pi, Pi?" she called.

The goat was not there. Lilly's legs felt hollow as she spied the rope and hauled it in. The end had been untied from Pi's collar.

There was a crash inside the caravan.

"Es? Esmeralda!" she mounted the back step up to the wagon door. There was a struggle going on inside, and the door was locked. Lilly pulled and twisted the latch, but it would not give. Then she remembered the key and found it lying quiet as an egg on the inside hub of the left wagon wheel. Another crash inside flogged her back to the door and she fuddled the lock open with trembling hands, wanting to pull off her bulky gloves but knowing she mustn't. At last the lock yielded and she threw open the door.

With the curtains drawn it was dim inside but Lilly could see the interior was in a shambles. There was a clunk and a stir on top of the bunk, and there stood Pi with a copper pot hanging from a bail-wire over one horn. She gave Lilly a bland look, as though it was perfectly natural for her to be standing on a bed with a pot on her head.

Relief loosened all of Lilly's ligaments and her laugh was only slightly tinged with hysteria. "Oh, Pi, you are in so much trouble!" she scolded. Bless sensible and reliable Esmeralda, who had taken the time to shove the goat into the safety of their caravan before she ran to see about the fire.

"Come here, you."

Pi held her ground on the bunk-bed-for-two and wagged her tail to drop a cascade of pills onto the covers behind her.

"Oh, now why did you have to go and do that?"

Pi sneezed, shook her head and the pot clattered to the floor. The goat looked down at it and calculated her descent, and hopped just past it in what would have been a graceful move if not for the udder swaying from her undercarriage.

"Nice," Lilly said. "Now get over here so I can beat you."

Outside Spitfire erupted in a frenzy of barking, the likes of which Lilly had never heard the old dog muster before. She and Pi both took it to heart. Pi jumped back up on the bed and Lilly peered out the curtain. When Spitfire's alarm cut off abruptly without even a yelp, the silence that followed was even more disconcerting.

"Let's have that goat, then."

Lilly spun around. The doorway was empty. The voice had come from outside. It was a woman, but it was neither Es nor Idee.

"Bring it out. Step around to the driver's side."

Driver's side?!?

Oh hell no. Lilly's racing heart doubled its pace. "Who are you? Are you from Wardenclyffe?" She looked around for something with some heft. There was no way she was going to hand Pi over, no matter who it was or when she was from.

Lilly was sure the Gypsies would be armed, but not in plain sight. The caravan was one-third bed, one-third closet and one-third kitchen. She was standing in the kitchen. She settled for a heavy ceramic rolling pin and reached with her other hand to grab the door to pull it closed. She put all of her weight into it, but the other woman's hand shot out and caught the door and wrenched it open.

Holding tight to the doorknob, Lilly went with it and tumbled out.

She wasn't cleanly knocked out, but when she hit the ground she *grounded* as her face planted in the dirt. The contact pitched her mind-over-heels. Her perceptions sparked and fizzled as she tried to gather her wits and failed; Thoughts skittled beyond her reach like so many marbles dashed on a plank floor. She had no motor control. All she had was fury and frustration.

Lilly saw the woman had the goat by the horns. They grappled together until she got a grip on Pi's collar, and it was easier going after that. Pi could not resist the loop around her tender neck. Giving in, the goat hopped over Lilly, rolling her eyes mournfully as she was dragged away.

Lilly could do nothing but wait for the polarity of her vertigo to spin down while anger and despair rose up. She chose anger, and nursed it into a big strapping righteous rage. But it was not enough to get her limbs working any faster. She scrabbled a few feet in the dirt and fell back in exhaustion. Then tried again. And again. Each time gaining in some minute way, but the goat thief was long gone, and already she felt the first nagging sensation at the front of her tongue. That vague hotness: The slightly sticky feeling of thirst.

CHAPTER TWENTY-FÖUR

"What you see and what you think you see are just two layers of a many layered blindfold."
— *The Chairman's Notes*
Wardenclyffe Foundation Archives

∞

The Power Station

There was a disagreement at the front doors of the Power Plant. A half-dozen Columbian guard barred the way from the service technicians come to see about the power. Now that the Ferris wheel steam tunnel was mended and the emergency of the fire was winding down they meant to turn to the next crisis, but they were being prevented.

"Orders, you see," a guard insisted. "No one shall be admitted until Mr. Tesla gives the *all clear.*"

"I am Mr. Tesla's assistant!" Sunner said, threading his way through. "He sent for me!"

"Orders are orders."

"Nonsense!" A big-bellied man pushed forward. He had the demeanor of being in charge, and he was. He was Mr. Burnham, the superintendent of the fair. He wore a plaid suit, vest, jacket and hat that gave no ground to the early autumn heat. He chawed an unlit cigar, and his face was a florid pink.

The sabotage of the Ferris wheel proceeded a very suspicious fire. But before any of that the power had gone out, and it still was not restored. The timing was portentous with Chicago Day nearly upon them. He blamed the Unions. Calls for a strike had echoed all summer. The Pullman workers were growing restless and while the recession cut back on wages and jobs, they staged slowdowns that snarled the train schedules to and from the fair. Now they were attacking the fair itself. That's how Burnham saw it, except he was wrong.

"You open those doors and give Mr. Tesla any assistance he may require, but you open those doors." Burnham bellowed. "The power must come on, see? We have three hours until sundown and this fair must not be dark. *–Will not be dark*. Do I make myself clear?"

They opened the doors. The technicians streamed in and fanned out, staring up at the turbines, which were humming along as they should be. Nothing seemed out of order.

Sunner hung back at the door. *Hell's bells.* He looked at the giant machines that pulsed with electromagnetism. He could not enter. He *must not* enter. He looked down at his cork-soled shoes. They were ragged and worn down from his run across the gravel paths. He doubted they mattered. He doubted there was shielding inside. Sunner checked in with his passenger and learned that for all Sergei knew about how things *would* work, he knew little for certain about how they worked *right now*.

Sunner and Sergei wrestled a moment with their options and then took a collective breath and stepped inside. If the Wholly Roller with the trident tattoo set the fire and had his bead on Tesla, neither one of him would be caught dithering on the sidelines. He launched into a jog and went the length of the building, calling out: "Mr. Tesla!" He circumnavigated the room and looked in every niche and crawl space. His worry was as loud to him as the turbines, and his feet sped up to match the cadence of his heart. In minutes he'd worked himself back around to the entrance where Mr. Burnham stood chewing his cigar to shreds as he conferred with the workmen. They were shaking their heads. The turbines were fine. The trouble was elsewhere.

"Where is the switch room?" Sunner asked. They pointed. It was one of the doors he'd already tried. It was locked. But looking at the closed door now made his hackles rise. "Didn't you check the switch room?"

He received blank stares. The men were mechanics. They kept the machines maintained. They were not electricians.

As a group, they moved to the switch room door and made a hemisphere around it. Sunner stepped forward and tried the knob again. "It locks from the outside," he was told.

"Key, then?"

"*Ah.*" The man who just spoke looked bothered.

Sunner clearly read that the key was missing. "You have a master, right?"

Burnham bellied up to see what the matter was.

"Is there a master key?" Sunner pounded his gloved fist on the door in frustration. "Your trouble is in there. It's ... It is where the switches are."

He pounded on the door and yelled, "Mr. Tesla?" and he nearly put his ear to the door to listen for a response before he remembered himself.

Tesla's voice could not be heard over the roar of the turbines. But there was an answering thud against the back of the door. A thud that sounded quite like an expensive shoe full of urine had been chucked at the door. Exactly like that.

"The Administration Building," Burnham said. "The master keys are there. Make haste!"

One of the Guard peeled off from the group and sprinted away to get the keys. The Administration Building was only just across the Court of Honor, but it would take some minutes.

"What about the hinges?" Sunner asked. They were on this side of the casing.

The mechanics set to dismantling the door. The doornails were pounded out and two men took hold to lift out the door. The latch gave them trouble and tried to stay engaged, but they worried it loose and pulled the heavy door away.

Sunner and Tesla shouted simultaneously, "Wait!"

The sandbags at the threshold held back a still pool of deadly water.

Marooned in the center of the dark room, Tesla was perched on a stool in his stocking feet. One of his shoes was capsized near the door: That was the one he had signaled with.

The other was hanging from his hand at the end of a length of necktie and shoestrings. Tesla's vest was torn in two and wrapped around his hands. He'd been casting his other shoe to close the switch on the wall. In the dark he had no way to know if he'd succeeded. It was his intent to keep at it until he toppled over, which would happen eventually if he weren't rescued. It was only then that he would learn if he had succeeded. To say he looked relieved at his rescue would be a gross understatement.

"Beware!" he cried. "The floor is electrified! It is the doings of a madman!"

He was believed. They all took a couple of steps back.

"Mr. Tillman!" Tesla called to Sunner. "The maniac's name is Mr. Lauder. He is dressed as a member of the Columbian guard. He may also masquerade as a Salvationist. He is Brown's man: Edison's electrocutioner. Do you hear? He is a dab hand at electricity, and he is after you."

Sunner heard.

"And there is more. I may be mistaken, but I believe he may be *as you are*. Something about the accent, you see. Something about his manner."

Sunner appeared to stand in a trance, his eyes ticked back and forth as he and Sergei compared notes. Neither of them knew a Mr. Lauder, but they suspected he was the one with three tattoos on the back of his hand.

"What about the lights, man?" Burnham frothed. "Can they be put to rights?"

"The switches are only closed, Mr. Burnham. I have but to open them again. However, at present, I am *indisposed*," Tesla pointed out. "If you wish me to be of immediate service, I require a pole, with a loop on the end..."

"Nicky." Sunner interrupted. "He burned down the Cold Storage,"

Tesla went very still.

"Our friends?"

"They made their escape."

"Our equipment?"

"Gone. All gone."

Tesla looked down and his posture deflated. "I am very sorry. That is most unfortunate." It had every nuance of condolences for someone bereaved.

Sunner took his meaning. There was no easy path back to where they were this morning. Perhaps no path at all. Tesla's magnetic resonator was the result of years of work, and now it was gone. That they were able to make use of it at all had been a miracle. Replicating the results from scratch – as was the goal of all scientific pursuit – was never easy and frequently took longer the second time around. Sunner knew the score.

"What is this you say?" Burnham demanded. "The same conspirators lighting fires? It is the Pullman strikers, is it not?"

"No," Sunner managed. "I seriously doubt that." A whisper was all he could put into this. His energy had drained away with his hope. "The Wardenclyffe Foundation, maybe. I don't know. Have you heard of them?"

"No," Burnham said.

"Yes," Tesla said.

Sunner dredged up just enough energy to be surprised.

"Go talk to Sam. The Wardenclyffe Foundation is his ..." Tesla nearly said 'benefactor' but decided to be circumspect for the sake of his friend, and started over: "He received tickets from them to the fair as well as for the train."

"I see," Sunner said. But he still didn't. Wardenclyffe had given him tickets once as well, and more. They'd sent a small fortune to his parents. *Who the hell were they?* To his surprise, Sergei didn't know either. He'd once thought they were on his side; His own personal secret society of really helpful anonymous donors. Now he felt manipulated. Orchestrated. Fated.

Tesla and Sunner fell to silence, busy with the working of their minds. It very much resembled worry, in that it brought no satisfactory conclusions to either of them, but it was something to do while waiting for the Columbian Guards to return with the necessary tools to drain the room and rescue Tesla.

Sunner kept looking at the door, shifting from foot to foot and raking back his hair.

"Mr. Tillman, there is nothing more you can do here. You should go."

"I'm sorry," Sunner said, "I have to see to Lilly."

"Yes, I think you should."

"And you?"

"Once extracted from this predicament, I shall return to Victoria House. I could use a little rest before we reconvene."

Sunner nodded distractedly.

"Mr. Tillman. We *shall* reconvene," Tesla said with confidence.

Sunner faltered on the brink of wanting to believe.

"*Mr. Tillman. Attend my words.*" Tesla said and insisted a third time, "We *shall* reconvene and overcome this setback." Sunner shifted toward the refuge of his conviction, and was caught up in the full furnace of his gaze. Tesla was still and unwavering, like the patron saint of science granting absolution to one who had doubted.

And damn, if it didn't refuel Sunner with some hope.

"Thank you," Sunner said, and he discovered he *did* believe him. "Yes, we *shall*."

CHAPTER TWENTY-FIVE

"Our virtues and our failings are inseparable, like force and matter. When they separate, man is no more."
— Nikola Tesla
Wardenclyffe Foundation Archives

∞

The Train Yard

Lauder sat on the ground. He wanted to dig a hole, climb in and pull the hole in after him. He sat in ashes, as was appropriate. He heaped them on his head, as had the Old Testament prophets, but it did nothing to alleviate his suffering. It would not bring back the dead.

Men had died, because of him. Men who wouldn't have died otherwise. Good men, brave and true, and he was responsible. Even when he closed his eyes, he saw them, embracing in the flames, slapping one another on the back, gripping hands, briefly and strongly. They had shouted, "It's been good to know you!" and then hurled themselves together off the tower. He saw it in their faces. They had not hoped to live and they did not, and it was his doing.

In starting the fire, Lauder had killed them, and their sacrifice was for nothing because he had also at the last moment unbarred the door, the same door he had only just barred, because the Murderers had pounded upon it and he could not bear their cries. One had assayed his guilt and even called *him* the Murderer of the World. They'd also called out to his same

God and in their voices he recognized the same anguish he had felt when he lost his Arlee. He could not do it. He let the Murderers escape, and the Chief Murderer hadn't even been among them. He spied him later, along with his compatriots, who ministered to those who survived and even helped fight the fire. Lauder was dismayed by their actions. He didn't understand what he was seeing, except he did. He'd doomed good men. They were all good men.

The trouble he went to, to save that oily inventor Tesla, had been for naught. The dummy wires trailing from the jaw switches in the Power Station control room were dead of course. He had no intention of dividing the world over its precious innovator, no matter how irksome Lauder found him. He'd played it perfectly: He marooned him on a stool, and he'd switched off the light to prevent Tesla from examining the wires and working it out. It kept him out of harm's way for the time being. But it was for nothing.

The world was rent down a new course anyway and it was by his very own hand. Lauder himself was now the Murderer of the World.

CHAPTER TWENTY-SIX

"Nothing that grieves us can be said to be little."
—*Mark Twain*
Wardenclyffe Foundation Archives

∞

The Gypsy Caravan

When Sunner returned to the camp, he needed every ounce of hope Tesla had granted him.

The evening was still and the pall of smoke from the wreckage of the Cold Storage building layered over air that was already clotted with the stench of the stockyards, makeshift latrines and trash. The elm hunkered down in the funk and didn't lift one saw-tooth leaf, where it sighed over the Gypsy caravan.

It hardly seemed the same day Sunner and Lilly had picnicked overlooking the wooded island under a perfect blue sky on a lawn that sparkled green and gold in the full swell of Indian summer.

Sunner approached to Idec's soft crying, and saw soon enough it was not for the loss of their belongings in the fire. Her mangy little dog Spitfire was dead, and she was clutching him to her breast.

Sam stood three measured paces away, and was actually smoking his cigar for once. His head was bowed, his hands in his pockets and his hat tucked under his arm. His wild thatch of hair hid his downcast eyes. He was practiced in the art of polite mourning. He knew just where to stand; close enough to be beholden to offering comfort without imposing, and far enough away to permit the expression of grief with dignity. He demonstrated how to avert his eyes when they were not needed, and how to employ them to utter sympathy when they were.

"Why oh why would someone murder my poor lil' doggy?" Idee wailed. Her eyes were fixed on Sam, demanding he make some sense of this for her.

"My dear Mrs. McIntrye," Sam said gently, "There's not a mark on him. He just gave out, that's all. Same as all God's creatures. Same as will happen to you and me, by and by."

Idee wasn't hearing it. Her grief turned to rage. "Sech wicked goings on! We was nearly burnt up, then Spitfire was murdered –and that ain't all! Theys after us, sure as the devil! Who'd ever have such meanness in their heart?"

Spitfire's head lolled lifelessly over her arm, his tongue hanging grotesquely from his mouth. Idee's face crumbled into a renewed fit of weeping. "My doggy ain't done nothin' to nobody 'cept to love on 'em. He ain't done nothin'!"

Sunner was sorry to return to such a scene as this. Idee needed hugging, but not from him. He looked for Lilly, that he might comfort her instead. After all he'd been through, he hoped he still retained enough of the calibrated resonance to take her in his arms and... But no. He was the one who needed comforting. He really needed her to tell *him* everything was going to be all right, just this once.

Esmeralda was sitting dejectedly on the wagon step. When she saw Sunner her face crumpled, and she ducked her head, hiding her face in her hands under a tent of hair.

Vladimir rose up beside her, protectively. His face was ash-smudged and sorry, but his eyes blazed out a warning: *Whatever happened here, Esmeralda felt responsible. Maybe she was responsible, but Sergei had better-by-God not make it any worse than it already was.*

Sunner had only one thing on his mind. "Where is Lilly?" he asked. He was answered by a bang on the side of the caravan. He frowned. "She's inside?"

Vladimir swallowed and shook his head. "As far as I can tell, she's out."

"Oh," Sunner said.

A riff of tapping answered. It signaled nothing in particular but told Sunner everything he needed to know. Their worst fears had been realized.

"Oh, Lilly. *My Lill.*" Neither Sergei nor Sunner wanted command of the vessel at that moment and he began to sway. His joints loosened as if the pegs that held him together had all been pulled. It was only habit that kept him upright.

"There is more." Vladimir was still standing protectively over his wife. He squared his shoulders a little more. "Pi is gone."

The words hung in the still air. The only sound was a quiet snuffling from the Gypsy's wife, who had been in charge of keeping the goat safe. Pi was Lilly's only remaining lifeline. Out of phase, Lilly couldn't even stomach water. It was Pi's milk or nothing, and *nothing* afforded only a few days more before Lilly would die of thirst. But before that, she'd endure unspeakable suffering.

"Lauder." Sunner arrived at the wrong suspect with the wrong conclusion: "He killed Pi." And he also thought, *He's killed Lilly.*

And as he said so, he wanted to return the favor to Lauder in person: Slowly. Over a low fire and with rusty instruments. Sunner's humanity crouched low and made room for something else. Something he'd sealed in a barrel and drove the bunghole closed on many years ago. But such things don't die. They just wait.

Lilly's double bang said *no.*

"He *took* her?" he asked.

One desolate thump, closer now, like she had banged her shoe on one of the stumps set around the fire ring for seating.

"Why in God's name...?" Unless Lauder *knew.* Somehow he must *know.* The Wholly Roller with the three tattoos wasn't through laying traps for them.

Sunner sat down hard on the near stump and flirted a little with despair; he introduced it to the dark thing that was at that moment ripping out his heart with its teeth. And then he realized all eyes were on him, presumably even Lilly's. So, he bucked up. He took a deep steadying breath. He stood. He squared his shoulders to match Vladimir's, and he recycled the hope Tesla had given him.

"Let's go find Pi," he said. "How hard can it be? A man dragging a big white goat would be pretty conspicuous, yeah?"

But Sunner's entreaty was met with blank stares. There was unfinished business here. Sam gave him a freighted look and cleared his throat.

Of course.

"We need to dig a grave," Sunner realized aloud.

Idee looked at him, full of red-eyed woe and gratitude.

Esmeralda rose to her feet and undid her shawl. She handed it over to Idee with a teary smile that made the old woman start to cry all over again. Taking the shawl, Idee tried to tuck it around the dog, but her hands shook and she seemed suddenly feeble with age and grief. Esmeralda helped her, snuffling back her own tears until they managed to wrap Spitfire and make him decent again

Vladimir produced an axe and a spade, and handed the latter to Sunner. Together they hacked their way through the roots of the elm, to make a little niche to lay Spitfire in. Sunner pulled off his gloves for the task. He didn't need them anymore.

While they worked, Sam produced a pocketknife and pared away a patch of bark and then carved in the trunk a brief epitaph: *Fido.* Not the name of the dog, but to indicate he had been *faithful.*

After lowering Spitfire with care, they stood in a silent circle while Idee plucked up her courage to bend down and drop the first handful of earth on the sad little package. And then they stood a while longer while she bawled with all her heart.

Not one of them thought it was a waste of time or misdirected effort. The universe owed them a moment of grace. On the one hand was survival, but on the other was a *reason* to survive, where the rituals of love were required to make sense of it all.

Lilly sidled up to Sunner: At least he thought he felt her near. He did not try to mask his anxiety. He was itching to set out in search of Lauder and Pi, but he held fast in the congregation of his friends. He hoped she understood.

He felt something touch the back of his hand.

It was Lilly, surely, but there was no shock from her touch. He didn't keel over. It was only a touch, tingling a little, but as light as a feather. He looked down, startled. He saw her hand, barely brushing the back of his. He traced the graceful disturbance of her fingers to her delicate wrist, to the curve of her arm, the slope of her shoulder to the willowy neck, up until he was looking straight into her eyes.

In a quick motion, moving fast as to not lose the moment, he reversed his hand so they were palm-to-palm.

Lilly remained.

His fingers intertwined hers in a grip that might have made her recoil in pain, except that she gripped his back just as hard.

"Can you see this?" he asked no one in particular.

They did. Even Idee hiccupped and stopped her blubbering to stare. Lilly at last had stabilized, and it was from his touch.

The first thing she told him was, "It was a *woman* that took Pi, and she's a time traveler, like us."

CHAPTER TWENTY-SEVEN

"All time travelers are crazy. It takes a discrete and persistent insanity to shift one's perceptions while retaining continuity of a particular aspect of oneself."
—*The Chief Engineer*
Wardenclyffe Foundation Archives

∞

In the years 2158/1893

The big awful thing is the reality, the time artist thought. *The really-real, here and now, sunshine and bowel movement everyday-ness of it all:* Your breath expands the same rib cage it always has. Mirrors report what you rely upon them to and if you sit too long, your neck aches in that one place where it always has, but ... *But.* Everything else that should seem different is so-much-the-same, that it throws you.

The brain expects respect of the convention of cinematic flashback devices. You want to see this world through sepia filters. You want it to be black and white and every shade of gray: a soft-focused flickering film with projector marks and bulb-burns streaking past. The imagination wants to flatten to affix the past into 2D FX, but it doesn't cooperate like that.

Not this. This is more than just a costume drama, or a fancy-dress ball. Today, it is 1893. Period regalia only, or no admittance.

And no exit either. Not ever. Leastways, not back to where you came from. Not exactly.

She always had trouble adjusting to the weird normality of it: The way humanity blithely disregarded two-dimensional type casting which is the best imagination can do. What does a 19th century man look like? What does a 19th century woman sound like? How do they smell? Like a room full of anybody at all, with the crazy-quilt slap-stitched randomness of people everywhere and everywhen. Watch out for the dichotomy between what you expect and what is. You're on an anthropologist's acid trip, but never mind that now. Hitch up your britches and boots on the ground!

Everyone's here except who you might expect, because who you expect can't begin to rise to the task of being a full-blown human being. That's an unquantifiable sum and no one's imagination is equal to the task, not the Elder Engineer's. Not the Chairman's, and not even the Artist's. And certainly not the technicians of the Wardenclyffe Foundation.

Each person is a magnificent conundrum that boggles the mind. Every man, woman and child contains their own multi-*versities* in ever-shifting kaleidoscopes of possibility.

Managing just one 'verse is complexity beyond measure, and it takes an artist to finesse a bare approximation. Time travel is crazy-making because it's so damned normal you lose your way and speak to yourself in cliché.

"Pinch me," you say. "I must be dreaming."

Don't you just wish you were? Did you ever have buyer's remorse with no receipt?

Once you get the hang of it, you can pick out the other newbies: novice travelers and tourists alike. They sit, wide-eyed and gazing and are always touching something: Petting walls, plucking the leaves off trees, tracing their fingers in the dust. You name it. It comes up short, the imagination does. The brain wants sensory input. The kind of constant reassurances that say, "This is real, and so is that, and this thing here? That's real too..." You can't get too much of that on your maiden voyage.

Watch next time you are in a restaurant. Look for the spacey loner tracing the rim of his goblet and staring as though upon the sweating glass was writ the date and time of his death. *Ah.* Those yokels you thought were stoned? Maybe. Maybe they are stoned for a reason. Turns the time-travel juice down a bit, a good stoning does.

It softens the contemplations that you aren't going back. You can jump around all you like but you are *not* going back. This is *your* world now, Bub. *Uniquely yours.*

The best you can do is try not to muck it up so you can at least return to a facsimile future. If you are careful, it will be similar enough that your dog won't bark at you, and the kids won't stare. Find a nice apartment recently and mysteriously vacay'd by someone a whole lot *like* you, but *not you.* Not exactly, but close enough to proceed with a sense of continuity. If, that is, continuity is important to you. If it isn't, what the hell? Knock yourself out and have a good time doing it. That's the motto of the Wardenclyffe Foundation. Well, not the official motto. The official motto is, "If at first you don't succeed..."

Yeah, that may indeed be the first corporate motto with an ellipsis at the end, but what are you going to do?

I'll tell you what you're going to do: You're going to get in, tweak the tuning pegs of God's fiddle and get out. Hopefully before God notices, and most especially before the babysitter goes on overtime. (Or a babysitter very much like the one you posted over the kiddies, who very much resemble your own and accept your *Mommy's home* kisses with the same milky-mouth sleepy time nuzzlies you've come to expect.)

Yeah. Timing is everything, and art has its price.

The artist moved through the crowd and was chock-full of déjà vu. She tugged the collar of very-nearly-the-same persnickety old goat that kept muttering question marks and insisted on frequent stops to sneeze out of pure cussidness.

It doesn't pay to rush a goat. That at least hadn't changed.

She had nearly as hard a time walking in the long skirts as the goat did walking with her strutting udder, and never mind the crowds. Poor thing missed her milking, but there was no time to stop for it now. There was a junction just up ahead and he was waiting for her there, because 'close enough' and 'very-nearly-the-same' wasn't good enough for them. They'd made a vow a very long time ago: *Whither thou goest, I shall go*, and they kept it. It wasn't something they could justify, and no data-sheet bore it out. – Every moment spun off universes after all. But there it was. It was their own business, they had their own reasons, and they kept their promises to one another. Seniority had its perks, after all. If it didn't, they'd find a nice little farm in the Commonwealth of Arkansas and retire to travel no more. They would find something else to do. There was always something else to do — Infinite verses of *something else.*

But today, her task was laid out and her course was set. She checked her trans-dimensional mod, and then also checked Hector's wristwatch that dangled from her forearm, and hurried up the goat.

CHAPTER TWENTY-EIGHT

"There are many scapegoats for our blunders, but the most popular one is Providence."
—Mark Twain
Wardenclyffe Foundation Archives

∞

The Administration Building

Mr. Burnham gave the order: All catwalks, balconies and rooftop widow's walks were to be closed. That included the popular promenade atop the Peristyle, and the fifth-story sight-seeing deck that encircled the interior of the 1,000-foot-long Merchant Building. Both of these were hugely popular, and it gave him heartburn to issue the command.

Burnham was spooked by the Cold Storage fire and deeply affected by the sight of the firemen leaping to their deaths from its tower. Word had just come that the Fire Chief who had saved himself from immolation by riding down the hose until it broke free, had perished in the night from his injuries. The death toll was up to 16. It was a terrible business, and one he would not repeat.

Burnham's night was spent touring every dead-end at the fair and entertaining visions of visitors trapped in flames at each one of them. He considered issuing smoking bans as well, but knew that was unenforceable and unlikely to do any good against conspirators who would not limit their arsenal to pipes and cigars.

He called Mayor Harrison from the telephone operators' switchboard on the ground floor of the Administration Building and asked for reinforcements from the city's police force and fire brigades. He got neither. The police were busy with a show of force at the company town of Pullman, along with a small army of volunteers against a larger force of potential strikers. The struggle had not yet turned violent and the Mayor had his hands full keeping it that way. As for firemen and pumper trucks, Mayor Harrison would not leave Chicago unprotected, especially with arsonists afoot. Most of Chicago would be attending the fair the coming day, leaving the city vulnerable to mischief and never mind the usual sorts of mishaps like candles flames and cooking fires left unattended. With fewer people to raise alarm, it was unconscionable. No. Mr. Burnham and the fair were on their own.

The Columbian Exposition's superintendent sent word to all his staff. The crews responsible for removing the waste and putting the grounds back in order each night were to pull a 24-hour shift. All hands on deck, and no arguments. He sent the crew-bosses around to the tenements to roust everyone out. Each man was to attend a section of each building and keep sharp for smoke. If they had sons, they were to bring them to act as runners to carry messages.

He considered closing the wheel as well, but there would be a riot if he did and they needed the ticket money it would bring.

The morning dawned to a fair as secure as it could possibly be and still remain open for business. Masses of people were already queued at the gates, waiting for them to be thrown open where all could pass for once without forfeiting a full day's wage on the price of admission.

The pier bristled with every manner of craft, from yachts to rowboats, and their discharged passengers and crews were rushing in along the movable sidewalk, which was out of order. *Again.*

When the first train of the day arrived and spilled a mass of humanity on the platform with a *hurrah!* — Burnham was still worried, even though he had gone so far to have all the service doors locked, especially those on the roof of each building.

None of this deterred Lauder. He had copies of the keys he needed.

CHAPTER TWENTY-NINE

"No one recognizes the prophets among them, do they?"
—The Artist
A retrospective of 4D works from the Wardenclyffe
Foundation

∞

The Electricity Building Rooftop

Lauder's prayers were swept out of his ears by the tsunami of tens of thousands of voices. He heard the thunder of their surge when they overran the grounds through gates that weren't opened so much as they were breeched. It was Chicago Day.

He knelt before the electric chair. Its seat was his armrest. The perforations that had once drained away the piss and blood and sweat and shit and bile and fear of Arthur Kennelly and a dozen others, deckled the skin of his arms like a pox.

He sat back on his stiff haunches, his eyes feverish. His forehead bloomed in a pink bruise where his clamped hands had dug and beat against it. His fingers were slick with sweat and blackened with ashes, so he was obliged to dry them thoroughly on his trousers before he rechecked his wiring, as he had done already many times before, and each time he disintegrated into a fit of loose-bowled prayer when he reached the jaw-switch.

Below him, the crowd roared.

Lauder and the electric chair were atop the Electricity building; on the service landing that gave him access to the wiring panel. The wires leading from the box powered the building's nighttime illumination and also fed the four arc searchlights atop its four corners. These played across the sky each evening in concert with other searchlights atop all the buildings facing the Grand Lagoon along the Court of Honor. Lauder had inched along the edge with his nippers until he had enough wire to connect to the chair with ample slack to reach the wide decorative ledge below.

He was sorry he was without a transformer to boost the power. Six hundred volts of alternating current were all he had to work with. Given enough time, the chair would be fatal, but it would be a prolonged and gruesome spectacle.

— A spectacle more easily seen from below once he lowered himself to the ledge along the hemicycle alcove that sheltered the 18-foot-high statue of Benjamin Franklin. The location was perfect. Most of the buildings were so monumental that their viewing decks and service porches — like the one he was on now — were too high to afford a clear view from the ground. Though great for looking across the whole panorama of the fairgrounds, they were not suitable as a stage.

The ledge he selected was only 35 feet above the promenade, facing the Court of Honor. It was wide enough to accommodate the chair, and its proximity to the hemicycle was ideal. Lauder could use the curved walls as a makeshift amphitheater. With the assistance of a bullhorn, his voice boomed when he shouted into it.

Lauder's plan was to lower and position the chair to where the gaze of Benjamin Franklin seemed to rest, next to the inscription: *He Wrest the Thunderbolt from Heaven and the Scepter from Tyrants,* which was nearly as good as the inscription along the Peristyle: *Ye Shall Know the Truth, and the Truth Shall Make You Free.* The Peristyle however, was a kind of bridge connecting the main lagoon with Lake Michigan, and so high he'd be a speck atop it, and would be lost against the host of heroic statuary. Besides, most of the searchlights were on the Peristyle, and these he meant to employ, as there was a clear span between them and where he was now.

Lauder wobbled to his feet to look out over the sea of humanity packed bustles-to-britches across the Court of Honor. The crowd was so thick that the walkways and bridges that sustained them could scarcely be seen. Across the canal he could see the entrance to the colossal Merchant building already clotting with lines to get in. The queue below him into to the Electricity building was also at a crawl. Boats out on the lagoon were casting off over-capacity and riding dangerously low in the water. But the real jam-up was in the wide avenue that intersected the Midway, and not for the Ferris wheel or for the Menagerie or to watch the Turks do mock battles in the streets with their elaborately curved swords. *No*. It was the shortcut to the biggest and most storied spectacle today at the fair: The smoldering ruins of the Cold Storage building.

Let them look. Let them remember. Let them see and be held in thrall at the sharp contrast between the black ashes and the White City. And most of all, let them *understand*. Lauder desperately wished he could make them all understand that the lives he'd sacrificed were lost in their behalf, though not even that would lessen his guilt.

Lately, Lauder had come to realize that the real purpose of the fair was to serve as a gilded mirror: It cast a reflection so beautiful it transformed the context of the gazer, and having once looked, a person would evermore see himself differently. Gazing on the fair worked a permanent alchemy, after which no one could go back to the way things were. Change a man's perspective and you change his understanding of the world and his place in it. Once an idea arises, it changes the course of a life. Lauder knew it to be true for himself. It was one thought as a boy that triggered his goog, that opened his eyes and planted an idea. It set his feet on his current path. Everything since then had led him to this moment.

An idea could alter destiny. This Lauder understood and counted upon. It was his last shot. He would give them an idea they would never forget.

He looked down at the multitude with ice-water anticipation. They were plowed fields: furrows awaiting his seed. He had but to get their attention. Many of their faces were up-turned already, pulled heavenward by the astonishing white architecture, which reminded Lauder (and no-one else) of travel by jetliner through mountains of massive clouds.

He'd spent the early morning with his purloined keys visiting each rooftop that bore a searchlight. He aimed each light by dead reckoning and trained them to focus where Benjamin Franklin's gaze was also fixed. Afterward, he nailed shut the access doors, just as he had nailed shut this one. Except that here he nailed from the *outside.* Now there was nothing to do but wait until evening, for the magic hour when the buildings would disgorge their overheated visitors and they would press together in delirious and exhausted rapture, to watch the lights come on and follow the Cycloptic gaze of the searchlights come to rest upon the chair and its unfortunate occupant.

There was justice to be done.

Lauder shuddered and let the exquisite ejaculation of adrenaline bathe him in cold sweat, and he fell to praying again.

CHAPTER THIRTY

"One train of thought is there are no branching 'verses at all, but one for each of us. They pass through and bunch and separate as so many bubbles foaming the sea. We show up for each other and where our ''verses touch, we participate in one another's lives: we learn, we instruct and most of all, we love. This train of thought makes Nicky roll his eyes, but I rather like it."
    —*The Chief Engineer*
    Wardenclyffe Foundation Archives

∞

Victoria House

After the ordeal in the switch-room of the power plant, Nikola Tesla retreated to his rooms at the Victoria, where he threw his windows open to the lakefront breeze. He wanted it to sweeten the stench of the fire and diffuse his bitterness over equipment lost and hopes cast down. He dropped across his bed fully clothed and soon fell into a deep dreamless sleep that lasted nearly 10 hours. He hadn't been so mentally fatigued since he was hiding in the mountains as a youth to avoid the Ottoman war. Fearing for one's life took its toll, even when, as it turned out, he needn't have. The wires in the water hadn't been connected to anything at all.

He awoke in the wee hours, still alone. Sam Clemens had not returned; The other half of the bed was unrumpled. Though Mr. Tillman had assured him his friends were safe and accounted for after the fire, the sight of the smooth bedclothes and the pillow that bore no indent of normalcy nurtured malignancies that something was amiss, and so he would need a clear head. Reason was the anecdote for chaos.

Tesla sprang up to prepare, pounding the floor with calisthenics until he felt elastic and the blood throbbed hotly through his brain, and now needed cooling. In near darkness he followed the path to the beach and swam out beyond where the ducks still dozed on still water in the gathering mist. He breaststroked along the shoreline and swam out around the pier to the other side where the caravels were moored.

Fully invigorated, Tesla got out and walked the shoreline back again, dignified in his union suit, cuffed at the knees and elbows. Americans, he'd learned, bathed fully clothed, even in the dim light of dawn. And they called *him* queer.

Refreshed after a breakfast in the Victoria's dining room — poached pear and tea — he felt recovered enough to apply himself to today's crisis. It began with a newspaper at his breakfast table. The rag published for the fair at the Administration Building had the same headline as every paper for as far as the telegraph relay-chain had reached that night. It was all about the fire, of course. An etching depicted an engulfed tower from which figures fell. Or jumped. Upon the figures were little wavy lines signifying that the flames had already kindled upon them.

And it was Chicago Day. Sensibilities flared at the irony; it was the 22nd anniversary of the Great Chicago Fire.

The pear turned over in Tesla's stomach as he read the words: *Calamity Strikes the Columbia Exposition! Electrical Fire Attributed to Faulty Wiring.*

Preposterous! An electrical fire, indeed! Any fool could see the fire began in the super-heated chimney, and further the power had been off at the time. Yet Tesla knew the influence of the press. Once publicized as an electrical fire, the dye was cast and damn the truth. —And never mind that his reputation hung in the balance.

Tesla nursed the kind of rage that galvanizes quiet men to a lethal stillness.

It was Lauder's fault.

This fire put at risk the chance he and Westinghouse had of winning the commission to harness the river at Niagara. Tesla had once even dared to question Sergei Tillman about that, and was told his work would be worthwhile, and that at Niagara in particular. When he pressed, Mr. Tillman responded by shaking his head, and Nikola prudently dropped his inquiries.

By his own reckoning and up until yesterday it was looking favorable: Even Edison and Brown's campaign to link electrocution with alternating current had little effect, and neither did Lauder with his hideous dog and pony carnival of death. In spite of all that, Americans were won over after witnessing the dazzling illumination of the White City. America would have its lights, by God, and Westinghouse would bring it to them. —Not sputtering weakly one mile at a time, but surging along tremendous courses, over hundreds of miles, erupting out of Tesla's massive turbines churning in the Niagara.

But now this fire.

Reported to be an electrical fire unequaled in history, in a building wired by his diagrams and furnished with alternating current from turbines of similar design proposed for Niagara. The very same building in which his own equipment was recently up and running. This could tear asunder their tender hopes. Public opinion, capricious and fickle like water, always sought the lowest course to follow.

In spite of what Mr. Tillman said, Tesla felt the possibilities pulling apart. He felt it as though each of his limbs was tethered to a horse galloping in a different direction. Mr. Tillman spoke of alternate universes (an idea Tesla found astounding), and if true, then he could be on any course at all, and not the one Mr. Tillman remembered.

A messenger interrupted his brooding and handed him a crisp white envelope embossed like one Sam Clemens had shown him.

Tesla slid his long narrow fingers under the flap and broke the wax impressed with a W signet, and carefully removed a single folded sheet of paper. His eyes slid over the text, down to the signature, and back up to read a second time. Then a third. Then a fourth.

A few minutes later, Tesla walked in a daze out onto the manicured lawn in front of Victoria House and found a large chestnut tree to sit under, right on the ground and never mind his trousers. There he sat for the rest of the day, letting time proceed without any interference from him. He stirred only periodically to check his pocket watch, or re-read the letter. The rest of the time he just starred vacantly ahead, a bemused look on his face.

Sometimes when the breeze shifted, he caught the acrid scent of the smoldering ruin of the Cold Storage building. Mercifully, that was not very often, and it wasn't enough to interrupt his marveling that the signature on the letter from the Wardenclyffe Foundation had been his own.

CHAPTER THIRTY-ÖNE

"The first hurdle is to overcome the falsehoods of limitations."
— *The Chief Engineer*
Wardenclyffe Foundation Archives

∞

The Livestock Pavilion

"Pi, Pi, Pi?" Lilly called. Her throat was hoarse from the calling, and she'd been calling since the night before. This new day now was growing long and the shadows nudged in with the promise of another rough night if they didn't find the goat soon. As tired as she was, Lilly wouldn't stop; She gripped Sunner's hand and pulled him onward and he let her. He was hers to command.

Hand to hand, it was she who tethered *him,* though to him she still felt as unsubstantial as a helium-filled balloon and his fingers less sure than a toddler's sticky grip on a cotton string. He *would not let go,* though the muscles up his backside twitched and tingled with the vertigo inducing thought that he *might*, and might not be able to help himself, and might even *have to* if he thought about it too much. He wished her fingers were string, that she might tie them around his wrist with a mother's double knot and he could stop worrying about it.

Although his grip had hauled her across that tipping point Tesla had prophesied, and was no longer necessary, he didn't care. Sunner would not let go. And neither would Sergei.

Alignments. Currents. Resonances. Entrainment. Could any of that be trusted, really, with something as precious and essential to him as breathing? Sunner visualized himself as sine waves and set all his determination to wrap her up in them as securely as in his arms. Intention and imagination might be all there was at the end of the day. That and love. Everything else was so intangible and changeable it might be said not to exist at all. If the 'verses were evermore expanding and branching and dancing in and out of focus, then all he really had was this.

Lilly was growing more substantial moment by moment. She drank and ate untreated food. To boost her energy he bought her Cracker Jacks and fed them to her as they kept walking. (They were not as they remembered, but they were after all, the first of their kind.) Midday, he made her take a time-out to sit long enough to be served a warm beer alongside a plate of bratwurst, kraut and bread. All the time he clasped her free hand across the table and watched her closely as she took careful bites and sipped the ale. She managed to clean the plate and grinned tipsily at him over the empty beer mug at her noteworthy accomplishment. He grinned back under cascades of relief.

The real test came when it was necessary for her to pry off his fingers and enter the ladies comfort pavilion. She didn't vanish; She just pushed through the door like the other women did. While she was gone, Sunner paced outside, and then realizing he was drawing stares, he stopped to chew his knuckles and resisted the mighty urge to burst in and ask if she were all right.

When she emerged, she gave him a sarcastic 'thumbs up' and then submitted to his crushing hug.

"You're going to have to get over this," she chided him.

"I know," he agreed. But he took her hand again anyway.

She didn't need Pi anymore. To continue was nothing more than a wild *goat* chase. It also no longer mattered that they lost the resonance cage and the other equipment in the fire. She was okay now. It was going to be all right. She should rest. They should lie down together and sleep for hours and miss the train to New York with Tesla. Instead, Lilly would take the train with him and Idee back to Arkansas and put the fair behind them. They'd leave Tesla the hell alone so he could get on with what history required of him. There would be time and plenty of it to find and rig the Hadron Cell for the journey back to 2123 or 2010 or where ever in time Lilly wanted to go. He was sure he could make another QET his own damn self once Sunner and Sergei put their minds in order. *Two heads were better than one,* his internal companion agreed.

But Sunner didn't say any of this. If she required it, and she did, he'd turn the fair upside down until they found that damn goat and exacted justice on Lauder for stealing it, to say nothing of paying for his other outrages. Even though Lilly persisted in saying it had been a woman who took Pi, he didn't think so. She'd been knocked senseless and he reckoned maybe she misremembered, though she agreed that Lauder must be behind it. At the very least if it turned out there *was* a woman, they were surely in cahoots. It had to be Lauder. Sunner wanted *very badly* for it to be Lauder. He wanted one more reason to relish the moment when he finally caught up with him.

Sunner kept his thoughts to himself and let Lilly tow him along. If she wanted to search for the goat until he had to carry her, then that was fine by him. She was the least of his burdens.

On and on they trudged. Sunner looking right; Lilly left. They coveted every flash of white, willing it to materialize into a flick of a tail, a curve of a horn, the wagging beard of Pi.

There were over 650 acres of fairgrounds. Over 750,000 people crowded in on this one day, the busiest so far and perhaps the most attended single event in the history of the world, at least up until this point. It took them hours to wend their way across and down to the southernmost end of the fair, until they found themselves where the farm exhibits and stockyards were.

Sunner and Lilly trod up and down the barns, with renewed hope to find Pi stashed with others of her kind, but goats did not warrant their own exhibition, except for the longhaired Angoras which held their own division among the endless pens of sheep. Hand in hand, they waded through each enclosure to be certain Pi wasn't down among the flocks of white shearling lambs. She wasn't.

They resorted next to the beef barn where short red Herefords stood in ranks as far as their eyes could see. The cattle drove them mad with the flicking of their white-tipped tails that flung off mirages and hoaxes of goats.

Sunner repeated their story to each farmer who camped with his stock in the barn. To a man, they were sore sorry the couple had been so careless as to misplace their goat, and pulled off their straw hats to mourn with them and then stood out in the barn alley and watched alertly and sadly after them, shaking their heads to show they were steadfast in the company of tough-luck-all-around.

Pi was nowhere in the livestock pavilions.

Sunner could feel Lilly's strength faltering so he pulled her to a bench and made her sit. She rested her head on his shoulder, said nothing to save her voice, and needed not to. In silence and in dread together they pondered Lauder's motives: *Brown's man,* Tesla had called him. *Edison's dog killer.* It didn't take much imagination to figure what he was up to.

"Maybe we should head back to the Electricity building?" Lilly suggested.

"Got it covered," Sunner sighed.

"I know. But there's like a million people here today. The Columbian guard have their hands full, and he'll need *electricity.*"

"Not hard to come by."

"He'll need an audience."

Sunner said nothing.

"He'll need *relevance*. He'll need Tesla, too. Yeah?"

"He *had* Tesla," Sunner said quietly. "If he'd meant to kill him, he would have. Something else is afoot."

Both of them elected to remain silent on what that 'something else' might be, though they shared the same awful vision of Pi with electrodes clamped to her and Lauder throwing the switch.

Their dark thoughts were interrupted when one of the ubiquitous white pigeons of the fair dropped down on the walkway in front of them and came bobbing up to beg for scraps.

"*Huh!*" Sunner burst out. His exclamation was loud enough to startle the bird, which throttled the air with its wings and took off again. A flash of Day-Glo orange on salmon-colored legs flicked by.

"Did you see that?" Sunner asked in obvious excitement.

"What'sit?"

"That pigeon's leg band."

"No. And neither did you," she warned.

"It's our 42."

"Is not! You could not have read that from here."

"Didn't have to! *Orange plastic band.*"

"So what?" She grumbled.

They both knew pigeons were a part of the décor: White birds for the White City. They were everywhere, they flew in great wheeling flocks all the day long over the fair, and leg bands were not uncommon. If he was suggesting it was their same white pigeon that time-traveled with her, that had circled the farm, flying an endless ellipse between 2010 and 1893 — well then, that was then. That was *there*. In Arkansas.

Pigeon 42 was the same age-fixed bird Sergei had made his test pilot for the QET in 2123. It also appeared in 2010, and 1893: marking three time travel events at the same location. This pigeon was not remarkable in that it homed, but that it did so riding the currents of time as easily as other birds rode currents of air. Time meant nothing to that particular bird. It could home from anywhen. But the point was, it *homed*; Pigeons didn't fly to new territory, not unless they were taken and released and even then it would wing for home, stopping only to eat or drink or rest along the way if necessary.

None of that seemed to matter when Sunner repeated: "Orange *plastic* band." This time he gave it the right inflection for it to register.

"Oh," Lilly let it soak in. "*Plastic. I see.*"

They sat a few more seconds in absolute silence while they both mulled this over.

"I guess that's our cue to leave, then," Lilly said when the cobwebs and pixie dust cleared her head.

"I guess so." Sunner heaved to his feet to help tug her upright.

"Follow the birdie?" she asked.

"Thataway. Back to the Court of Honor, I think."

"Where the Electricity building is..."

"Well. Yes. Incidentally."

"Wish I'd thought of that."

"You did."

"I know. Do you think Pi is there?"

"If she's still in this universe at all, yes I do."

"Why now? Little birdie tell you that?"

"Pigeons *home,*" he said, "but what is home, exactly? A place with a particular vibe. They follow the vibe. Everyone knows that."

"I'm not sure everyone does."

"It seems to me, we've got us a *home-vibe,* somewhere here at the fair. Enough for a pigeon to squeeze through. Maybe enough for a goat to squeeze through, too. Maybe we can catch the wave also. Maybe Pi already did."

"Pi was stolen," she said firmly.

"Yeah," Sunner agreed, but the appearance of the bird introduced other possibilities. He reluctantly took his focus off Lauder to consider them. These other possibilities weren't so dire, and were intriguing as hell. Sunner even felt a bloom of excitement as he told her, "We really don't know for sure who took Pi, do we? And we don't know why ... But if I wanted to scatter and distract a merry band of travelers, sending them on a wild goat chase might be a good tactic."

"I'll be damned," she said, fully in earnest. "We've been played again, haven't we?"

"Yeah. The bastards." He grinned at her. He was enjoying this again. "And I'm putting my money on the likelihood it's someone with the same home-vibe as us."

"You don't mean..."

"I think you may be about to uncover another Pia Stiller. Not a painting this time, but the artist herself."

"But *I'm* Pia Stiller," Lilly insisted.

Instead of arguing, he just stood there grinning like a fool. He knew it would come to her in time.

CHAPTER THIRTY-TWÖ

"If there wasn't anything to find out, it would be dull."
—*Mark Twain*
 Wardenclyffe Foundation Archives

∞

Buffalo Bill's Wild West

Sam and Idee searched for Pi at Buffalo Bill's Wild West and Congress of Rough Riders, on account of there was plenty of fodder there to entice a foraging goat. Almost immediately, they fell into a quarrel with Indians who were roasting mutton, not goat, on a spit behind the mess tent.

How were they to know it was the carcass of a sheep? Honest mistake.

A small and lean woman shouldered her way into the fray predetermined to up the side of the indignant Indians before she knew what was going on. Then she saw Sam and recognized him, and hustled them off to her place: a prairie schooner with *Annie Oakley* painted on the canvas top. There was also a mural of her standing steely-eyed in the face of charging buffalo and descending red-skins, holding a dainty rifle to her cheek. She seemed girlish as in the paintings when they first saw her. This did not hold up close and in person, in spite of her gushing enthusiasm.

Annie was proud to show off her shootin' irons to the esteemed Mark Twain. *Shootin'.* Without the 'g'. Sam was pleased to indulge her. He tutted his admiration under his mustache, pursed his lips and splayed its prickly fringe at her. He fawned over the mother-of-pearl handles, as was his obligation.

"You shoot?" she asked him.

"Harrumph," he answered. "I shoot off my mouth, but even then can't hit the side of a barn."

Annie squealed and then hoo-hawed and slapped her leg. Horse dust rose from her riding skirts that were slit right down the middle and sewn up again like britches. The dust cloud softened her ropy edges, and settled back down.

"That's a jape if I e're heard one," she declared. "I'll wager you're some stripe of a war hero. Did you go up for the war between the states?" It was not polite any longer to ask which side. Or at the very least, not prudent to back a Southerner into a corner.

Idee reared up. "'Course he did! All our fellers did, and no exception!"

Sam pulled back his hat and scratched distractedly at his abundant thatching. "I had the dubious honor of being second lieutenant in the Marion County Rangers for precisely two weeks," he allowed. "We had us a skirmish up east of St. Louie. I defended a cane break from the invasion of a wondering mule that was unfortunate enough to have the sun at his back as he imitated a brigade of northern aggressors. We rained hellfire down on that poor creature and yet he managed to escape unharmed, that is to say, without consideration for his dignity. But that t'weren't the only action I saw. I saw plenty from afar and over my shoulder. I was a prodigious retreater, perhaps the best in the entire Confederacy, but all in all it was not to my taste. Having filled my craw with the business of war, I decided instead to take up the art of peace and I lit out for Nevada."

He gave Idee an apologetic shrug that did nothing to lower the volume of what she left unsaid.

He tried to make amends with claims of roughing it. "Went as far west as a body could go without going east."

"California?"

"The Sandwich Isles," he corrected.

"Westward ho!" Annie crowed. "What arms did you carry?"

Sam mumbled something and decided to admire nothing in particular in middle distance, giving it his full attention. He did not succeed in changing her focus.

"What's that then?" Annie demanded. "Speak up."

"I said; *a 12-pound Oxford.*"

"A 12 gauge, you mean," she corrected. "Oxford ... " It was a struggle between admitting she didn't know that gunsmith or to pretend that she did.

"I meant pound, not gauge. An Oxford is not a gun, Miss Oakley. It is a dictionary. I was otherwise unarmed."

Annie looked appalled, and Idee cleared her throat. "My Magnus had hisseff a right nice pistola," she said. "Toted it off to war, so's I nary had a crack at it, but gimme a squirrel gun and from way off yonder, I can pick a tick off a coonhound and his'un nary flick an ear."

"Haw!" Annie howled. "You an me, we're a pair! We could team up and be Granny and Annie!"

Idee liked that.

"You sharps done jawing, perhaps we should commence finding that goat," Sam grumbled.

"I seen a goat," Annie Oakley volunteered. "Last e'vnin. After the ruckus over the fire. Big white critter."

"Well, that'd be our Pi!" Idee exclaimed.

"Dare we hope you corralled it?" Sam asked.

"Weren't mine to catch, was it? It was follerin' along with that gal."

"Gal?"

"That little ol' gal I seen t'over by the Gypsy camp, and always that goat tagging alongside, purdy as you please."

"Not last night," Sam said. "Not a gal."

"Sure as shootin!" Annie insisted. "As much a gal as I am!" and then she hoo-hawed again and rose another cloud of dust.

Sam and Idee didn't know what to say or who to say it to.

CHAPTER THIRTY-THREE

"How many courses are there to sail upon the same ocean?"
— *The Chief Engineer*
Wardenclyffe Foundation Archives

∞

The Gypsy Caravan

Midday, when Esmeralda finally dragged herself from bed, she chased Vladimir from the caravan and set to work. Last night she had found and cried over the goat-berries left behind on the quilt that covered their bunk. She gathered the quilt up by the four corners and shook it outside in one expansive *whomp*. The berries hailed down across the campsite and Esmeralda hung the blanket to air on a low branch of the elm tree. On her way back to the wagon, she paused, bent down, and reclaimed one of the berries. She carried it like a jewel back inside and set it at the north position on her round table where she sat and drank until she was very drunk, and the trace of the goat would no longer come into focus.

Now, she took up her broom and swept every inch of floor out onto the step, and then swept the step, and then swept the dirt path leading up to the step, and all the way to the edge of what felt like 'theirs'. That is, everywhere the dirt had been trod by the soles of the feet of their extended family until their footprints herringboned with the footsteps of strangers. There she stopped, and made three rounds of that perimeter, counterclockwise and swinging her broom in the air, like one might shoo a flock of chickens.

"Two and fro, Maggery go," she sang over and over with each swipe of the broom-straw, until she was finished. Then she backed into the van and laid the broom carefully across her threshold, and closed the door.

She poured a pitcher of water over her dusty hands and wiped them on her skirt.

"There," she said, and sat at her table in a shaft of sunlight and slipped her tarot deck from her silk purse.

She held the deck gently as an egg and whispered her prayers, ending with *Pi.* Then she shuffled seven times, cut the deck and began dealing.

She laid out five cards in a cross; face down. She inhaled deep to clear her head and set the remaining cards aside.

"Where are you, Pi?" she asked and turned over the card at the bottom of the cross.

The Tower.

"Obviously," she sighed. The card showed a castle turret struck by lightning in a storm. From its toppling ramparts two figures fell. One to the left. One to the right. She'd been chased by that image all night. It was seared into the underside of her eyelids. Those poor brave firemen, leaping to their deaths from the top tower of the Cold Storage building to escape the flames. Vladimir had pressed a glass of whiskey to her lips each time she awoke with a cry. He did not sleep at all, but sat all night at the table with the bottle in hand, red-eyed and haggard, not daring to sleep because he had been near enough to the ladders to have seen them shake one another's hands in farewell before jumping.

He had heard their calls to those below. "Nice knowing you, boys!" So heartbreakingly civilized. Not one survived the fall, and it was a mercy. One man's face was as black as a Negro's, charred and fissured and crisp.

"Where are you, Pi?" Esmeralda turned over the second card.

The Hierophant. The resolute priest seated on his throne. Except this card was reversed. The chair and its occupant upside-down.

"Where are you, Pi?" The third card at the top of the cross was the Magus. A magician holding the philosopher's stone in one hand and on the table before him the four elements. He traced a lazy eight in the air with the wand in his other hand.

"Where are you, Pi?" Es turned over the right arm of the cross of cards and started to sweat. It was the Lovers. Thus far, every card was in the Major Arcana. It was like drawing a royal flush: None of the 56 cards that made up the courts so far had presented. No coins or swords or wands or cups, kings, queens, princes or princesses. Just the Powers.

"Where are you, Pi?" the left arm of the cross was *Fate.* Another Major.

One card remained. It was at the center of the cross. It was the one at the center of the issue.

"Where are you, Pi?" she asked one last time and eased it over.

The Fool.

Esmeralda got up and walked around, her hand to her mouth. This was all 'behind the veil' work. This was all thought and no substance. It was as if Pi had vanished into a thought-stream. Into the world of the spirit, into a world of no substance and all possibility.

She made herself sit down and work the layout, as though she were reading for a client, wishing someone read for her instead, who could reach across the table and pat her hand and give her comforting reassurances, like "*The Death card never means someone is going to die,*" and other gentle fibs.

She took it one at a time.

The Tower: At the root, we begin with catastrophe; the tower struck by lightning, cracking it in half. It is the crisis that precipitates change, followed by sudden and unanticipated enlightenment. Two people tumble down into the abyss. Too late to choose. Committed only as someone in the middle of a fall is committed to hitting the ground.

Esmeralda didn't like this at the root. There were no options here. This was beginning with the consequences. And there wasn't a clue as to where the goat might be.

The Hierophant: The voice of God on earth, the stone-faced priest seated in his golden chair, but the card was upside-down. Not the voice of God, then. A deceiver, or worse, one who was himself deceived. The earnest believer in a false god. *The sorrows,* she thought. But of Pi, there was nothing.

The Crown card is the Magus, the *Magician.* "Who are you?" she wanted to know. The card showed him conjuring the lazy-eight of infinity over his head. She could think of only one candidate, and there was no comfort in the thought; It was too obvious. Too straight-forward, and if it were so, then all was duplicity.

The right and left arms were the *Lovers* and *Fate*, or, *The Wheel of Fortune,* as the Fate card was sometimes called. Were these material aspects, the Lovers were easily cast. But in the immaterial? What were the dual forces at play? What was the hidden alliance? What events awaited the turn of the great wheel of fate? And where in blazes was Pi?

At the heart of it all, at the transept, was *The Fool.* The blithely innocent traveler, the dreamer gazing at the stars as he steps off the cliff, unmindful of the little dog at his heels, barking its warning. She couldn't help but think of Spitfire.

Esmeralda rubbed the heels of her hands deep into her eye-sockets. She was hung-over. That was the problem. And these were her friends. Her emotions were muddling her thoughts. The imagery was so obvious. No subtly. No nuance or art. It was a cast of characters, but not the play. The script was missing. All motive and no action. The stage was set but she'd be damned if she knew what the first act would be.

She picked up the remaining deck and rifled absently thorough it, realized what she was doing and firmly put it down again. You could cheat at solitaire. You cannot cheat at tarot. Nevertheless, she peeked at the top card. It was *Death.*

The door of the caravan banged open and Esmeralda dropped the card with a guilty fright.

"How goes it?" Vladimir asked. He was taking a calculated risk. Nothing fanned Esmeralda's temper as effectively as interrupting her at work. She spun in her chair, flushed with scarlet fury that he should stick his head in the door and presume it was a good time. But the clock in Vladimir's head was reliable. He knew it was a good time. If she was stuck, she needed a bit of *passionate mad* to get her juices flowing again.

He braced himself for the screaming, while in his head he began the drinking song, the one that starts with Skol! Skol! Skol! It sounded quite like the stammering prelude to the aria of her wrath and it sustained him when he stood as his wife's jousting dummy, so that she could sharpen her lance.

She did not disappoint him, she leapt to her feat, scolding in Romanian, pacing in the narrow space and flailing her arms.

"Archetypes!" she screamed at the end of her rant and gestured rudely at the card table. "Nothing but empty nesting dolls!"

"Yes?" he asked. "Can I have a look?"

"A deck of tarot is not a picture book!" she shrieked. "You cannot just look at it and … and..." she wound down because she was looking at it now. Just looking at it. Her husband waited, keeping his grin to himself.

"Vlad," she said. "I know where Pi is."

"Good," he said. "Let us go, then." He bent down to move the broom out of the way. "Where are we going?" he wanted to know.

"Pi is in the seat of judgment atop the Hall of Electricity."

"Ah. But of course she is." He smiled. "After you?" and beaming with love, he held the door wide for his wife.

CHAPTER THIRTY-FÖUR

"Engineer Sergei Tillman's chief contribution was an idea. But once an idea of that magnitude took hold, everything changed. That idea was simply that there was enough, *and in that idea he lifted the lid and let off the pressure. –Let the steam escape, if you will. He didn't save the world as much as he released it."*

—*The Chairman's Notes*
Wardenclyffe Foundation Archives

∞

The Court of Honor

Seven hundred and fifty thousand people were in attendance on Chicago Day, and as many of them as possible were pressed into the Court of Honor and along the basin walkways or in the boats that plied it. All eyes were riveted on the man who sat in the electric chair. He was spotlit so intensely the fat rays of light from the search lamps along the Peristyle seemed to be discharged from his glowing form, rather than received by it. He was Christ on the cross and Christ transfigured all in the same moment.

But that's not how he felt.

The ledge wasn't so high that he was hard to make out. It was hard to look at anything else.

Lauder was louder than he'd ever been, shouting into the bullhorn. He aimed it to magnify his voice off the massive curved walls of the hemicycle. He was shouting the same phrase over and over, directing the cone differently each time, panning the expanse with his words.

The sea-sounds of the audience died in hissing packets as they shushed one another to hear.

He was crying "Chief Elder Enge! Chief Elder Enge! Show yourself and attend! Look upon your handiwork! What is done to me you have done to the world!"

Whaz... Whaz? The crowd conferred, translated, or tried to, and became a buzzing hive that drowned his words again.

"Chief Elderidge?" Lilly asked Sunner, "Sergei *Elderidge?*" It was the name Sergei had gone by when first he appeared to her and Sunner as an old man.

"Chief Elder *Enge,*" he told her, parting the syllables into separate words. "Enge is short for *engineer.*" His head was bowed so he could speak full volume into her ear just to be heard, but his eyes were locked on Lauder. He was attending. He was looking on his handiwork as instructed.

"It is a title," he told her. "It is my title. He is addressing me."

"*Sergei.*"

"Yes. *Me.*" Sergei said, and gave her *that look.* The one freighted with the mysteries of there and back again.

"He's a traveler. Tesla was right." Lilly hollered it loud to be heard among the din of speculation.

"Tesla is always right." Nikola said, squeezing in beside them. He gave them a brief smile that came and went like the flash of a camera bulb.

"How did you...?" Sunner shouted, but didn't finish as Tesla flicked a white linen envelope he pulled from his breast pocket.

"I received an invitation," Tesla yelled. "Very precise."

"Wardenclyffe?"

"*Precisely.*"

They all nodded together as though that made some kind of sense, which it didn't.

"What do we do now?" Sunner indicated the envelope.

Tesla shrugged. "Very precise. Very *brief.*"

"Come on," Sunner tugged Lilly's hand.

"You're not going up there!" Lilly shrieked.

"Hell no," he agreed. "I just want a closer look," and he pulled her, seeking a wormhole through the crowd. Lilly grabbed Tesla, who looked at his hand in astonishment when he realized Lilly was holding it. Skin to skin, and feeling like a hand should. That tingling he felt, that was just him.

They snaked and wedged and eeled their way closer, but not so close that they lost their line of sight for being too far beneath the ledge, and not so close they could be easily spotted. The spectators opened up a bit the nearer they got to the building. This was one attraction of the fair that no one wanted to be too close to. There was a definite boundary at the border of good judgment. Inside that ring were mostly inebriated young men too wobbly and full of beer to decline the dare. Them, and a couple of Gypsies.

"You are late!" Vladimir reproached them.

Esmeralda carried an extra shawl and dropped it around Lilly's shoulders. "You will be cold later," she advised her.

They didn't have to yell as loudly here, but they had nothing left to say. They knotted together and craned their necks. They were close enough they could see the laces of Lauder's Salvationist shoes, but he had not seen them.

"Don't that beat all," Sam Clemens said. He and Idee sidled up to their friends, arm in arm. "It's that hooligan with the electrification chair, ain't it?"

Lauder was ranting, but he couldn't be heard now. His face was pale and blotched and had that crazed look Tesla recognized from the war, the look of sustained panic and desperate determination. The look of imminent death. He had the look, frankly, of a man seated in an electric chair.

Nikola retreated a step and meant to pull Lilly with him, but she let his fingers slide out of hers.

She gave Sunner's hand a double squeeze to remind him they were there just to get a closer look.

Sunner's fingers twitched back, but without much reassurance.

Lauder spotted them then, and sagged back into the embrace of the chair when his eyes met Sergei's. He lifted his chin, and reached out for the jaw switch affixed to the arm of the chair.

"Oh, no," Lilly whispered.

But Lauder was interrupted by a sudden commotion on the ledge beside him.

It was Pi. *Pi* – who wasn't there an instant ago, but was there now. Along with a woman who had her firmly by the collar.

Lilly rebelled against 19th century convention and decided not to swoon, but it wasn't easy. She sagged against Sunner who himself was fighting a sudden weakness in his knees. The cigar fell from Sam's open jaw and Idee squeaked and then clapped her hand over her own mouth to keep herself from blasphemies. Vladimir was less successful and let loose a stream of curses and Esmeralda crossed herself, and thought, *The Magus,* and decided her gifts were fairly worthless if she hadn't seen this one coming.

Tesla stood very still and alert.

The crowd deployed many thousands of private reactions around them, which finally resolved into a smattering of applause that was joined with relief until it was a cheering roar of approval. It was a show, then, they all decided. Not a madman on a balcony, just a bit of theater; but they were wrong, the way crowds usually are.

CHAPTER THIRTY-FIVE

"If you knew for sure you would die tomorrow, what would you do today? If you knew for sure you would live forever, then what would you do?"
—*The Artist*
A retrospective of 4D works from the Wardenclyffe Foundation

∞

In the year 1893/1893

"What's the dealio, Brother Lauder?" The artist asked him.

"How did you get here?" Lauder cried. He could not see who spoke because he was strapped to the chair and the ledge was narrow and there was a good 35-foot drop down to the Court of Honor below. But he knew the greeting. He knew the accent, and he knew the age from which it came. He lost his grip on his bullhorn and it clattered to the deck and rolled off the edge of the balcony to be snatched up by some tipsy young men who pumped it in the air like a rugby trophy.

Lauder strained against the belts he'd already tightened around his chest. He fought against them, fumbled madly with the buckles and wrenched himself free. "Get out!" he demanded, and then stood on the precarious edge and saw she was not the engineer Nidhi come to fetch him back as he expected, but the magician's assistant — Sergei the Amazing's hidden mistress which of late he had seen wrapped as an invalid and pushed along in a wheelchair.

How could that be?

He glanced down at the leading edge of the throng below him and reaffirmed the woman was also *there,* standing next to the Chief Elder Enge.

Yet, the woman on the ledge was clearly the magician's assistant, dressed as the imagination clothed her from her shadow on the sail. She wore Grecian white: as white as the snow-white goat walking with ease and confidence on the ledge beside her. They were dazzling in the spotlights, and made him realize in that rational part of his brain that he too should have worn white for a better effect.

"Who are you?" Lauder demanded.

The goat bleated with the voice of Legion, which was also the crowd laughing at the goat bleating.

"I'm the one thusly saving your day-o, see?"

He didn't see. "Don't speak to me in the voice of that doomed age," he warned her.

"I'm the *artist,*" she clarified not at all. "I'm your archangel, come to provide a sacrifice in your place. A scapegoat, likey? You're the new Abraham, Lauder." She scratched the goat affectionately behind the ear.

"*Isaac,*" he corrected. "And it was a ram."

"Say-so?"

"Abraham was provisioned a ram for the sacrifice of his son Isaac. A scapegoat is some elsey which-what."

"*Ram. Goat. 'Let us compare and contrast.'*" She mocked the art critics. "All the same under the circs, lol-ha."

"Two hundred some-odds too short a notice for you to get it right?"

She was a traveler like him. It made him furious and it made him afraid. Now that the world was rent, the future was leaking into the past. The very idea of his cascading failures caused him to stagger along the narrow ledge.

"You can save your goat. There is no recompense for me," he cried. "I am a useless vessel. I cannot do what was required. Were you an angel of the Lord, I should not be delivered."

"But I *am* your angel, Lauder. We are all each other's angels." She stroked the air and white pigeon appeared but missed her outstretched hand and scrambled fluttering up her to her shoulder instead. "I am your angel, and I am your reaper; but not the way you think. I'm here to deliver you."

"Mocker! What do you take me for?"

There was only a smattering of polite applause as she let the pigeon walk up her arm to her hand. The crowd was loosening, its attention drifting. It had been a long day. They didn't have the capacity for another magician producing doves, no matter how dramatic the staging. Not after all the genuine wonders they'd seen. A loud whistle followed by a bang grabbed their attention as the pyrotechnics began over the Peristyle and reflected grandly in the lagoons.

Lauder saw his sea of witnesses begin to drift, saw the pale upturned faces wink out one by one, as their heads turned in the other direction. He was losing the moment, the only moment he had left, and if it slipped away he might even lose his nerve. He flung himself back into the chair and buckled up.

"You are coming down to it then," the woman said, and she turned the watchband hanging from her arm to check the time. "You don't have to do this. There are *always* options and I've got a better one for you. You need it. Really you do need it very badly."

"It is given unto men *once* to die, and after that the judgment!"

His emphasis was clearly on the *once,* and he was shuddering at the thought of judgment, for everything he had intended had gone terribly wrong.

"You don't have to kill yourself to prove your point."

"I am muchly dead already, girlie-girl. I'm the one trying to save *your* day-o, see? You and them-lot." He included all of those turning away in Court of Honor in his gesture. "Tried but failed," he clarified. "It's up to them now. Let them see. Maybe in their number is a better man than me."

"I admire your motives." She was entirely sincere. "But you are misaligned. You think bearing witness will set them against the chair, and by-n-by set them against the shunt? It will not. It did not and it never will. If history were heeded, shunts would be nary-no-mind and never needed. All that remains of you, Lauder, is a ghost story and a Halloween prop. You are a footnote to a fair that is nearly forgotten within a decade. The chair is but a little horror in a hail of coming holocausts. Trust me, Lauder. There is a better way. All the worlds are open at your feet..."

"Get thee behind me, Shunter."

"I'm not a shunter. I'm a *painter.*"

"Who are you working for? Why are you doing this? "

"I'm doing it for the Chairman of Wardenclyffe. I'm doing it for *you,* Chairman Lauder."

Lauder didn't hear. He pulled the buckles tight at his thighs and dashed a pitcher of vinegar over his head before pulling the metal helmet down and strapped it under his chin.

It was a crowd-pleaser. He was now in good competition with the fireworks. With his right hand he strapped down his left and then reached for the jaw switch recently screwed to the armrest.

"Lauder. You are a hypocrite." She said it gently, because there were tears running down his cheeks and hers as well. "Don't do this. Please. Electrocution is a fuck-all way to go. And besides..."

He glared at her and threw the switch fast as a snakebite.

There was a crack; the sound lighting makes right before the thunder, except —

The crowd was silent for a moment and then they started to scream —

— And elsewhere as the universe split

The crowd was silent for a moment and then they started to boo —

"... and besides ... it won't do you any good," the artist sighed and put a soft hand on his shoulder.

He sat in shock, as it were, but not electrocuted. Not at all. He was perfectly fine.

The crowd was booing. It was not at all the lightning show they had hoped for. He was no Tesla, that was for sure.

"Lauder," she said, and turned his chin so he could see her earnestness. "It can't be done. You can sit here killing yourself all night if you like, but I wish you wouldn't. It won't work. It never works — At least not from where you sit. You've got a future, Lauder. It's got you entrained and it'll just keep pulling you along, one way or another. You don't need a shunt to pull it off. Me, I'm rolling double or nothing, and I'm telling you there are enough of me already, so give it a rest and let's go get a drink and talk-talk, yeah? You've got a fresh start here. Think of it as being reborn if you like. *Born again.*"

"Don't mock me," he pleaded.

"I am not. I assure you I am not." Her fingers worked the buckles of his chinstrap.

He looked at her with total dismay. "You don't understand. *I murdered the world.*"

"No, you didn't."

"You can't go on halving a thing forever. It thins out. It breaks down."

"No, it doesn't. *It gets bigger.*"

But Lauder wasn't listening, or if he was, he wasn't hearing.

"I snuffed all those cobbers. All those good men." He was actually crying now. Big gasping lost-it-all sobs. *"That goddamn Schrödinger box!"*

"Quantum Suicide changes nothing. The options are always the same. You don't have a future as much as the future has you, see? You're not done here. Not by a long shot."

"You disconnected me!" he accused her.

"I didn't have to. You can throw it again if you want, but please give me a chance to clear. I don't go for the volts. I suffer a deep no-likey for riding the lightning."

He didn't throw the switch again. He just sat staring at her, needing more.

"What mayhaps, may hap." She shrugged. "Any one of billion little things can go wicketty to save your skin. You always gyp the reaper. Jackpot every time and never-no-mind the odds."

He just kept staring.

"Put it together, brother. It's *you*. Your will to exist. Dig it? '*To be or not to be*' may be the question, but '*To be*' is always the answer. Whatever it is you are, down in the deep, you find the loose gim-jack and push through. You marshal the lazy-matter into a supportable aftermath: You take *matter into your own hands*. You are your own black hole, and you pull the languishing 'verse into yourself and make it anew, in your own image and likeness, if you will."

"Get thee behind me," he wept.

"It's glory-glory," she crooned to him and eased his buckles loose.

"I want to die."

"Not on the menu, big guy."

"I deserve to die."

"Not so much."

When he was loosed from his belts he slumped forward. "I couldn't do it," he told her. It was like a confession. His voice was slurred, inebriated with despair.

"Lauder," she told him, her voice gently exasperated as she produced an actual paper tissue and wiped his face and dabbed his nose like he was a child.

"Your fail is your salvation, sweetheart. You failed to kill anyone you set out to kill, not even at the behest of God nor angels, and that's saying something: Really it is. It takes a grand humanity to do what you have done. Well, not counting the canines. We're going to have to work on that. — But see here: You have the mark of the beast on you. The *human* beast. Ain't no higher creds than that."

"Nidhi," he lamented.

"You never hit the trigger, slick. Nidhi is fine. Mad as a mink, but fine. We had to shuck the time-twister and snatch the schemas, and lemme tellsya, she was fit to bite the floor. But not dead. Not even close."

"Kemmler..."

She shook her head at the name of the first man to die in the electric chair. "His fate was in his own hands."

"Tesla ..."

"You mean that chum down there?" She waved at the crew on the ground. One of them tentatively waved back. The others just continued their slack-jawed stares. "Very clever non-booby trap." she said with genuine admiration. —And your murder-by-arson at the Cold Storage building went awry when you yourself turned back and un-sketched the doors. All that effort to barricade the exits, and you busted them out in the end."

"The Chief Elder Enge wasn't even there."

"Well no. He and I were on the Ferris wheel, weren't we?"

"But ... the *firemen.*"

"Yes," was all she had to say about that. An old pain flitted across her face.

"That they died by accident doesn't make a wit'o diff," he said for her.

"Not to this verse, true enow."

"There are consequences," he insisted.

"And you shall pay them to the utmost farthing. —And pay with your life." She looked at him squarely. "With your *life*, Lauder. Not with your death."

"That's the price, then."

"It be steep, and no mistake. Recompense without end, but on the other hand, the interest is high." She gave him an apologetic smile.

"Now let's look at why you are really here. You want to save the world, da? So do I. So does everyone when it comes down to it. Like I said, we are each other's angels. Given enough time and resources we can do it, too. Luckily, we have an endless supply of both. We *will* save the world, and we *are.* One person at a time and starting with you, if you don't mind."

He blinked at her, the whole of his expression asking *why?*

"We need *you*, Lauder," she answered. "You are re-sourceful and you have the creds of being *human*, if a bit bent; but being bent is part of the job description. Bent, split and full of best intentions –and really it's true: There *is* no greater love than he who is willing to lay down his life.

"I can't guarantee success, but I can guarantee we'll keep it up as long as we can, and *forever* is a long time, yeah? I can't tell you how many times we've argued up here on this ledge! I'm tired, Lauder, but I'm not giving up. Neither one of us is getting any older and the universe is younger than you think. In fact, *this one* just started when you threw that switch. Give me a break for once and let's get on with it. Are you in?"

He shifted then. Not in posture nor expression nor anything else he could put his finger on, but he felt it and felt the possibilities yawn open at last.

She saw it too.

"Welcome aboard, Chairman Lauder." Lilly said with a grin.

∞

One by one the spotlights swung away as their keepers broke down the rooftop doors to reclaim them. Yet even without the lighting, Lauder remained at the center of the artist's composition.

He was her patron, and he was her subject. He was the portrait at the focal point in her vast tableau, and he paid dearly for that privilege. He has paid for it with his life, over and over again. This time ... This time, they got it right, and so she called it finished.

The Artist looked out over the Columbian Exposition for what she hoped was the last time, and was moved by the beauty, the symmetry and the miracle of each moment unfolding in its perfection.

Time was her medium. But that's not saying much. Time is the medium of every human being.

The trick to being a great artist, was knowing when to lay down the brush and walk away.

EPILÖGUE

"Who was first? Who rescued who? Who started the ball rolling? If you think there is a logical, linear answer to that, you haven't been paying attention at all."
—*The Chairman's Notes*
Wardenclyffe Foundation Archives

∞

In the year 1909: Redding, Connecticut

It wasn't called 'The Pilot's House.' Not yet. The sign over the door simply said 'Tavern,' but Sam refereed to it as 'The House of Republicans and Sinners,' and Tesla, who didn't drink at all, referred to it only (and a bit tartly) as 'That Place in Redding.'

Idee had her own reservations. "Here now! It ain't proper!" she declared.

"It is quite proper, and we make it so," Magnus said and he took her firmly by the arm. "Miss Lilly holds no compunctions agin' it, and I'm inclined to let her hold sway. And look. Yonder's Esmeralda!"

From the corner on the other side of the bar, they heard Esmeralda's tinkling laughter. A man was seated ramrod straight in a chair in front of her, worrying the brim of a hat in his lap. Vladimir stood behind him and had a faraway look in his eye as he made his pronouncements. He was pressing his fingers into the man's scalp, reading the bumps on his head. Whatever he said made Esmeralda laugh again, but the subject looked as if he were in the judgment seat, and clamped his eyes shut in embarrassment. Esmeralda leaned around Vladimir and gave Idee a big wink as she fished a pocket-watch from the seated man's vest.

"Laws!" Idee said, "Like we'uns don't have enough to answer fer!"

"Ida Mae..." Magnus said with a look. She sighed and let him steer her right up to the bar where he ordered a pint for both of them, laying out a Morgan silver dollar.

As the draft was pulled, Magnus unslung the equipment that he had balanced over his shoulder and set it down. He carefully unfolded the legs of his tripod and righted the wooden camera box on its swivel and tightened down the pivot clamps. With the toe of his brogan, he nudged it around to where it aimed at the table in the back, where Sam Clemens was already holding court with the rest of the Lazy Eight, as they were wont to call themselves.

The name was first coined because that's what Esmeralda called it on tarot card with the magician describing the shape of infinity with his wand. Since the addition of Magnus, there were now nine of them, so the pun no longer held, but the name stuck, the way names do, and he took no offense. Magnus thought by the drawn looks of old Mr. Clemens, they would be eight again, soon enough, and it made him sore sorry to see it. He wanted it to be otherwise, but Mr. Clemens would not be dissuaded from his fate: not since his wife and daughter passed on. Well, Magnus couldn't blame him for that. The others accepted with varying degrees of resignation that Mr. Clemens was bent on grabbing the tail of the comet (as he put it), and that was that.

Another time, maybe. Another place.

Lilly kept assuring Magnus that things went other ways in other places, but he couldn't quite get his head around it. Every time he got close he felt seasick and his thoughts got clumsy.

For a while, Magnus had been obsessed with checking the listed dead at the Battle of Pea Ridge wherever/whenever they went. Sometimes his name was there. Sometimes it wasn't. Once, he saw Vlad and Sergei's names there as well, so he stopped looking and kept to his own memory of the two of them striding out of cannon fire and chaos to spirit him away. At first he'd thought them Yankees and figured himself a goner. Then he thought them angels, and when he saw Ida Mae as young and comely as on her wedding day, he knew he must have died and gone to heaven. He still tended secret thoughts that he'd been right on that account, no matter how insistent his rescuers were.

Magnus didn't have a fondness for photography as much as he had a requirement for it. It pinned things down and anchored him as nothing else did. This started when he stood for his first portrait back in Bentonville before enlisting under General McCulloch. He felt then he had affixed himself somehow: attained a permanence that stood fast against the uncertainties of war. That was one portrait he'd never seen, at least not before it was defaced and that was too bad. He'd traded his Pap's pistola for it. He considered it a dear price at the time, but it turned out to be the best bargain of his life.

Idee sipped the ale through the foam of her mug to calm her self-consciousness as she watched Magnus set up his camera. She felt conspicuous, and kept smoothing her dress. No one called her Granny anymore, except in affectionate jest. When she looked at her reflection in the glass behind the bar, it was like looking at one of her daughters. The bartender gave her a wink and she scowled at him, but it didn't have the same effect it once did. He just grinned and winked again. Youth had its advantage, but age had its privileges. She gulped at her beer until her blushes were indistinguishable from an alcoholic glow that flushed her all the way to her toes. It 'twern't as good as her own hard cider, but she was a long way from the Ozarks, so it would have to do.

There were times and places where anything was possible. Sunner told her so on a train ride many years ago. She'd believed him and held him to it. Now that Magnus was back by her side, and the two of them restored, her fussing was mostly for appearances. Mostly. But when Magnus also winked and nodded at her peevishness, and reached out to pat her on the bottom, she gave a little yelp. She gave him her most ferocious scowl, gave up, and bumped him with her hip. When his grin got bigger, she tutted and rolled her eyes, but she was smiling.

The Chairman was the last to arrive. He always drew stares when he entered the (somewhen named) Pilot's House. Patrons tended to drop their heads and look guiltily at the drink in front of them when they registered his uniform. Even the regulars couldn't quite adjust to a Salvationist amongst them, though he wore his collar unbuttoned, his tie loose and his cap set at a rakish angle. Strictly speaking, Lauder was no longer an officer in the Salvation Army, although he kept up his dues and was known to make large anonymous donations whenever they went.

"Brother Lauder!" Sam Clemens cried. "You are just in time. I was remonstrating on the perils of vanity and youth."

"Am I to take that personally?" Lauder asked.

"Youth has its advantages," Sunner remarked, not looking up. He and Tesla were flipping through a small notebook that had Tesla's full attention.

"How can an estate which is not earned, be envied by those that have bent their backs and labored long years to escape it?" Sam wanted to know.

"Perhaps you should sample it before you establish your conclusions." Tesla suggested.

"I have sampled it, sir. I barely escaped my own youth by the skin of my teeth. Many who were wiser and luckier than I, did not. It is a folly to delay one's mortal fate, just as it is a folly to grow old. All life is folly and I see no argument against it. The curtain must fall, the final chapter must be written. Life, as literature, is improved by brevity."

Lilly, who was looking over Sunner's shoulder, bent to the side to plant a kiss on Sam's wooly head. It was a concession. She didn't agree with him, but she loved him just the same.

Sam Clemens gave out a great theatrical sigh. "You see, if I were once again young and full of spunk, I should require a proper kiss, and what then would befall our companionable troupe?"

"You'd get no argument from me," Sunner said absently, and tapped a page.

Tesla said "Hmm..." and sat up a little straighter. He took the notebook from Sunner and held it at the best focal distance, peering down his long nose. Leaning back, he crossed his legs and was now totally absorbed.

When Lauder asked him, "How's it coming at Wardenclyffe Tower?" Tesla didn't answer.

"I ask you," Lauder said, shaking his head and gesturing to the Serbian. "Is there any talk-talk to be had once he gets work in his grippers?"

It was a rhetorical question, requiring only nods and fresh swallows of beer in reply.

"Oh look! Magnus has his camera ready!" Lilly said.

Magnus gave her a little salute. "By your leave, ma'am."

"Don't ma'am me, you Rebel. Just say 'when.' We have some loose ends to tie up."

Magnus was done adjusting his camera. "Anytime, Miss Lilly," he drawled. "I reckon I have pert-near 'nough flash powder for a take or two. You'uns ready?"

"Great Scott, not another infernal photograph." Sam grumbled. "I shall sit this one out if you don't mind."

"Oh no you don't!" Lilly said and pushed him firmly into his seat with both hands on his shoulders. "This is for posterity."

"That boy must have a hundred of me already."

"Not like this, he doesn't."

Sam twitched his mustache, cocked his head and regarded her. He had to hitch around in his seat to do so, his movements stiff and elderly. "This is one of those jimmy-whatnots you are always going on about, isn't it?"

"Potential point," Sunner offered.

"Just think of it as tying up a loose end," Lilly repeated.

"Madame, at my age, all my ends are loose. Why don't we just see what happens if I don't? Just this once?"

"Nothing doing, Mr. C. This is critical to history."

"I suppose Michelangelo said the same thing to Christ when he made them pose for the Last Supper."

That brought a grunt of amusement from Tesla, and Sam struck the Jesus pose, with arms outstretched on the table and his head slightly canted to his right.

Lilly grinned at him and stepped away from the table to stand with Lauder, so it was just Sunner, Tesla and Twain in the shot. Lauder didn't step quite far enough, however. His tattooed hand dangled in the foreground edge of the view-frame.

"Let 'er rip," Lilly told Magnus. And then she squeaked, "Wait!" and ran back.

Lilly slid Hector's watch from her arm and handed it to Sunner. "Loose ends," she whispered, and gave him a quick peck on the cheek as he pulled it over his hand and onto his wrist.

"It'll be something to show the kid, in about eight months or so." With her shining eyes locked on his, she backed away.

Sunner's jaw went loose and he gazed at Lilly with wonder and astonishment and love. He had the look she'd seen before: The *'I get you'* look, the *'Do you feel this too?'* look. That startled look of daring to believe something amazing was happening: that *they* were happening, and that their child was happening too. It was the look that everyone has but only their lover sees. Sunner was caught in the transition of a realization; He knew what this photo meant. It was their future and their past. It connected them. Lilly saw that he loved her in this moment and this moment was forever more.

There was a crack as the flash-powder ignited, like lightning just before the thunder rolls.

It was me, Sergei thought, thinking of the first time they saw the old photo hanging on the wall in the Pilot's House Pub.

"No, it was *me*," Sunner said. And then he leapt to his feet, grabbed Lilly and danced her around the room, the three of them laughing.

∞

Author's Note

I hope you enjoyed this book. If so, you'll be doing me a tremendous service if you could say so in ratings and comments online. For indie authors, ratings are the coin of the realm.

It is astonishing to me that so few people outside of Chicago know anything about the 1893 World's Columbian Exposition, or how important it was. Up until I began this book, I was in their number.

It came as a bit of a shock, because I always thought of myself as a 'Gilded Age Geek'. Some of my earliest memories go back 120 years. Yes, *really.* My great-grandmother had a spare bedroom in the upstairs of her house in Kansas City, Missouri. She used it for storage, and she was a packrat. The room and its bed were piled high with boxes and trunks and bags full of things she'd collected over her lifetime, as well as artifacts from her family that went back to the mid 19th century.

When I visited her, this room was my playroom, and the treasures in the boxes, my toys. I didn't know it at the time, but incidentally, this was also the room I was conceived in when my parents were first married and couldn't afford a place of their own. I point that out, only to underscore what a fateful room this was for me.

I especially loved the oldest things I found. I knew this by instinct, I think. There was a magical weight of time on them: the faded ribbon rosettes, souvenir medals and copper tokens, cardboard advertisements stapled to fan handles, commemorative tin pins and elaborately engraved postcards and newspapers so old and brittle they'd break in my hands. These items from a bygone age were elegantly and sometimes even hysterically overwrought; Like the image of a heroic bare-breasted woman holding aloft a torch with the words "Hail Columbia!" embossed on a sash across her chest.

These amazements impressed me so much that my earliest memories are askew with images from that bygone age, as though they were my own.

It is not surprising that all my life I've surrounded myself with relics of the past, even as I reveled in science fiction, time travel and speculation about the future. Yet it was my son who introduced me to Nikola Tesla, and I immediately accepted the label as a Teslaphile. I'm also a Twainiac. The fact Nikola Tesla and Mark Twain were friends just gives me *squees* of delight.

None of these things caused me to pick up the book, *The Devil in the White City*[2]. It just happened. I grabbed it at an airport simply on the weight of the award medallion stamped on its cover. (It won the Edgar Award for best fact-crime writing, and was a finalist for a National Book Award.)

I hadn't heard of the book before then, and I had never registered The World's Columbian Exposition, although in retrospect I am convinced some of my Great-Grandma's artifacts were from there. I was more than just enchanted with the account of the fair. I became possessed by it. When the author Erik Larson noted –far too casually, to my mind– that Mark Twain traveled to see the fair but fell sick and spent two weeks in his hotel room in Chicago before *leaving without ever seeing it;* I didn't believe it. I still don't. That's not the Mark Twain I've come to know and love.

I mean, come on. For *two weeks* Mark Twain was *right there.* And he just left? Really?

A lot can happen in two weeks.

Those two weeks started to grow in my imagination. *I wonder what he might have been up to? And what about Tesla?*

Tesla was likely at the fair at the same time, and he *was* more than just an acquaintance of Twain's: in fact the night Tesla died, he was in a desperate state to get a package to Twain, who had by then been *dead for 30 years.* Yet he swore Twain had just visited him the night before.

Hmm.

As Lauder might say, "Doesn't that just tweak your mod?"

And don't even get me started about Tesla's white pigeon.

Thus was seeded the Wardenclyffe Trilogy.

Even though fiction is a license to make stuff up, I tried not to abuse it too *much*. Events like Tesla's talk at the Electrical Congress, the fire at the Cold Storage building, the deaths of the firemen and the stupendous attendance of Chicago Day all happened, but they did not occur on the dates or in the same order as appear in this novel. If you read Devil in the White City, you may have recognized the event on the Ferris wheel where a terrified man was pacified under a lady's skirt. I take it for granted it was a true event, although I dare say there are no records as to whether or not the woman was a time traveler.

Buffalo Bill Cody's Wild West and Congress of Rough Riders (such a mouthful, that), was outside the fairgrounds, but I could only speculate about the 'tent city' that sprung up behind the Midway Plaisance along the road that lead to it. It seems likely, but it is a product of my imagination. Sometimes a story informs itself and you just have to go with it.

I also tried to be faithful to the architecture and exhibits. The electric chair was indeed on display, but so was pretty much *everything else,* and I do mean *everything else.* What a sight it must have been!

As I was completing this third and final volume of the Wardenclyffe Trilogy, I visited Chicago. I was delighted to meet the fireman who graciously opened up the Chicago Fire Museum to me on an off day and let me stroke and photograph the statue of Columbus that was pulled from the entryway of the Cold Storage building when it was ablaze. Imagine my thrill when I saw Columbus held a white dove! This was pure coincidence, but it knocked my socks off. Google it. You'll see.

Later, I went in the Science and Industry Museum, hoping to get a feel for the building, as it might have been when it was the Palace of Fine Arts. The exterior was magnificent, but I was disappointed that the interior was thoroughly modernized and the only reference to the Columbian Exposition was in a single glass case by the bathrooms (oh dear God, no) and a couple of posters. I was also hoping to see more old technology to get my steam-punk groove on, but those displays were also set aside for flashier and more exciting exhibits meant to capture the imaginations of school kids. I can't think of a more worthy reason, but I was sorry, just the same. I did get a kick out of the giant Tesla coil affixed to the ceiling, and my husband and I reclined for over an hour on uncomfortable plastic seats just so we could watch it fire off *twice*.

Afterward, we roamed Jackson Park, and the wooded island and tried to plot from a map on my iPhone where the various buildings in this book once stood. While doing so, we came across an enormous and elderly tree that had recently been uprooted by the wind. Beneath it was a huge root ball and a deep hole where it once stood. I climbed down into that hole. *I had to.* I chipped away at the deepest sediments and came away with several inch-thick fragments of what looks like porous cement that was smoothly painted white on both sides. Were these remnants of the white chaff buildings of the White City? I could get it analyzed I suppose, but I'm not going to. When it comes down to imagination or reality, I'll go with imagination every time.

—*Dana Reynolds*

∞

10% of the Author's proceeds
from this edition will be donated to the
Tesla Science Center at Wardenclyffe.
(This book is not otherwise associated with the
Tesla Science Center.)

For more information, visit
http://www.teslasciencecenter.org

[1] Cheney, Margaret. (1981). *Tesla, Man out of Time*. New York, New York: Prentice Hall, Inc.

[2] Erik Larson, (2003) *The Devil in the White City: Murder, Magic, and Madness at the Fair That Changed America* Crown Publishers

www.ingramcontent.com/pod-product-compliance
Lightning Source LLC
Chambersburg PA
CBHW061517020726
47502CB00006B/2116